GHOST LIGHT DARK GHOST

outskirts press

Ghost Light Dark Ghost
All Rights Reserved.
Copyright © 2023 R K Johnson
v2.0

This is a work of fiction. Names, characters, businesses, places, events, locales, and incidents are either the products of the author's imagination or used in a fictitious manner. Any resemblance to actual persons, living or dead, or actual events is purely coincidental.

The opinions expressed in this manuscript are solely the opinions of the author and do not represent the opinions or thoughts of the publisher. The author has represented and warranted full ownership and/or legal right to publish all the materials in this book.

This book may not be reproduced, transmitted, or stored in whole or in part by any means, including graphic, electronic, or mechanical without the express written consent of the publisher except in the case of brief quotations embodied in critical articles and reviews.

Outskirts Press, Inc.
http://www.outskirtspress.com

ISBN: 978-1-9772-5698-0

Cover Image by Rick Johnson

Outskirts Press and the "OP" logo are trademarks belonging to Outskirts Press, Inc.

PRINTED IN THE UNITED STATES OF AMERICA

— dedications —

The Little Golden Book, "The Little Fat Policeman" probably doesn't count as a mystery novel. I don't actually remember the plot, but I remember my mother reading it to me. Last spring, I read my first mystery novel to Mom. She couldn't read it for herself. Now, I feel her spirit reading over my shoulder. Thank you, Mom, for giving me the gift of loving books among all the other gifts of love you gave.

Jean Carlysle represented everything that is wonderful about the Cedar Falls Community Theater. She was a real pro. In the theater world, that means she did things the way they were supposed to be done. Whether on stage as an amazing actress or backstage working on costumes or props or whatever needed to be done, she was a true artist. Her greatest art was as a kind, joyful and loving person. I may not work with her again, but I will keep her smile in my heart forevermore.

– acknowledgements –

As always, I am indebted to many. Thank you, Shelby Davis, for your photography. You have a wonderful eye. Thank you, John Lusaich, for allowing me to roam at will throughout the intriguing theater that you have managed so well. It has been such a pleasure to work with you, not only on these pages, but so many times on the stage. Thank you, Gary Kroger, the first to read the very unfinished manuscript, for your encouragement, for sharing your creative spirit with me, and, most of all, for your friendship.

Thank you, Paula Dean Johnson – my patient proofreader, editor, straightener, prodder, and nurse. You are also the one and only love of my life and for eternity.

— prologue —

His name was Geoffrey Christopher, but everyone called him "Doc."

I don't know why. It might have been because he seemed to know a lot of things about a lot of things. No matter what the subject, if you were missing a piece of information, or were you were just idly speculating about something, Doc seemed to know about it.

One day, at the theater, some kids were talking backstage. They all loved nachos and were thinking about making a stop to get some after rehearsal.

"Boy," one of them commented, "I sure hope they gave the guy who invented them a prize or something."

"They named it after him," Doc tossed in as he was passing by. "A cook in a little Mexican town. His nickname was, 'Nacho.' Early 1940's, I think."

Doc turned the corner into the hall, and went out the back door, the stage door, leaving everyone in awe.

They found his body the next day. He'd been hit by a train.

— one —

Once again, I find myself struggling to find the right place to begin to fill in the gaps. Every story has so many roots, all leading to the same trunk.

The Cedar Falls Community Theater was deep into rehearsals for their Christmas play: the now classic, *Miracle on 34th Street.* As always, we had a great cast of all ages.

Paul Gregory, playing Kris Kringle, was in his early seventies. From his sometimes childlike attitudes, many would guess fifty at the most. He's been in many productions over the years. Here, no one ever looked more the part. He doesn't need any make-up or padding.

Madison Everhardt is six. She sits on Santa's knee and sings with him in Dutch. She didn't know Dutch before the show and has perfect pitch. I expect to see a lot of her in future years.

In between those two extremes are "children of all ages" as the Ringling Brothers saying goes.

I've already been getting a pretty good work-out as part of the stage crew. There are several scene changes that must be done quickly and with precision. Some of the set pieces, even those that are unfinished, are on wheels, which don't always want to go in the direction they need to go. It will get worse as they get a little heavier as we continue over the next month to opening night.

There is something about theater that many theater-goers do not know: almost every time you see a play, you are watching a magic act. You don't see the magicians or even realize the tricks, but they happen. A city street turns into an office which turns into an apartment and back again, all because someone you don't see closes and opens a curtain. The magicians – set designers, costume designers, lighting designers – have plotted and conspired beautifully. The magician's assistants – carpenters, painters, electricians, tailors – have turned dreams into realities which takes the audience into the dreams. Magic!

Doc Christopher was a part of this, too. For nearly ten years, he'd been our resident character actor. By that I mean that he was never a lead role, or even secondary role in a play. He played the smaller, but necessary, character who sometimes was the linchpin of a plot. In *Miracle*, for example, he played the campaign manager for the judge who is to hear the sanity case concerning the man who claims to be the real Santa Claus. Because he is up for reelection, the judge must find a way to render his rulings without upsetting people, voters, on either side. The campaign manager reminds him of this in no uncertain terms. It is his only scene. Doc did it perfectly.

One of Doc's specialties was dialects. He played a tough New York cop, an opinionated German writer, a very proper English colonel, a comical French diplomat, a sinister hillbilly. His appearance matched this. He was very average looking — height, weight, build. His face was pleasant and plain. There were no real distinguishing characteristics. He could be anybody.

As to his own origins, he was very hard to pin down. He kept to himself a lot. Some, who only met him on a limited basis, thought him aloof. Since I'd been around him more than most, I thought he was just reserved. I hesitate to use the word "shy," but, well, as I said, he was hard to pin down.

He was always pleasant, cordial. He just didn't like to talk. Like, the nacho bit, he might offer a snippet and move on. More than once he a had a suggestion about set construction that saved us a lot of time, trouble and expense, but he never once, that I ever saw, picked up a hammer or screwdriver.

He made me feel like something of a failure as a private investigator. I thought I had developed a knack for getting to the bottom of things, especially with people. In the ten years I'd known him the total of what I knew was very small.

In the playbills for a production, there is a short bio of each of the players and crew. His read: "Geoffrey Christopher is a retired businessman living in a pleasant retirement community. He is a familiar face to our audience. He is very glad to be working with these talented people once again."

I didn't know much more. The "retirement community" is about twenty miles from the theater. When I asked him directly what business he was retired from, he replied, "Oh, I did a lot of different things over the years."

"Any family around here?"

"No. The kids are scattered from Spain to South Dakota."

"Oh, really?" I hinted, hopefully.

"Yes," he said, flatly. End of family history.

"Married?" One last try.

"Divorced," he said, again, flatly. "Long, long time ago."

He didn't seem sad or upset. I wanted to feel sorry for him – no real family; no friends that I could discern – but there he was. Polite. Cordial. Even content.

"As solitary and self-contained as an oyster." That is how Dickens describes Ebeneezer Scrooge. So was Doc, but all seemed pleasant and smooth with him. That left less of an opening for inquiry than Scrooge.

Even when Doc answered questions that required at least a sentence or offered one of his pieces of helpful or trivial information, he disguised himself. He had a practice of speaking in character. Whatever character he was playing in a production, that was the voice he used off-stage as well. And not just his voice, but his mannerisms, his gestures, even his way of walking. Whenever he was in the theater, he was "in character." Since I never saw him outside the theater, that was all I saw.

In most community theaters, it was customary for the cast to help strike the set. That means disassembling all the set pieces and putting away all the ones that can be re-used, and putting away furniture, props and other things. That is sometimes a big task. Most of a theater's total space is a vast warehouse. The square footage for the stage and audience are usually less than a third of the total.

Doc never stayed to strike the set. He never attended the cast parties following closing night. He did not socialize with any of the cast and crew. He was not the only one and some allowances were always made for his age and travelling at night. He offered his apologies occasionally to directors and left by the stage door.

Parking has always been a problem for Main Street in Cedar Falls. On busy nights, particularly Friday and Saturday, whether you are going to the theater or a restaurant or a club, you have three choices: get very lucky, have a designated driver (not the non-drinking kind, but one to drop you off), or be prepared to walk. I've walked as many as six or eight blocks to get to the theater, and there are times when that was lucky.

I discovered, by accident, that Doc parked farther away than that. Even at times when parking close would be relatively easy, he parked at least half a mile away.

The Cedar River in Iowa is said to run north to south. Through Cedar Falls, it makes a bend and runs nearly west to east. Going north on Main Street you cross the river, but you are technically going from the west side of the river to the east. It gets confusing. And, because the streets start being numbered south of the river (First Street runs parallel to it), most of Main Street is officially South Main. North of the bridge, on the east side of the river, you are on North Main.

There isn't much on that side of the river north of the business district. North Main only extends for a little more than one hundred yards. North of that is woods and then farmland. The street turns to the east, and, although you are now traveling east, you are still on Main Street – East Main Street. Even some natives of Cedar Falls don't know East Main Street exists. With the woods on the north side and only a couple of construction company complexes along the way, it is hard to miss.

It has some traffic. The street leads to Big Woods Lake. I know people who go to the lake a lot, who don't know what street they take.

Halfway between the bridge and this phantom street is Lincoln Avenue. This used to be the main thoroughfare for a busy little neighborhood. There were thirty or forty small family homes here. Most of them were built in the 1920's in the boom following

World War I. There was also a drug store, a small family-owned grocery, a gas station, and, I think, a small variety store. Except for three houses, they are all gone.

Not far from the Main Street bridge to the west, is a railroad bridge. The tracks continue to curve before straightening out to head east. They run nearly equally distant from East Main and Lincoln Avenue.

Flooding has always been a problem along any river, very much so in that neighborhood. The businesses, many of the people and insurance companies got tired of dealing with it. Eventually, so did the city. The city began buying up and tearing down everything, one by one. Now the area is, for all intents and purposes, one large park. Two of sections are officially designated parks, but all of it seems to be.

One of the remnants is a house purchased shortly after World War II by Floyd Thompson, by father's older brother. He lived there for nearly fifty years before his death. His wife, my wonderful Aunt Meta, continued for another dozen until a stroke forced her to go to a long-term care facility. It wasn't that long.

The house I grew up in is gone, too. It was nearly a mile south of Floyd and Meta's, and was taken, not by flooding, but by an expanding car dealership. The house I own is several blocks west of Main, near the university campus.

One day, I was headed to the theater. This was

for a previous production, not *Miracle*. On the way, I realized I had misread the clock and was very early. On a whim, I decided to drive down Lincoln Avenue.

I don't know who lives in the old house now, but it is obviously occupied. There is a much newer garage, I suppose built by the present owner, far back from the house. In fact, it seems, at first glance, that it might have belonged to another house which has since been torn down.

Continuing east on Lincoln Avenue, you come soon to the city limits. Once you cross this invisible line, you are in Waterloo and the name of the street is Airline Highway. At that point also, the river tends more to the southeast getting farther away from the street. Airline Highway has had very few flooding problems. The woods and empty spaces of Cedar Falls become warehouses and related businesses of Waterloo.

Driving on the edge of any city is a little strange. That is particularly so here, especially in recent years with high-speed highway systems going around and above the old streets. On Lincoln, it's empty of most buildings, but it isn't farmland. The woods are on one side, but it isn't woods. It is and is not a park. It most certainly isn't residential anymore. Uncle Floyd's house and the two others just seem lonely.

These thoughts and lonely feelings filled me just enough for me to miss turning into an actual park area where I intended to turn around. A dump truck had come up behind me, so I would have to continue east for a while before another opportunity presented itself.

As I came back near the old house, I saw someone emerge from the garage by the side door. It was Doc Christopher. I slowed to say, "Hi." To be honest it was more from curiosity than courtesy.

He seemed to take a long time locking the door. His movements appeared almost mechanical, as though the process was complex. He finished and walked to what used to be Logan Avenue which intersects with Lincoln. It still is listed as Logan Avenue, but since the only thing there is the entrance to that garage, whose address would be Lincoln Avenue, the name seems irrelevant. Christopher turned toward Lincoln, where I had stopped.

"Hello, Doc!" I hailed him, with a smile and a wave.

He froze. The designation "deer caught in the headlights" didn't really apply. There was something more predator than prey in his face. A wolf caught in the headlights? I was more startled by his reaction than he had been at my greeting.

"Thompson," he said, matter-of-factly without changing his expression or his posture.

Christopher always had a business shoulder bag with him. He carried his script, rehearsal schedule, note pads, pencils, and other things he might need. Most actors have something similar, whether a backpack, tote, or something. I assumed he had some personal items, as most other actors did, but I only occasionally saw the "theater" stuff, and nothing more.

After he had locked the door, he had put the keys into this bag, and kept his hand in it as he walked. It was just one of those absent-minded gestures that most people do from time to time.

His hand was still in the bag during the greeting, a pause, his recognition of me and another pause. I noticed. It made me extremely uncomfortable.

"Can I give you a lift?" I said, trying to sound casual. I'm pretty sure I failed.

"No," he said, flatly, still not moving.

"My Uncle Floyd and Aunt Meta used to live here," I continued. "I was just seeing if it was still here. Not much left around here, is there?"

"Not much," he said, with a slight reduction in tension. Maybe five percent.

"Thanks for the offer," he said, after another slight pause. "I like the walk to clear my head before rehearsal." His voice and posture had changed. He was now in his character for the play.

"Sure," I said. "See you at the theater."

I waved again and drove away, wondering at his attitude, and why heart was beating so fast.

When we were told of Doc Christopher's death, that scene on Lincoln Avenue immediately came back to me, and some confusion.

Although the train tracks run near the garage, they are on the north side of the street. The house and garage are on the south. The only sidewalk is on the south side of the street. Christopher would have to walk all the way to the bridge before turning south on Main. Even if he crossed main before turning, he would not have come withing twenty yards of the tracks.

So, how could he have been hit by a train?

That question was not the only complication his death would cause me.

— two —

The night after Doc's death, rehearsal was cancelled. I went to the theater in the afternoon. I knew Bob would be there. He is head of the construction crew, and work helps him cope with things.

Bob Carpenter was a carpenter. That was his profession. Whether he followed it some deference to his name or not, he was very good. He also enjoys when people refer to him as "Bob, the Builder," like the children's TV show.

Over the years, I've gained some proficiency with tools, especially working on scenery. To refer to me as a carpenter would be demeaning to the word and real carpenters everywhere. Bob, on the other hand, was a master.

I never ceased to be surprised by people who work with their hands when they make the impossible seem ordinary. For example, I've seen Bob nail some disparate pieces of lumber together in ways that never would have occurred to me. If I hadn't seen it with my own eyes, I would have believed it possible.

Bob, now sixty-one, had grown up in the business. His father and, probably, grandfather had been carpenters. The business was known as "The Family Carpenter." I liked the double meaning. The business will eventually be in the hands of another generation, Bob's daughter, Lori Carpenter-Jenkins.

Most of the backstage area is the "shop" where most of the set construction takes place. On the south wall of the shop are two doorways: one, on the east, leads from the make-up room; the other, west, is to the basement. In between, is a steel sink whose main function is cleaning paint brushes and such.

The back wall, west, has a freight door. Most of our furniture pieces are in storage several blocks away. They are brought in through this door. There is one other door to the outside. It is in the extreme northwest corner of the building. I suppose it is intended as a fire escape. I only hope the fire marshal is okay with how small the access to this door is at times.

In addition to these openings, the wall to the main stage has two others. On the north end, stage left, is a door similar to the one which leads to the make-up room. It leads into the shop. In the center, is a very large opening, taking up more than twenty-five percent of the whole wall. There is a metal door which rolls up nearly at the ceiling, not unlike some garage doors. From floor to ceiling here is two stories. This is how the work in the shop and on the stage is moved and coordinated. Unless it is needed to move set pieces, or for actors entrances and exits, the doorway is closed.

When the work is done, and the show opens, tools are put away in cabinets, lumber is piled on high shelves, even work benches are stacked on top of one another. The shop then belongs to the actors as a gathering place before the curtain opens and a passage from one side of the stage to the other.

Bob was on the north end of the shop where most of our lumber of one kind or another is stored. He was searching through odds and ends of plywood. He seemed angry. He was banging one piece against another, loudly.

"Hey, Bob," I announced my presence as I came in through the make-up room door. "What's going on?"

"It happened again!" he complained without turning around, obviously annoyed. "Somebody moved my board."

"What board?" I asked. He almost always had a board in his hands or in front of him.

He turned to explain.

"You know how we were going to make that holly wreath cut-out to put over Kris's chair in the opening? I had a piece of underlayment just the right size. Now it's gone."

Underlayment, I had learned, was plywood less than a quarter inch thick. It is not strong enough to support much weight. We usually use it to make walls. It got its name from its use between weight bearing lumber and carpeting or other flooring.

"Oh, no," I sympathized.

"I still think it was Gary," Bob said. His craggy face showed both his annoyance and resignation.

Gary Emory was new to our crew. He is in his early twenties. He's about six one, with brown hair. He is handsome, in a quirky kind of way. That is, his face is not quite symmetrical. A lot of people have crooked smiles. The only time Gary's mouth is not crooked is when he smiles. He smiles a lot. He is quick and strong and learns new tasks easily. I'm sure his boss is always happy to have him. He works just across the alley at a tire business.

Gary's biggest fault is that he is just a little too eager to please. He wants to keep busy all the time. He is always putting things away, even if we aren't done with them. If I make a quick run to the men's room, my hammer or screwdriver or whatever will be gone. He always puts things back exactly where they belong. At first, it was kind of funny. After the fourteenth time, not so much.

Bob, as an independent contractor and the boss of his own company, could be flexible in his work hours. Also, as winter approached, those in construction trades had less and less work to do. Bob had one more advantage – his daughter could take over anything that needed to be done.

I have some of the same advantages. As an early, semi-retired private investigator, I'm my own boss. I set my own hours. Except for two big insurance companies that still keep me on retainer, I can accept or decline almost any job. And I had recently acquired an assistant/apprentice: Frost.

During the unfortunate business in Georgia concerning his father, I had told Frost – Forrest Duane Jackson – that he would make a good investigator. His father, Tom, was a truly repentant, cooperative witness for the state and a decent man who had just gotten caught up in things he couldn't handle. Even with that and other mitigating circumstances, he had to go to prison – three to five years, minimum security.

Frost, who had been working with the local police, settled his father's legitimate business affairs and showed up in my office one day. He wanted me to teach him my business. So, for the past year, that's what I've been doing. In truth, he's been teaching me as well. He seems to have a natural, some might say super-natural, way of seeing into people. He reads them in a minute and knows the questions that need to be asked to jump past whatever tricks and façades they may be using to hide certain facts or truths.

What I've been teaching him is timing. Frost, for all his easy-going manner and southern charm, is impatient. He wants the truth immediately. Many people, no matter how honest they are, do not. If you push too quickly or too soon, they may stop talking. Some will walk away. Some will disappear.

Our relative freedom put me with Bob in the theater shop a lot. We work together well. He is still the master carpenter. I am still the semi-skilled assistant. But we've also become friends. We rarely see one another outside the theater, but our personal bond is deeper than you might expect. In our first show together after my wife died, Bob walked over to me, put his hand on my shoulder, and looked into my eyes. Neither of us said a word, but he spoke to my heart. It lasted five seconds, then we got to work. It will last a lifetime.

"It had to be Gary," Bob said again, but I thought I heard a note of doubt in his voice. "But what the hell did he do with it?"

Gary has to work during the day, but often comes directly from the tire place to the stage door to help out. The stage door is at the back of the theater, naturally. It opens to a hallway on the south side that runs all the way to the audience seating. At that east end, there is an archway with a curtain. The hallway, in a sense continues as the far-left aisle of the house. That archway is sometimes used for entrances and exits for a production.

At first, coming in the stage door, you go up four steps to get to the stage level. Then, you walk about twenty feet to another doorway on your left, which leads directly to the stage. From there, you can get to the shop either through the make-up room or the big door in the middle.

If the stage door is locked, Gary can assume that

no one is there. He will sometimes come in the evenings to do some things, if it doesn't interfere with rehearsals. Early in the process, rehearsals are in a large room on the third floor of the theater so the construction crew can do their work. If Bob can't be there, he will sometimes leave the door unlocked for Gary, having left him some notes. Gary usually follows those notes exactly, except for the notes about not moving things. If the stage is being used for rehearsal, which means the stage door may be open, Bob will leave a note telling Gary not to do anything. He does it anyway. He straightens things up. He picks things up. He sweeps the floor.

This was the reason for the note of doubt in Bob's voice. Gary puts things where they belong, even lumber we will be using: two-by-fours, plywood, odd pieces. They have a place among like things. The piece Bob was looking for should have been easy to find.

Such pieces are kept on edge in a kind of slot. There are a variety of thicknesses, lengths, widths, and shapes. This is where they stay until they are used up. Some remnant of the original four-foot by eight-foot sheet of plywood may still be around for a generation after it was purchased. Community theaters cannot afford waste.

Gary knows and understands this. He had put things in that stack many times. It would be odd for him to put the missing piece anywhere else.

This was the latest in a string of strange

occurrences over the month in which we had begun this production.

Bob, like all good workers, keeps careful track of his tools, or the tools he uses. He can tell you the exact size of a Phillips-head screwdriver from across the room.

"Hey, John," he said one day, "Have you seen the Phillips with the green handle?"

We have a drawer in a standing tool chest with two dozen screwdrivers. Half are flat heads; half are Phillips. The handles are a variety of colors. There is a only one green one, dark green, almost black.

Gary was there that day. It was a Sunday afternoon. Bob and I and Jim Banks, another volunteer – a retiree from John Deere – kept busy with constructing a "wall." Gary spent two hours carefully looking for the missing screwdriver. He looked over, under, around and through everything. He found nuts, bolts, nails, and other small things. He found an orange golf ball. And he found a screwdriver: an extra-long flathead with a yellow handle that no one could remember having.

A couple of other times, Bob would get to the shop and find things moved around. Tools were out of place. A waste bin moved from one side of the freight door to the other. A work bench with locking wheels not as far back in the corner where Bob usually put it. And it wasn't just in the shop.

As far as anyone could tell, nothing of real value was ever missing, but several things were found out of place, moved slightly from where people remembered putting them.

The front part of the theater building, facing Main Street, is three stories of old brick. It was first opened as the Cotton Theater in 1910. That information is carved in stone above the marquee. Most of that front, on the ground floor, is large plate glass windows. There are double doors, the main entrance, in the center, and a door at each end, north and south. Each of those leads to a staircase to the second floor. They were built mostly as emergency exits.

The main part of the ground floor is the lobby. Continuing straight ahead there is another set of double doors which, one way or another will lead to the seating. There are wide staircases leading to the balcony and four arches. The arches lead to aisles sloping rather sharply all the way to the orchestra pit. The archways at the far ends lead to other archways. On the south, the audience left, is the one which eventually leads to the stage door that I already mentioned. On the right, is a hallway that leads another stairway to the basement.

Just before you turn to the right-side aisle, at the end of the hallway, are curtains which conceal a fire escape door. There is another escape door halfway down the hallway that leads to the basement. This makes three doors on the front, the east side, two on the back, to the alley, and two on the street level on the north side. That north side has one other door: a fire escape from the second floor. There are also two doors to the roof, or I should say roofs – the building has two levels of roof. There is one more door, sort of hidden, on the south side of the building. There are twelve doors in and out of the building. The double doors are unlocked during business hours and rehearsals. The stage door is unlocked only for rehearsals and performances. The others can only be opened from the inside.

The far north end of the lobby area is the main business office. It is blocked off from the rest by a counter and windows to the ceiling. The center of this counter has a cut-out for ticket sales or for answering questions. The end toward Main Street is open for access. On the other side of the counter is a desk and chair, a combination printer/fax machine and some small filing cabinets. There are file drawers under the counter as well. This is Shirley's office. Shirley handles ticket sales and answers the phone and other day-to-day business. She does it well and with a smile that you can see whenever you come in and you can hear if you call.

Mike Coppola is the General Manager. His office is on the second floor. Mike is in charge of everything. He is especially good at fund raising, whether that is special events, letters, flyers, phone calls – whatever is necessary. It is a year-round task.

Behind this office, with access on the other side of the counter is the public Ladies' Room. The Men's Room is on the opposite side beyond the small concession stand and the elevator. In front of the elevator and concession stand is the main waiting area.

Just to the left of the Men's Room door is another door which leads to a second basement. This basement runs under the whole of the front of the theater, the lobby and the seating. This door and stairway are the only access. This basement meets the one at the back of the theater at the wall of the orchestra pit. It is this basement that houses the main furnace. Naturally is also used for storage, little of which appears on stage. It is mostly cleaning supplies and paper products. There was once rack or two of donated furs, real and not, but it was decided that it was too damp for those. There are still a couple of long rows of old military uniforms. I think my Uncle Floyd's Air Corps uniform is there.

During our recent string of odd occurrences, the chair in Shirley's office was moved. She is usually careful about putting it under the desk. It was moved, but nothing seemed to be missing from the office.

In a utility closet, the vacuum cleaner and some brooms were not in their usual places. Nothing seemed to be missing.

That was the continuing pattern: things moved; nothing missing. It happened in the concession stand, in the basement, both basements. Although some places are rather cluttered, it was apparent to those most familiar with those areas – custodian, manager, props supervisor – that something was not where they were sure it had been.

The biggest problem is human nature. Being what it is, after the first stories of moved things, everyone began looking at every little thing and wondering, "Has that been moved?" Most people have certain habits about their everyday lives that they take for granted. They put their keys, purse, cell phone down in the same general place day after day. If you stop and stare at it sometimes, it will seem somehow strange to you.

All the movement stories were not quite the same. The second floor of the theater is rather oddly arranged. There is a kind of zig-zag narrow hallway connecting to the south stairway to the lobby, two restrooms, the elevator and the costume shop. The main door to the costume shop has a key-code lock. The other doors with access to this shop are also locked. The one near the north end is to offices.

The one door in this area which is not locked opens into another narrow hallway which it not seen or used by the public. At the far north end of this hallway is a stairway leading to the street-level door on Main Street. On the south end, where the doorway near the costume shop, is a stairway leading up to the third floor. I assume this passage was built as an emergency exit.

There is one other locked door on this floor. At the top of the south stairway, you turn right to enter the balcony. You turn left to get to the restrooms or elevator. At that point is the mysterious door. I say mysterious because it is on the south outside wall of the building. On the other side of that door, one is in another building. On the first floor, there have been a variety of things from a butcher shop to a boutique. The second floor belongs to the theater. It is the main storage areas for costumes. There is a narrow hallway along the length of the building on the north side. The rest is divided into one larger room on the Main Street end and six nearly equal size small rooms going to the alley end. The two in the center used to be rest rooms – now, no longer functional. Each of these rooms, including the former restrooms, has different clothes hanging there. One has men's suits. The next has other men's clothes. Then there are women's clothes, including hand-made period dresses. And so on. It is quite a sight. At the back of the building is a door to a long wooden stairway to the alley.

Even the locked doors did not keep out the stories of things being moved.

The third floor of the building is mostly just one large room, about thirty by seventy-five feet. The door to the indoor escape stairs is in the far northwest corner of the room. There are large windows along the north and east sides. There are storage closets along the west side. These hold tables and chairs for dinners and other gatherings. The room is mostly used for rehearsal space until the stage is ready. On the south end of the room, on the far east side, is a short hall to the restroom. On the far west side, a hall – really just a space leads to a stairway down to the second floor. The elevator is located here as well. Usually, the room is only accessible by this elevator. The rest of the south end is a small kitchen. The door is in the hallway on the east. There is a counter opening, with a roll-up door that takes up most of the wall. Behind the kitchen is a small room that has the blower for the roof-top air conditioners. An occasional case of wine, for the dinners, is kept in there.

Like many old theaters, the over-all lay-out is both simple and complex. Everything is just as is necessary for efficient operations, including emergency exits. However, getting from one place to another, even in and out of the building can seem to be a labyrinth rivalling the Minotaur's of Greek mythology.

That brings me to the ghost.

Legend, or tradition at least, says that every theater has at least one ghost. There are as many explanations of this as there are theaters. I know of a small college where plays were performed in the chapel. The woman for whom the chapel was named objected. It was claimed that she could be heard playing the organ late at night to cleanse the place.

My personal favorite is the one about the actor who died, perhaps even in the theater, before finishing a performance. They had never quite gotten it the way they wanted and keep coming back to finish, or to get that final round of applause. They didn't get the final laurels to rest on.

Pop says our ghost's name is Laura.

Harold James "Pop" Barnes is nearly a ghost in his own right. Now, nearly 100, he first "walked the boards" in Cedar Falls before World War II, just before the theater changed to a movie house. Just before the theater was changed back, Pop was one of the leaders of that process. Now he sort of haunts the place. He comes to an occasional rehearsal, usually on a Sunday afternoon, and usually with a care giver to help him.

Even though his body is failing, his mind is sharp and his memories clear. Directors covet his advice. Actors, too, but, being actors, don't always follow his advice as much. He knows this, and laughs, knowingly. I just like to hear him tell the stories of the theater's history. Every theater should have a Pop.

One of the stories was about Laura.

Laura St. Michaels was a young actress who died on the stage of the theater, in Pop's arms. It was one of the last stage plays to be done before the cinematic transformation.

There was a noise. Laura looked up. A falling stage light caught her directly in the chest. It is unlikely that even today's medical procedures could have saved her. Pop, only known as Harold then, was standing in for the leading man during the rehearsal. He was the first one to reach her. She was in great pain. Almost literally with her last breath, she finished the line she was to deliver, her last line in the play.

"I was very much in love with her," Pop would say. "I was sixteen and she was a beautiful woman of twenty-one." He always said this a bit wryly, but with a deep sadness evident behind his smile.

I've seen pictures of Laura St. Michaels, who was with a traveling troupe and just beginning a professional career. There was an ethereal look to her even before she took up permanent residence in our theater. She was quite lovely. She is eternally twenty-one.

Pop says she isn't noticed often. "Occasionally, if you're the last one to leave, just as you turn away, you'll catch a glimpse of her in the wings, waiting for her cue. Or you'll feel her brush by you. She isn't cold, like you hear about in ghost stories. There is a warm, kind feeling. You don't know where it comes from or even how you feel it. But you notice."

Pop has told this story often. Sometimes, in parts of it, there is a suggestion of a mischievousness wink. Most often, there is a smile as if remembering an old friend or a lost love.

"What about now?" I asked, concerning the moving things. I had talked to him a few days before Bob's board went missing.

"I don't know," he said, thoughtfully. "Costumes and props, I understand. I never heard of anything in the shop before. From what I remember, I don't think she would know one end of a screwdriver from the other."

He often spoke of Laura as though he'd had tea with her just last week.

"I'll tell you this: She seems to love this old place. She's very protective of it and everyone in it. Usually, it's a quick thing, some kind of warning, so what happened to her won't happen to anyone else. If she's around for more than a second or two, it's not something; it's someone."

He sounded so sure. Then he smiled. Did he believe what he just told me? Or did the old actor want me to believe it?

Bob puzzled over his missing board more than he usually did with missing things.

"I don't know if it will help," I said to him, "but Pop is sure it isn't Laura."

Bob was caught between laughing and being annoyed. I knew he would be.

Just then Gary burst on the scene. We were not surprised. Gary is not a quiet person. We knew who it was as soon as he opened the stage door and started up the stairs and down the hall.

"Hi, guys," he hollered, more boisterous than usual, which is to say a lot. "What a beautiful day!"

It was pretty nice for November.

"What did you do with my board?" Bob confronted him, pointing to the workbench where it was last seen.

"What board?" Gary replied, with unfeigned innocence. He usually responded to such questions in the manner by immediately going to the missing item.

Bob pointed again. "The one that was right there the day before yesterday."

"I don't know," Gary said with a smile. "I'll find it for you." He started for the plywood stack.

"I've already looked there," Bob stopped him. "I've looked everywhere I can think of. What were you doing in here last night?"

"Last night?" Gary seemed genuinely stumped.

"Didn't you come over to fool around in here last night?" Bob's tone was more fatherly than angry.

"No," Gary said openly, "I just got back in town this morning."

"Back in town?" Now, Bob was stumped.

"Yeah," Gary explained. "I had a couple of days off. I went to Newton to see my grandparents. It's Grandpa's eightieth birthday!"

There was a pause. No one knew where to go next.

"Okay," Bob said, getting his boss face on. "You haven't been here for a few days. I haven't been here for two. John?"

"Jim and I were here during a run-through," I answered. "Mostly we moved furniture around along with two college kids that help out. We were in and out of the shop. I don't remember anyone near the bench or moving any lumber."

"Basement!" Bob exclaimed. "Actors are always playing around with stuff. I'll bet one of them took it down there." He had begun to move almost as soon as he began his revelation. Gary and I followed.

Bob flipped the light switch at the top of the narrow stairs and started down. We turned at the bottom and stopped short. Nothing.

Well, not nothing. Chairs, small tables, desks and other odds and ends as usual were pushed back in corners and against walls. It created floor space where a dozen or less guys could change into costumes. In community theaters, even the idea of dressing rooms is adapted to necessity. During a production, a clothes rack would be there with the costumes neatly divided and marked for each character. Now, there were no racks. The cast would not be getting into costume for at least two more weeks.

Bob's idea that some actor had carelessly or playfully carried the missing square of plywood down here while heading down to change was blown away. Actors often wandered around down here even before costumes were ready, mostly out of curiosity, but it would be a long shot that they carried a board with them.

We looked around anyway, not only in this first area, but throughout the basement. We didn't go back into every corner. Some are hard to get to without carrying anything.

We returned to the shop empty handed.

Chucky was waiting for us.

Charles P. Wemyss was the director of the show. He had taught speech and drama at a community college in Missouri for fifteen or twenty years. He had directed plays there and at the local high school.

Ten years ago, he left that profession to join his brother-in-law in the real estate business. He is very good and has been very successful in that.

Memyss has a pleasant, broad, open face and a nice smile. Although beginning to thin in the front, his dark, wavy hair is very becoming. His body is a little odd. He dresses well to compensate for it. He usually wears long sleeves, even in the warmest weather. Once, when the air conditioning was off in the theater, even he was forced at last to remove his sport coat. The short-sleeved, white shirt underneath was nearly transparent from perspiration. Two things were revealed: First, he has a very doughy body from the neck down. This was not a big surprise. But, second, his arms were so thin in comparison that it was almost startling. I sort of pictured a snow man made by a child who used sticks to represent the arms.

He is a good director for our community theater. He knows what he is doing. Actors recognize that and respect his judgement. He likes to sit rather far back in the theater, just under the balcony as he watches rehearsals. From there, he yells to the actors. Of course, it isn't really yelling. It's projecting.

"Projecting" in the theater is a technique for making and actor's words heard clearly. For those who have perfected it, they can be heard as well in the last row in the balcony as in front of the stage, and that person in front will not feel they are being yelled at. It is a form of breath control and enunciation. In many places, it is a forgotten art because of the advent of sophisticated, individual microphones and computer controlled sound systems.

In personal interaction, Wemyss spoke much more quietly. However, it always felt like he was standing at least six inches closer than was absolutely necessary.

Chucky. He insisted that everyone call him "Chucky." And, annoyingly, he returned the favor.

"Johnny boy," he greeted me when I came from the basement. "There you are. I really need to talk to you."

After I reached puberty, no one still called me "Johnny," except my great-aunt Minnie. Her, I didn't mind. From "Chucky" I tolerated it.

Bob, of course, was "Bobby." Gary got lucky, since his name already ended in a "y." He tried to call Martha "Marty," but one look from her ended that. Some names threw him completely, "Jonah" for example. That always seemed to disappoint him.

Bob and Gary decided to work on another part of the set while "Chucky" and I went out on the stage area to talk.

"Well, Johnny boy," he began. His voice was soft and pleasant, but right in my face. "We've got a real problem."

"You mean because of Doc," I replied. I always studiously avoid saying, "Chucky."

"Yes. Terrible thing. Terrible," he said sincerely.

"Sorry for him, but I have to admit I have mixed emotions."

"I think we all do," I commiserated. The saying, "The show must go on," is almost always true, even when it almost seems callous.

"But, when we get right down to it, Johnny," he went on, "that's what we're faced with."

"So, what does it mean?" I said, suspicion suddenly sneaking up on me, as I felt Wemyss was doing.

He put his hand on my shoulder. "I need you, Johnny."

"What?" I had figured out that's where he was going, so my surprised tone was mostly self-defense.

"I've been on the phone all day." He was beginning to sound desperate. "There's no one out there who's available. Johnny, you've got to help us out."

If he'd said, "help me," I might have had more room to wriggle. He said, "help us." That tapped into my sense of being a team player. I always have been. It makes me feel good. I tried to argue anyway.

"I'm not an actor," I tried not to whimper. "I just push scenery around."

"Let's look at this logically," he countered, softening his tone even more. "You've been on the stage before. I know. They were just walk-ons, but you did them. This is just one scene. A few lines. You've already been around some the rehearsals, so you know what's happening."

"Now, wait a minute," I thought I had a way out – a straw to grab at. "That scene takes place on the apron. I'm behind the curtain setting up the next scene."

"That's how I know that you know the timing, Johnny," he said, with just a hint of triumph. "You know you don't have much time backstage, because the scene is so short."

"What about the crew? I can't just let go of that." I knew that sounded lame. Many of the actors already helped with scene changes. One replacement would not make a lot of difference.

Wemyss just looked a me. He knew I was out of arguments. He was gracious enough to pause to give me one last chance.

"I'll try," I said weakly.

"I know, Johnny," he said calmly. "We start back with rehearsals tomorrow night at seven." He handed me a script. "Thank you. Thank you very much."

He smiled and walked away. I thought I heard him let out a long sigh of relief.

My breathing had become very shallow.

The phrase, "everything is relative" became very clear.

Several years ago, my wife and I took a trip to Florida. We flew from Waterloo to St. Paul a day early because of an impending storm front. The next day when we the plane took off, the wind chill was minus forty. When we landed in Orlando, they were having a bit of a cold snap as well. Some people were running around in parkas. It was in the mid-fifties. We were in short sleeves because it was nearly 100 degrees warmer than where we had been. Relative.

I have a nice fire pit in my backyard. On a cool autumn night, it was a wonderful place to be. It was forty-eight degrees, but with my good neighbor, Alan, and a glass of very good bourbon, it was the warmest place I could want.

My heart rate and breathing returned to normal.

— three —

The days following my move from backstage to front were complicated, to say the least. I spent more time in my office that I had in years. Frost had gone to Georgia to visit his father and finish some business. Alone, I studied the script over and over. I walked up Main Street to stumble through rehearsals. Because my one scene involved just one other actor, Jim Butler, playing the judge, it wasn't as difficult as my mind had made it.

Unexpected complications came from Doc Christopher in two different ways.

The first involved the investigation into his death. The official theory seemed obvious and logical. An older man, walking at night, somehow wandered in front of a freight train. The train hadn't stopped. Fortunately, railroad companies keep meticulous records. The train and its crew were easily located. No one had seen anything. Even at a slow speed, at night, the incident would happen in a split second.

Sergeant Murphy, who was looking into it, called me. That was somewhat routine. I'm known to the department and Murphy. I'm an investigator.

I knew and worked with, so to speak, the victim. Preoccupied as I was, I'm afraid I blew off the phone call a little. All I said was that Christopher always parked his car "up that way," and that he went there after rehearsal that night. I had forgotten to mention the garage. I went back to my script.

I was on my third time through my scene one day, when the phone rang. It was Norman Corrigan.

Corrigan is president of Iowa Agribusiness Insurance, a wholly owned subsidiary of a large company headquartered in Des Moines. The parent company has me on retainer. I saved them several million dollars in a fraud case several years ago. They are still grateful. I usually dealt directly with Norman. His office is in Waterloo.

"Hello, John," came the big friendly voice. His voice belies his size. He is a smallish man, not quite completely bald, although he is a few years younger than I am. When you first meet him, you almost expect a squeaky, meek voice to come from his sweet, but rather comical face. His happy, nearly baritone voice startles you.

"Hello, Norm!" I nearly sang. I welcomed the interruption.

"Well," he said. "You're in a strange mood."

"It's complicated. I'll try to explain it to you sometime," I replied. "What can I do for you?"

"I've got a complication, too," he said. "Halleck called me from Des Moines. Wants me to ask you to look into something odd."

"Can't be any stranger than what I've gotten myself into," I laughed, without much humor.

"Unless you're looking into flying saucers, I've got you beat," Norm said. I heard confusion in his voice.

"Okay," I surrendered. "Mine is personal and more annoying than strange. What have you got?"

"I've got a beneficiary who doesn't want half a million dollars," he said with understandable astonishment.

"Who?" I joined his wonder. "Bill Gates?"

"Nope," he went on. "A welder. Just getting by from what I hear."

"What's his story?" I asked.

"The whole thing is strange from beginning to end," he began. "A guy just died a few days ago in an accident, and bang! There's this thing he put in the policy that says beneficiaries are to be notified immediately. You know, it usually takes up to a month, maybe two, if they aren't close by. The guy even called his agent a lot – like two or three times a year – to check on things. Most people buy insurance and forget about it except for paying the premiums. Of course, Halleck says he was suspicious from the beginning."

"Why is that?" I asked.

"Two million dollars! Divided equally among four people. Two brothers. Two sisters."

There was a pause. It was stunned silence on my end. Norm knew it would be and gave me the chance to catch my breath.

Most insurance companies are almost identical. It is in their little differences, for the most part, that makes one company better for each individual client. The other major difference is usually that client's relationship with a particular agent.

One similarity that I've seen in every company I've dealt with, big or small, is that they don't like surprises. That's why they have actuarial tables. Life's circumstances very often fall into neat categories. A grandmother passes away in her sleep at age 103? No problem. A man gets hit by a train at 10:15 p.m., on a Tuesday night on a seldom traveled street? Things like that don't fit the tables. They want more information.

"Anyway," Norm finally continued, "the first one we contacted, this welder, Anthony Davenport, says there must be a mistake. He never heard of the guy and doesn't know anyone who could possibly have that much money."

"Never heard of the guy?" I couldn't keep this one in. "Who leaves money to strangers?"

"I know! Right?" Norm laughed. "So, Halleck wants you to look into it. We can't seem to find out much about the guy, let alone his connection to the Davenports."

"Davenport. Is that the family name?" I was beginning to organize facts in my head.

"Yes. That's right," was the response. "Let me see."

In the pause, I could hear the rustling of papers through the phone.

"Okay. Here we go," he began. "The brothers: Anthony Davenport. A welder in South Dakota. Michael Davenport. A truck driver in Ohio. The sisters: Bonnie Davenport Williams. Housewife in Nebraska. Laurel Davenport. Secretary in the U.S. consulate in Spain."

"Spain?" I pretty much shouted into the phone when the light went off in my head. I certainly startled Norm. I heard him on the other end: "What the hell!"

"Sorry, Norm," I apologized quickly. Then I added slowly and carefully: "Was the dead guy's name 'Christopher?'"

Silence. I was sure that I had surprised him. More than surprised him.

"Now, wait a minute, Thompson," he said. I knew he was very serious if he called me "Thompson" rather than "John." "Don't tell me you knew this guy?"

"Geoffrey Christopher. With a 'G', right?"

"Okay, now. This was weird enough before." Norm did not like being perplexed. "How the hell did you know that name?"

I explained as calmly as I could, especially the part about the conversation where Doc had mentioned "kids scattered from Spain to South Dakota."

"Are you telling me that this guy, Christopher, was these people's father and they never knew it?" Norm's voice was full of amazement and doubt.

"If not, it's an amazing coincidence," I said.

"Two guys named 'Joe' walk into a store back to back and buy the same brand of coffee is an amazing coincidence," Norm said, logically. "This thing? No. Can you look into it?"

"Of course, Norm," I replied. My curiosity was raging. I would have looked into it even if Norm hadn't asked.

"Good," he said with an air of finality. "I'll tell Halleck and get in touch with the Davenports again."

We exchanged some cordial back and forth for about twenty minutes. Norm did most of the talking, but it was brief, for him. He and his wife, Willa, have four kids, now grown and with kids of their own. They also have two foster kids in their home at any given time. Over the years, they've personally changed the lives of more than a dozen, all of whom keep in touch. They are the kind of people who change the world for the better.

I called Sergeant Murphy. It had been nearly a week since we had talked. I wondered what else they may have found out about Geoffrey "Doc" Christopher.

The answer was not, "nothing." It was less than nothing.

"Man, oh, man, Thompson," Murphy whispered, "who was this guy?"

"What do you mean?" I asked, more puzzled than he.

"We can't find out anything," he said, his voice rising. "His house is locked up tight. We can't find his car. We can't find any records. Even his driver's license seems to be phony."

"Phony?" I expected a surprise or two. I didn't expect a man who never was.

"Yeah," he said in amazement. "There's no record of it. It looks like every legit license I've ever seen, and I've seen a thousand. In the system, it doesn't exist. I even called Charlotte. She came up empty."

"Charlotte!" I was stunned. If Charlotte can't find something, it had to be buried deep. Maybe, even literally underground."

"Didn't you tell me," Murphy continued, "that Christopher, or whoever he was, parked his car on Lincoln, near where he was killed?"

"Oh, shit," I gasped. "The garage."

"What garage?" Murphy shouted into the phone.

"I'm sorry, Murphy." I really was. "I was kind of preoccupied when we talked, and I didn't think it would be complicated. Christopher kept his car in a garage up there. Actually, the house used to belong to my Uncle Floyd. The garage was built long after it changed hands."

There was silence. I know Murphy was cussing me out, but he was good enough not to do it out loud.

"Do you have the address," he asked, at last, very calmly.

"I'm afraid not," I answered, more than a little sheepishly. "But you can't miss it. There's not much there anymore. It's the farthest east and the oldest of the three houses that are left there. The garage is set kind of far back of the house."

"Okay," he said, thoughtfully. "I know the one."

"Can I meet you there?" I didn't know what I could do that would be of any help, but I thought I should offer.

"Yeah. Okay," he replied. "I've got to check on something else, first, so I'll be there in about an hour.

"Good," I said. "See you then."

I sat for a few minutes trying to clear my head. It was no use. I decided to walk up to Lincoln Avenue. I put on my jacket and headed up Main Street.

The crisp November air certainly perked up my senses, physical as well as mental. The sky was bright blue with a few small, fat clouds cruising by. Main Street wasn't particularly busy, but it would likely pick up in a few minutes as the noon hour approached. As I passed the theater, I tried to wave at Shirley in the front office. With the glare on the glass, I couldn't see in. I hoped she waved back.

As I crossed the bridge over the river, I realized I had a problem. With no more buildings to stop it, the wind was trying to cut my ears off one piece at a time. I could see very clearly, lying on my desk five blocks behind me, my nice warm stocking cap.

Rather than turn at the north end of the bridge, I continued on to the railroad tracks. They lie twenty yards beyond where Doc should have turned to get to his car. Why didn't he turn?

I saw nothing on the south side of the tracks. I didn't want to look on the north side. I hadn't asked for any details, but I couldn't imagine how a man could be hit and killed by a train without leaving, well, a mess. I'm not particularly squeamish about such things. I investigated several accidents. True, I don't usually show up until a few days later, still, I've seen more than an average person would. I once found a missing hand ten days after it had been lost.

Mostly, I just wanted to speculate on the "how" and "why." Did Doc have a sudden urge to use the substitute men's room of the trees beyond the tracks? Did something or someone draw his attention such that he wanted to see what it was? Either way, why was he so unaware that he walked into a moving train? Had he tried to beat it? What was his hurry?

To Doc's cautious nature that I had witnessed the day I saw him come from the garage, I would now add, with the new information, secretive. What ever drew him to the tracks could not have been something too common.

I crossed the tracks. I saw nothing.

It had been a week, but I expected to see some signs. Even if the authorities had cleaned up the scene, there would be traces of the clean-up. I had to assume that it did not happen here where the sidewalk ended just before the tracks. I decided to follow the tracks east, in the direction of the garage that Doc used.

I walked slowly in the biting wind, looking carefully on both sides. Still, I saw nothing unusual. When I finally, looked up, I was twenty-five yards beyond the garage.

I stood staring, blankly, at the garage. Then I looked back down the tracks to the west. Still a blank. I know recent days had been confusing, but how could I miss this?

I started toward the garage. I was nearly to the corner of Lincoln and Logan when I saw the police car coming down the street. I crossed Logan and waited on the corner. The squad car turned, passed me and parked in the gravel driveway.

"They" were Sergeant Murphy and Officer Isaac Jakes.

Murphy is a twenty-year veteran. He is a medium sized man with brown hair tending toward reddish. He keeps rather fit, but a little paunchy. He's a good cop and has the respect of all on the force and the citizens of Cedar Falls.

Isaac Jakes is something of a local legend. He was not only the team leader in four sports – football, basketball, track and baseball – but was one of the best in the state in all four. He had scholarship offers for each from several colleges, in state and out. There were betting pools about which he would choose. He choose the U.S. Army.

He had promised his grandfather, who had gotten a Purple Heart for his service in Viet Nam, that he would continue the family tradition that went back to the Civil War. Colleges may have been disappointed. United States citizens were not. He continued his leadership: Sergeant, Bronze Star, two Purple Hearts.

Six years after leaving high school and with shrapnel wounds in his legs, he decided he would limit his athletic endeavors to coaching kids. He also chose to continue serving others by joining the police department.

He is still amazingly fit. He is also one of the smartest people I know. No matter what he chose to do, I know he would be one of the best.

Jakes is African American in a town where that minority is one quarter the national average. His celebrity and race make him in demand for many things. He knows that some of that is a form of tokenism and lip service, but he always uses it to make people aware of the truths they try to gloss over with tokenism and lip service.

Did I mention he is one of the smartest people I know?

I walked down to meet them.

"Out for a little stroll?" Murphy greeted me cordially.

I'm sure I would have come up with the perfect come back if my ears weren't ready to fall off. I just shrugged.

"We have to notify the owner," Murphy said nodding toward the house. "Why don't you wait here. Out of the wind."

I saw the smile he tried to hide. Jakes didn't try.

I stepped between the car and the garage. Out of the wind.

Murphy and Jakes walked to the back door of the house and knocked. The door was opened almost immediately by a woman in blue jeans and a purple sweatshirt. She must have noticed our arrival and waited for the knock. I couldn't hear them, but I knew Murphy was explaining what was going on. The woman reacted strongly once. I assumed that was the first she had heard of Christopher's death. I more than assumed that Murphy handled it as kindly as these things can be handled. Just before the end of the conversation, a girl of about five suddenly appeared clinging to the woman's leg. They continued talking for several minutes.

"She doesn't know much," Murphy reported when he returned. "They virtually sold the garage to Christopher. He rented it for two hundred dollars a month. Pays them three years at a time, in cash. $7,200. No questions asked. They just started their third three-year deal. It allows her to stay home mostly. Two young kids. The husband was able to take his time changing jobs. Has a pretty good one now. Paid off their car. Kids have had better Christmas. They're doing better than they thought they would for years. Probably move to a better neighborhood next June. One with more families anyway."

He looked at my face.

"Who was this guy, Thompson?" he asked, not expecting an answer.

We went to the side door of the garage. It was locked, twice. Murphy bent over to look at one of the locks carefully.

"I've never seen a lock like this one," he said.

"I have," said Jakes, suddenly. "Don't fiddle with that knob too much."

Murphy stood up slowly and looked a Jakes very closely for a few second.

"What the hell are you saying, Jakes?" Murphy whispered sternly.

"IED training," he replied, coolly. "It was a lock we studied. Not all bombs were out in the sand by the roads. In some cities, offices and apartments might be rigged, too. 'Improvised' is a stretch when some are pretty sophisticated."

"Bomb!" Murphy grunted in a lower whisper.

I said the same. That is, my mouth moved, but I don't think I actually made a sound.

"If it is like what I've seen, just jiggling the knob won't do anything," Jakes lectured. "But turning it hard and trying to force the door might."

"With kids playing in the yard?" Murphy could not keep this down to a whisper. Threatened kids turned Murphy into another being. One you don't want to mess with.

"If he paid that much, in cash," Jakes continued, "it probably came with the idea of expected, complete autonomy. Privacy. And a warning. Not a waring about a bomb, just some sort of 'or else.'"

"Who the hell was this guy," Murphy's anger was

very evident. "Let's look around." Murphy and I went west; Jakes went east. The back, the east side was just a blank wall. We came around to the south side. There was a window, approximately opposite the door on the north side. It was about eighteen inches square. The bottom edge was about four feet from the ground. We both looked at it carefully without touching it.

Jakes was a little slower coming around from the east end where the bay door is. He probably looked without touching that as well. Murphy nodded toward the window. Jakes nodded in acknowledgement and went to the window.

With the sun mostly behind him, there was a lot of glare. He tried to block it out as best he could. Being six three helped a lot.

"There's a car," Jakes reported without turning. "Gray. Might be an older Impala."

"It's hard to see," he said, with a little disappointment, "but I think I see wires." He turned to us and continued. "Worst case: the door is wired and so is the window. It would seem a safe bet to say the car entrance is, too."

Silence. We all knew the answer to what needed to happen next, but no one wanted to say it out loud.

"What do we do about the family in the house?" Jakes spoke up first.

"I've got an idea," I offered. It almost surprised me as much as the other two. I was surprised that I could form words, but my idea seemed sound. They looked at me.

"I'll tell them I'm an insurance investigator. You two are here at my request to take care of any legal questions. Something about the car. Then I'll say we think there may a fire hazard, so, just as a precaution, maybe they should go somewhere for a couple of hours. She might buy it."

"She's pretty sharp," Murphy said. "If she buys it, it's because she wants to buy it. She'll do it for the kids."

"Yeah. I know," I said. "I'm going to lie my best anyway."

"Do it," Murphy authorized. "We'll be in the car."

I came back in less than five minutes.

"Her mother will be here in half an hour," I reported.

"We'll wait to call it in," Murphy said. He paused, looking at me.

"For the kids," I confirmed.

It was less than half an hour when an old blue Saturn pulled up behind us. A slender woman with bright, white hair was driving. When she got out, I noticed a pink streak in her hair. I also noticed her scowl when she looked at us. She was wearing sweatpants, tie-dyed in pinks and yellows, and a University of Iowa hoody. She pulled up the hood and walked quickly to the house.

Five minutes later, she, the younger woman, the little girl and a smaller child, wrapped up, were gone. Murphy called the hazard team.

Murphy clearly told them no sirens, but a fire truck,

an equipment truck with flashing lights, and two more squad cars are not unnoticeable. For the first time, I was grateful that this neighborhood was nearly deserted.

After some discussion, Isaac Jakes was put in charge. Bombs are not as common in Cedar Falls, Iowa as they were where he had spent considerable time. As he and two others began examining the garage, officers were sent out as a kind of perimeter guard. They were told, and would tell any curious neighbors, that there were some illegal fireworks that had to be removed.

Jakes found a small hole in one wall. He was excited. It would give them access via an important piece of equipment: a camera. The lens of the camera and a small light were on the end of a long flexible tube, about as big around as a standard pencil. Passed through the hole, it would give the team eyes on whatever was inside.

Jakes had been right about the door. The car blocked much of the view, but part of the window frame could be seen as well. There were wires. They were unsure of the bay door, but it was a safe assumption to believe it two had wires.

It was Jakes opinion that the safest entrance, would be through the roof. The booby traps were most likely aimed at someone trying to gain entrance at night. Even at night, it would be hard to cut through a roof and not be noticed. Bombs there would be extreme. Christopher wouldn't have needed that. Probably.

Now firefighters with axes were in charge. Getting on the roof was the easy part. A big guy raised his axe, then hesitated. He looked at Jakes. No matter how many times he might have done something similar, on the job or in training, this was different. Having a final nod from someone whose opinion he trusted was necessary. Jakes gave it to him with a confident look. The axe bit into the roof. Everyone flinched. The man on the roof hesitated again, took a deep breath, and struck another blow. Soon, he was working with a strong steady rhythm. Our breathing became more regular, too.

After a dozen or so blows, another man carrying a pry bar joined the first firefighter. Jakes went up, too. The two firefighters worked efficiently and carefully. Jakes supervised, but only a little. He had volunteered to go through the hole and wanted it to be right. No one was surprised. No one questioned it. It was an assumption in the same class as assuming the sun will come up tomorrow.

After about twenty minutes, the three men on the roof stopped. They looked at the hole and beyond for at least a minute. Jakes looked a Murphy and nodded. Murphy nodded back. The man with the axe said something to Jakes that I couldn't hear. Jakes shook his head. He got on his hands and knees and bent down until his head passed through the hole. He straightened up and removed his jacket, still on his knees. He took a deep breath and with grace and agility disappeared through the hole in a single move.

The only ones who could see Jakes now were the two companions on the roof. They watched intently in an attitude that said they were ready to go to his aid in an instant. The only problem I could foresee would not leave any room for anyone to aid in any way, least of all the guys on the roof. But then, these are the kind of people who think of saving someone first, and other consequences after. Thank God for them.

All the rest of us had to go on was sound. We heard the thump of when Jakes landed on the car and a swoosh that we supposed was his sliding to the floor, gracefully, I'm sure. Then it was mostly silence. It's a strange feeling. Silence gives you the fear of not knowing, but at the same time the sound you're afraid to hear makes you more anxious.

After several minutes that felt like hours, there was a scraping sound followed by a series of clicks. The side door opened, and Jakes walked out. Everyone felt like cheering. It came out as a long, united sigh of relief.

Jakes was relieved, too.

"Not as bad as I thought," he told Murphy, as though he was commenting on the weather. Chief Moorman, who had arrived just before Jakes had gone through the hole, clapped him on the back.

"It was rigged about as I expected," Jakes continued, "but it was made to be loud and flashy rather then deadly. It would probably only injure the first one through the door. It would certainly wake up the people in the house and maybe the other houses, too. It was aimed at the legs. It would have made it real hard for that person to get away on their own."

"What about the others?" Murphy asked quickly. "The window and the car entrance."

"They're wired, too." Jakes answered. "I haven't looked too closely yet."

"Alright," Chief Moorman took command. "Let's get this..." he stopped himself from saying bomb out loud. "...stuff out of there and get it boxed up."

Of course, he was referring to special boxes made to hold explosives.

It took two hours of careful movements. The window was rigged in a similar manner to the door: a very loud blast would blow up in the face of anyone trying to get through it. The car bay door was different. There didn't seem to be any way of opening it from the outside. Inside, the bomb mechanism – pretty well hidden – was designed to fuse the door in place so it couldn't be opened at all. Additions to that were also intended to be loud, rather than deadly. Everyone admitted that it was both ingenious and cruel, despite the care to avoid hurting innocent by-standers.

The obvious explosives only took a few minutes. Most of the time was spent looking for things they could not see. Had Christopher installed some other surprises in case someone breeched the main entrances? Special care was given to the car, which would seem to be the main target of an intruder.

Except for the booby traps, it was the only thing in the garage. It was the last thing removed.

There had been no bombs or other dangers in the twelve-year-old Chevy, but there were some surprises. If officers hadn't been looking for surprises of some kind, they would have been missed. First, two nine-millimeter Barettas had been concealed in very clever pockets, one on each side of the driver's seat. Under the back seat, there was a sawed-off shotgun, a box of shells, and a bag containing very carefully wrapped ten-dollar bills. One thousand of them.

While they were loading the car on to the back of a trailer, I called Dorothy Nicol, the mother of Mariah Patterson, the woman of the house. I told her everything was fine now and repeated the fireworks story that I'm sure she would not believe but would not ask for another. Chief Moorman would stay to greet her and give her an official word or two along the same lines. At least the now empty garage might give her some peace of mind.

Murphy offered me a ride back to my office. I gladly accepted. I had already spent most of the afternoon in his squad car, out of the wind.

We drove down Main in silence. It was necessary for any of us to mention the same question one more time: Who was this guy?

Although we did not know it then, some answers were coming.

– four –

Most of the rest of the day was a wash as I tried to file away in my mind what I had seen. I had no usual categories for some of it. I also shuffled through papers on my desk concerning other matters, hoping the change would clear my head. It was hard to bring the printed words into focus. When my phone rang, it startled me. Then, I felt a sense of relieve to be interrupted. It was Norm.

"John," he boomed, "I thought I might get lucky. Working late, huh?"

"Late?" I puzzled. I looked out the window. The street was lit up for the nighttime. I glanced at the clock on my desk: 5:27. The early darkness of November had come unnoticed.

"Yes," I finally said. "It's been a hell of a day."

"Sorry," Norm replied. He had recognized my strange tone. "I hope it won't be too inconvenient, but I'm coming to see you tomorrow. I'm bringing Tony Davenport with me."

"Tony Davenport?" I asked, stupidly.

"Wow. You are out of it," Norm said, kindly. "I

should have cleared it with you before I made the arrangements. Anthony Davenport. The welder from South Dakota. Beneficiary of Geoffrey Christopher."

"Oh, yeah," the recognition kicked in. "What's going on?"

"I've been on the phone all day," Norm explained. "Called Davenport. Called Halleck. Called Davenport. Made arrangements. Hallack wants you to talk to him face-to-face. I told him you couldn't get away right now, but he insisted. You know how he is. So he said, 'Bring the mountain to Mohammed.' Who the hell says that anymore?

"Turns out Davenport isn't too busy right now. Where he works is having a big downturn. Hallack is sending a company jet to get him.

"Davenports never even been on a plane before, so it took a little convincing. Also took a little juggling to find an airport. A lot of space between airports in South Dakota, especially ones that can handle jets."

"If he really doesn't know Christopher, what good will it do to bring him here?" I asked, when Norm took a breath.

"Hallack," he said, explaining it all, "he says you have a way with people. You can fill in the blanks better than anybody. And the two million makes him nervous. The policy is fine. The circumstances are making him crazy."

"I hate to tell you this, Norm," I said carefully, "but what I found out today is going to make it worse."

There was pause as Norm tried to work it out in

his head. Then he asked, nervously, "What the hell could make this worse?"

"We're pretty sure the name 'Christopher' was an alias. The business the guy was supposedly retired from was probably crime. In a big way."

A longer pause. "What do you mean 'we'?" Norm asked.

"Cedar Falls police. I was with Murphy all afternoon." I explained. "We found his car along with guns and cash. A lot of cash."

"Who the hell was this guy?" Normed whispered more to himself than to me.

"You, too?" I smarted off.

"What?" he snapped into the phone.

"I think Murphy asked me that question four or five times today," I said. "I've asked myself a hundred times."

"Well, get ready to get asked a hundred more times!" Norm doesn't like twists and turns. He's pretty casual in his personal life. In business, he's an information neat freak. He wants things in a straight line whenever possible.

"What time tomorrow?" I asked.

"Early. We'll be there at nine." Norm was all business now.

"The plane will get in that early?" I was a little amazed.

"The plane is due here in less than an hour," Norm explained. "I've got them checked into a motel already, and I'll take them to dinner."

"Them?" I asked.

"Oh, yeah," Norm went on, "The whole family's coming. Wife. Two kids. Part of the deal. Davenport's still convinced we got the wrong guy. I told him it would ease our minds to give his family a little vacation. Our way of apologizing for bothering him with something this big or celebrating if we have the right people."

Norman Corrigan is a great salesman.

"That's fine." I answered him. "I'll see you then." Our good-byes were brief.

I hadn't eaten since early morning and I had a rehearsal, a complete run-through, at seven. Between my office and the theater there is a wide variety of possibilities. I didn't have time for the more delicately prepared cuisine and something heavy wouldn't sit well right before rehearsal. I decided on a chef's salad and chose the closest place that served one.

Dinner went well. Rehearsal went well. The rest of my night did not. Christopher haunted my thoughts. I dozed off and on and finally gave it up around five a.m. I made coffee. I puttered around with breakfast and odds and ends in the kitchen. I checked the weather, both on TV and in person. I confirmed what the meteorologist had said. It was colder than yesterday and there were snowflakes in the air. The flakes melted as soon as they touched anything. After sunrise, they would probably disappear from the air, too.

When I ran out of ideas for killing time, I went

to the office. I was sitting at my desk before eight. More time to kill. More puttering around. I thought of using the computer to look up "puttering around" to see where it originated. I didn't.

At almost exactly nine o'clock, Norm appeared at my door. I'd left both the inner and outer doors open. He was wearing a dark gray overcoat and hat to match.

"Hi, John," came the friendly greeting as we shook hands. "Temperature took a nosedive, didn't it?"

"You've got to expect it," I replied. "It's November."

"That's right," he said, and turned to the man behind him. "This is Tony Davenport."

"Nice to meet you," I said, extending my hand.

"Nice to meet you," he replied in kind, rather quietly.

He was a man in his late thirties of average height with a strong face, even with his worried look. He wore blue jeans and a shirt with light blue vertical stripes, over which he wore a well-worn Tampa Bay Buccaneers coat. He had on a faded ball cap with an unfamiliar logo containing the word "Molton."

"You can hang up your things over there," I said, indicating a coat rack, and closing the outer door. "I've got a fresh pot of coffee ready."

I went into the office to start pouring. They joined me in less than a minute, taking the chairs I'd already arranged for them.

"Cream or sugar, Mr. Davenport?" I offered. I

already knew that Norman liked three packets of sugar, but I still cringed a little when I put them next to him.

"No," Davenport replied. "Just black."

I handed him a cup, grabbed mine and sat down.

"Mr. Davenport," I began as kindly as I could, "There's nothing I can say that can really put you at ease. We're just trying to find out the whole story."

"I haven't told him much of anything, John," Norm added quickly. "I thought it best if you filled him in first."

Norm was passing the buck. He and I knew it; I tried not to glare at him.

"If it helps any, Mr. Davenport," I continued, "we're all almost as confused as you are."

"Tony," he said, seeming to relax just a little. "Nobody calls me 'Mr. Davenport.' It sounds weird."

Okay, Tony," I smiled. "I like that. I'm John. This is Norm."

"Good," he said emphatically satisfied. "Now, what is this all about? What am I doing here?"

I liked the fact that he wanted to get right to it. At the same time, I knew there were some things that maybe we would not get to soon, if at all.

"Let's start with what we all know," I used my most business-like voice. "A man by the name of Geoffery Christopher died. His life insurance policy seems to have named you and your siblings as beneficiaries. I assume someone has tried to double check that."

I looked at Norm. He explained, "Yes. The policy had your full names and exact addresses. After you told us there must be a mistake, we went over it very carefully. I really don't see how there could be a mistake."

Tony just shook his head. "It can't be possible," was written on his face.

"There are two reasons you're in my office in Cedar Falls, Iowa," I went on. "First, I am an investigator for this insurance company and some others. Odd things happen from time to time. I check them out. Second, strange as it may sound, I knew this Geoffrey Christopher."

Tony jerked his head toward me, totally surprised.

"I didn't know him very well," I assured him quickly. "We crossed paths from time to time. He didn't talk very much, and I didn't press."

"Did he talk about us? My brother and sisters?" His voice had more concern than curiosity.

"Not exactly," I said, then, I decided to lie a little, or at least make a wide curve around the truth.

"We were talking one day. Well, that is, a friend and I were talking. Christopher was close by. I mentioned how spread out my kids are – one in Chicago; one in Los Angeles. Doc mentioned some brothers and sisters spread out from 'Spain to South Dakota.'"

"Doc?" Tony asked, naturally confuse.

"Oh, sorry," I apologized. "Some how he had picked up that nickname. It was what most people called him. I really don't know where it came from. Like I said, he didn't talk much."

"I see," said Tony, thinking it over. "Spain to South Dakota?" He was obviously stunned by that revelation.

"I'm afraid I just assumed he was talking about his own family," I said softly.

"Can't be!" Tony said emphatically, maybe too emphatically. "My father's been gone a long time." There was a strange determination in his voice. I would have to be very careful.

"I see," I tried to make it sound as if I completely agreed with him. "In that case, there must be some other connection. Perhaps through your mother's family."

"I don't see how," Tony explained. "My grandparents were farmers in Ohio, where I grew up. We lived with them after my father was gone. Then, they lost the farm during the farm crisis of the eighties. Mom married...."

He stopped himself suddenly. Was he about to say a name, or something else?

He went on. "Mom married a few years before that. Uncle Bill, Mom's older brother, did a lot of odd jobs trying to help out. He died about ten years ago. Never had a family. Uncle Jim, the youngest, was one of the last of the shade tree mechanics, as they used to call them. A jack slipped. He lived on disability for the rest of his life."

"And your mom," I asked quietly.

"She's dead, too." He closed that door so quickly and so hard, I knew it would not be opened easily. I looked at Norm. I had to go on asking questions, but how.

I pressed ahead as carefully as I could manage. "I can see this is a sore spot with you, but I have to ask. Can you tell me about your mother?"

His face softened a little. He obviously loved her very much. It didn't last long. His face got dark. Very dark. I knew he was having a struggle.

"He killed her," he hissed softly. I could tell he had wanted to say that out loud for a long time.

"That bastard!" he suddenly exploded, standing up. It was a primal scream. He started stalking around the room like he was looking for something to break.

Norm rose to go after him. I grabbed his arm. Davenport needed to get something out of his system. Needed it desperately. It took him a full two minutes before he could stop walking. He was shaking all over.

"Tony," I said calmly. He was staring at the wall. "Tony!" I was still calm, but just a little louder.

He turned toward me. The pain, anger and sorrow in his face were like an abstract painting done in bold colors, blending and contrasting at the same time.

"Tony," I said again. "You need to tell us what happened. Not for us. For you. Please."

Tony sat down. After a few deep breaths, he stopped shaking. Then, he began, low and slow.

"My mother died eleven years ago. She died

screaming in the night. She'd been hospitalized under sedation and close observation for years. She was always high strung. Fragile. It took most of her strength to get through raising her children until we could function mostly on our own. I've been working nearly full time since I was thirteen years old. Laurel is the only one of us who finished high school. Worked her way through college, too. It took her seven years.

"Mom kept getting worse. We were living with Grandma and Grandpa. Grandma could calm her down, but it took more and more. The nightmares in the night were the worst. As we got older and went out on our own, they got more frequent.

"Mike still lived at home, but he became a long-distance trucker. He'd be gone a week at a time. Sometimes longer. When he came home, Mom always greeted him like a soldier coming home from a terrible war. She'd cry for hours.

"Grandpa's lungs were giving out after a lifetime of smoking. Then, Grandma had a stroke. She went to a nursing home. Grandpa had to go a few months later. The day after he left, Mom disappeared. We found her two days later in the barn at the farm where she grew up. The deputy who found her said she threw herself at his feet, begging him not to kill her babies. They took her away."

Tony paused. He was seeing it all again right before his eyes.

I put my hand on his shoulder. "Stop, Tony," I

said, trying to keep it together myself. "This is too much."

"No!" he said, staring straight ahead. "I have to face it head on or it will sneak up on my like it did Mom." Then, in almost a whisper, "I need to tell it all."

He took deep breaths again and went on.

"When I was six – Mikey was not yet one – that was the last time I saw my father. He took us to Grandma and Grandpa's. Mom wasn't there. I never saw him again. When Mom got there a few days later, Grandma told us, me, mostly, that she was very sick.

"For a long time, I thought my mother's illness had driven my father away. No one said anything about him. Once or twice, in my childhood, I said something like, 'Mommy's not sick anymore. Can Daddy come home?' The looks I got soon put an end to that. It didn't take long for me to figure out that everything was just the opposite of what I had thought. One time Mom mumbled something like, 'He told me. He told me.' I stopped wondering what that meant.

"I think I was fifteen the first time she woke me up in the middle of the night. 'Tony! Tony!' she was yelling. When I came around, she grabbed me and hugged me tight, saying, 'Thank God! Thank God!' Grandma came into get her. Mom had an envelope in her hand.

"'He's trying again. He's trying again.' She cried.

'No,' Grandma said, 'No dear. He's gone. He's long gone. He can't hurt us.'

'Look! Look!' she cried again, shaking the envelope. 'He's trying again. He'll come back! He'll come back!'

"Then she stopped, looking around wildly and whispering, 'I've got to burn it.' Then she ran out.

"Grandma couldn't run, but I could. I found her in the kitchen. She had turned on the stove and thrown the envelope into the fire. I grabbed a towel and knocked it to the floor. I started stomping on it with my bare feet.

"When I yelled, 'Ow!' that seemed to snap her out of her daze. She got me to a chair and started taking care of my feet. Grandma had gotten there, turned off the stove and helped with my foot. I wasn't really hurt. After a minute or two, Grandma was able to take Mom back to bed. I heard her say, 'He always finds a way to hurt people. He always finds a way.'

"After a couple of other similar things, I was sure she was talking about my father. The envelope had a check in it. It wasn't the first one. It wouldn't be the last. She always burned them. She burned her fingers a lot doing that. Not always accidentally. I was an adult before I had the nerve to ask why she burned them. God knows we needed the money.

"She got hysterical. 'No!' she would yell. 'It's from the devil! It's from Satan. Burn it! Burn it! Don't let him get you like he got me! I'm damned! Damned to hell!'

"I never asked again.

"A couple of years later, I got a check for five thousand dollars. It was a cashier's check, so only the name of the bank. I kept it for a month before I burned it. The next year, I got another. I burned it right away. It happened five years in a row. I checked with my brother and sisters. They had the same. Twenty checks in five years from twenty different banks all over the country. We burned one hundred thousand dollars.

"The next year we each got a card, a plain blank card. Inside was printed, 'I won't send anymore checks.' And that was that."

Now, there was a long pause. Norm and I had to wait. There was nothing to say.

"You've got the wrong guy," Tony said at last. "One way or another, you've got the wrong guy."

"Tony," I tried to begin, "We aren't here to hurt you. Our job is to help people when we can. Geoffrey Christopher was a retired businessman. He was eccentric. He may have just picked your family at random."

Tony's expression and posture changed. There was hope, just a glimmer, but real hope. I had the feeling he had not had that much in his life. Even if it was only from a fairy tale that I had just invented.

"Look," I went on, "We've been operating on guesses. It isn't every day that someone leaves money to people he doesn't even know, but it does happen."

I turned to Norm. "You remember that guy in southern Iowa several years ago. Retired custodian at the courthouse. Had no family. Lived in a tiny apartment. Wore clothes until they wore out. He left a million dollars to some children's fund."

"Yes! Yes!" Norm perked up. Tony's story had nearly put him in a coma. Now he had that glimmer of hope, too. "And there was that school librarian! Oh, where was that? Out west somewhere. Wyoming, maybe."

"Wait, a minute," Tony interrupted, "I remember that." The darkness from his face was gone. Maybe it wasn't from his soul yet, but at least new life was coming to his face.

I grabbed it with both hands. "Like I said, we went where these things usually lead, the obvious way. These other things only happen about once every ten years. We didn't really think to look up who Doc really was."

I used "Doc" very intentionally. It would make him seem like even more of a quiet eccentric.

"I never thought of that," said Tony, both doubtful and hopeful at the same time.

"Now, look," I said, almost carelessly. I was careful to do so. "We just don't know who this guy really was. I'm sorry. It just seemed so obvious, so simple. I was busy with some other things, so I was just going through the motions. Norm, is putting you up for a few days – and that's the least we can do under the circumstances – isn't that right Norm?"

"Certainly!" Norm joined in heartily. "We didn't know we'd be putting you through so much."

"I know of a couple of events going on right now," I cut Norm off. I didn't want him going back down that hard road, even by way of apology. "You can have a little vacation. Take it easy. Enjoy yourself."

"You and Brenda and the kids," Norm prompted.

"Norm!" I jumped, without actually leaving my chair. Anything to seem to be other than what I was actually feeling. "You didn't mention the kids." I turned to Tony. "How old are they?"

"Maddie, Madison, is twelve," he began, caught a little off guard, as I had hoped. "Peyton is nine. Carter is seven."

"Great!" I beamed. "There's a place here in town where they bring in big shows. They're doing a Charlie Brown thanksgiving thing. You know, it's live but with people in costumes and wearing those big foam heads for the different characters. I won't promise – last minute, you know – but I'm pretty sure I can get some tickets for tomorrow night. I know a guy who's pretty good with that kind of thing."

"Hey," Norm jumped out of his chair in joy. "I know that guy. It's practically a guarantee!"

Norm was the guy. Because of his on-going work with children, he had a standing order for a block of tickets for such shows. He took a lot of kids who normally would have no chance to see such things.

"Tony," Norm went on with his hand on Tony's shoulder. "I can't help but think I've dragged you off on a wild goose chase. On top of that, I dredged up some painful memories. I know you've had a tough time in recent years. So, for the next few days, you don't worry about anything. The motel has a good indoor pool. I know every restaurant in town from burgers to steaks. And there's a couple of museums that have things for the kids, too. Come on. We'll go have some fun and let John do the work."

Norm grinned a me. I chuckled back. Even Tony smiled, a little.

They got their coats, went down the hall and down the stairs like two old friends who were having a reunion. In Norm's hands, Tony would be all right, or at least as right as he could be with his history.

A plan was forming in my head. It was complicated. I was going to need a lot of bits of information. Some of it I would get from Murphy. It would involve things he might not want to share with me very freely. I hoped it wouldn't take a court order. In this case, when I explained about the family involved, I thought he would go out of his way to get it done. Unofficially, of course.

For a lot of it, I was going to need some deep computer digging. Fortunately, I knew a computer wizard: Frost. He had a way of finding anything with a digital footprint, even things that other computer geeks couldn't see. I didn't ask him how he did it. In fact, I didn't even know how to ask. It was too far beyond me. I would talk with him first thing in the morning.

Too much information. Usually, people say that for things they don't want to hear. In this case, for me, it was all coming too fast. A week ago, an odd guy that I knew, but not even as well as I thought, died in an unusual accident. Today, that guy seems to have been a criminal hiding in plain sight who also may or may not have driven his wife insane and left his four children with years of trauma.

How was I going to handle it? Boone's.

Boone's is one of the last of the old-time beer joints. That's what people called them back in the day, a day that was getting farther a farther away.

"Beer joint" can be misleading to those who have not had the privilege of knowing one firsthand. They picture a dark, dingy, dirty old place filled with dark, dingy, dirty old men. There have been some like that. Most are not. I should say, "were not." Most of them are gone. The places were taken over by bistros and microbreweries.

The ones I knew were Boone's and Joe's Place. Yes. That was the real name. Where Joe's used to be is now a strip mall. Boone's is just where it has always been, as far as I know from the beginning of the town. Maybe from the beginning of time. And it's called a "beer joint" because it's pretty much the only thing ordered there. And the beers ordered have been around even longer than Boone's. No new or new-age stuff here.

I went there with my dad a hundred times, maybe two hundred. He went there to unwind, like a lot of working men. I don't say it that way to be sexist, I hope, but because, in my childhood, men made up ninety percent of the clientele: line workers for John Deere, auto mechanics, day laborers. They were occasionally joined by sons who tagged along. Let me be clear: in those one or two hundred times, I do not remember ever seeing a girl my age there. The sixties were like that. The only thing that has changed at Boone's is that the blue-collar workers include women, and the tag-alongs include daughters.

I wasn't going just for nostalgia, although that was going to help the pain I received from Tony's story. And I wasn't going there to have a beer, this time. Boone's also serves one of the best breaded tenderloin sandwiches in the state. That's saying something when the state's unofficial state sandwich is the breaded tenderloin. Besides, my drug of choice when I'm stressed out is fried food. Maybe better than a lot of other things. Maybe not.

— five —

After my nice, if unhealthy lunch, I intended to call Murphy. I didn't have to. I wasn't halfway back to my office when he called me.

"Hey, Thompson," he began, abruptly. "Can you meet me north of the bridge by the tracks?"

"Sure," I replied. "I'll be there in five minutes."

It was less than five. Two patrol cars were parked just north of the tracks. Murphy was standing by one of them. Jakes and two other officers were searching the ground between the tracks and the row of trees and brush just beyond them.

"What's up, Murphy," I asked. I wasn't sure I wanted to know the answer.

"Autopsy came back," he said, darkly. "It wasn't an accident."

I didn't immediately reply. Murphy went on.

"He was stabbed. Nicked the pericardial sack. Something long and round and very pointed. Like an ice pick." Then he raised his voice, angry. "Who the hell even has an ice pick these days?"

"Damn, Murphy," I said, almost to myself. "What's next?"

Murphy just shook his head.

"Is this where he was found?" I asked, indicating the general area where the officers were.

"Yeah," he answered. "Halfway to the bridge."

"What was he doing way over there?" I was truly puzzled. "He should have turned east at the end of the bridge to get to his car."

"Other than getting himself killed," Murphy said with resignation, "your guess is as good as mine."

I had no guesses left in me. Nothing about this guy could be guessed by the wildest imagination. He was more of a ghost than the lovely Laura at the theater. She at least had a real name and a real past.

"Sarge!" It was something more than a yell; something less than a scream. It came from Officer Myra Sebetka as she came out of the trees. She's been on the force less than a year but shows great promise.

Murphy started for her immediately. Jakes and the other officer got there first, of course. We got there just as Officer Jones, Colton Jones, came back out of the trees, turned sharply to his right two steps, and vomited violently. Sebetka nearly joined him but turned away and kept it together. Murphy kept up his pace, not quite a jog, into the trees. I slowed down. The tenderloin was very good going down. I was not anxious to test it in reverse.

Murphy returned. The look on his face defined the word "scowl." "We found the ice pick," he said in a low voice. "It's going to take some time to figure out who it's stuck in."

Other officers and personnel were called. A thorough search was begun. By thorough, I mean every square inch of nearly an acre of ground was examined closely, sometimes on hands and knees. Anything that didn't seem natural was photographed, tagged and bagged. Even some leaves and twigs joined the evidence log. The lab work would take weeks, maybe months.

Despite what you see on TV crime shows, DNA is not processed in five minutes, maybe not five days. Even when you have something concrete, checking data bases on-line doesn't happen in seconds. That, too, can take days. Identifying a body that's been lying in the brush and weeds for a week, unless there's some real identifying mark, can take a year. If a show like CSI had shown the real reality of investigations, their first case would have taken the whole first season.

I waited with Murphy, mostly in silence, for the first half hour. My standing around in the cold watching wasn't going to add anything. Murphy and Jakes offered me a ride back to the office. On the way, we were still mostly silent. It's hard to find answers when you don't know the questions and it's hard to find questions when you don't know where to start. In fact, the only real question we had is the one we'd been asking: who was Geoffrey Christopher?

We also didn't know that some men with some answers to questions we didn't know to ask were waiting for us.

A tall, thin man with a pale face and a rather large nose approached the squad car as we pulled up to the building where I have my office. He wore a nice brown suit. Murphy and Jakes watched him cautiously. He stopped a few feet away, obviously aware of their caution. Jakes lowered his window. The man's face and voice were pretty emotionless.

"Sergeant Murphy," he said, "We'd like to speak with you and Mr. Thompson. We've already spoken to your superiors. We thought Mr. Thompson's office would be best."

His manner was so confident and matter of fact as to negate the need for questions from most people. Murphy is not most people.

"Okay," he said, with some confusion mixed into his suspicion. "I'll just park up here." He indicated an available space several feet away.

"That won't be necessary," the man said in the same tone. "Officer Jakes can take the patrol car back to headquarters. Your chief will explain things to him."

It wasn't just that he knew our names that was disconcerting. He knew us well, on sight. His name and face were completely unknown to us.

All three of us got out. Since I was in the back, Jakes had to open the door for me before going around to the driver's side. Before he got in, Murphy stopped him without taking his eyes off the man in the brown suit. He paused, sizing up the situation. "Okay, Jakes," he said at last. "Go check in."

Murphy stayed in the middle of the street until Jakes drove away.

We headed for the entrance door like a little parade. I went first. After all, I had the key. The tall man was second, remaining at least six feet behind me. A smaller man in a dark blue suit and with rather dark complexion and thick black hair joined us. He'd been standing by the building wall. He stayed six feet behind his companion. Murphy brought up the rear. He stayed back, also. It felt very weird.

The street level door is not locked during business hours. It leads directly to a stairway. On the second floor of the old brick building are three offices. Mine is in the front facing Main Street. At the rear of the building, taking up more than half the available space is the accounting firm of Young, Ablen and Melchert. The small office between us in vacant. It has been occupied by diverse enterprises over the years. None stayed long.

I unlocked the door to the small anteroom and went in. My office door was unlocked and open. I went in followed by the two strangers. Murphy stopped at the outer door.

The tall man noticed, turned to him and said, "Please, come in, Sergeant. We want to be careful in our conversation."

"I'm careful, too." Murphy said, with meaning.

"I don't like closed rooms when I don't know what's going on."

"Of course," the man said with only the lightest change from his noncommittal tone. He reached into the inside pocket of his jacket and pulled out what I took to me his credentials. He showed them to Murphy. The tall man's back was to me, but I could see that Murphy was impressed. The man turned to me and took a few steps to show me what he had shown Murphy. I was impressed, too. The man was Special Agent Thomas R. Wheeland, FBI.

Murphy came into the anteroom and closed the door.

"Grab one of those chairs," I told him, indicating the two by the door. I still had the three from this morning in my office, but now we were four. When all were in the inner office, I closed that door, too.

"Before I begin," Agent Wheeland began, obviously taking charge, "Let me introduce Inspector Luciani from Italy. He's with Interpol."

Murphy and I froze. Impressed was not the right word now. I managed a mostly mumbled, "How do you do."

"How do you do," the Inspector returned, with a noticeable, but not thick accent. "We are sorry to have disturbed you so much with out unexpected arrival. Let us all be seated."

We sat. FBI? That was unexpected. Interpol? Deep into Iowa? It would take a few minutes for this to find the proper category in my brain.

"Your confusion is very understandable," Wheeland began anew with his usual unemotional voice. "I will get directly to the subject. We are here concerning the man you knew as Geoffrey Christopher."

He gave us a pause, a long pause, waiting for our minds to sort through the pile of stuff we had only recently gathered. "Sort" was not accurate. It was more like just pushing everything into pile away from the things of our every day lives. It's the same method I use for sorting laundry: pile of jeans there, pile of dress shirts here.

"Christopher," Wheeland continued, "I'll use that name for simplicity. He's had dozens of names. Christopher is a suspect in murders in seven states and four foreign countries."

The pile of stuff exploded. Wheeland let the debris settle.

Murphy spoke first. "This guy was a hit man?" he growled.

Wheeland's brow furrowed. A change in his face I didn't expect. In fact, I didn't expect a change. His companion's change in demeanor was more pronounced. He was having difficult keeping his emotions in.

"He was more than that," Wheeland said. His strong reserve slipped just a little, barely noticeable, but I noticed. "Many years ago the Bureau began calling him 'the Exterminator.'"

"What?" Murphy let that out in a long breath as he stood up.

"Yes," said Wheeland with a kind of robotic understanding for Murphy's reaction. "He was usually hired, not to strike a single target, but to wipe out whole families." Wheeland's bluntness doubled the shock of what he just said.

"He was a demon from hell!" shouted Inspector Luciani. If he had held that in any longer I think he would have had a stroke.

"One of Christopher's first big hits was more than forty years ago," Wheeland began his tale. "A crime family in New York hired him to take out a police captain. They wanted to send a message to the whole department. The captain, his wife, their twenty-two-year-old son and eighteen-year-old daughter were all found dead. The next-door neighbor disappeared. That house was scrubbed. We think that's how Christopher got to them.

"A couple of weeks later, the head of the crime family, his brother, his wife and four children were found dead. The youngest was a girl, age twelve."

"Jesus Christ," Murphy breathed out. We were both trying to breathe.

"At first, it was speculated that the crime family was taken out by some vigilante cops. What was eventually pieced together was that crime lord number one hired Christopher to kill the captain and Christopher made a deal with a second, rival crime boss to take out the first one and throw the blame in other directions. We think the whole scheme was Christopher's plan from the beginning.

"This was a continuing M.O. It was nearly the same plan for an incident in Mexico with two cartels and area federales. Then a few years later, it happened again in Italy."

Luciani mumbled in Italian. I don't know if it was a prayer or a curse. Maybe some of both.

"Many of the cases are guess work. Similarities. A couple of sloppy copy-cats. Exterminator moves in, blends in. In Mexico, people believed he was Mexican. Knew the language. Knew the customs. No one thought otherwise until he struck and vanished. Same in Rome. Chameleon. Changes with his environment.

"An actor," I added, almost under my breath, surprised I had enough breath to get anything out or my mouth.

"Yes," Wheeland went on, in almost a computer-generated voice, "By taking out an entire family, he shocks the whole set up. Makes it difficult for immediate revenge, or even who to go after. It's like dropping a large stone in a mud puddle. By the time things settle, all you see is the rock with no idea who dropped it.

"After that, he would disappear for years at a time. He'd blend in somewhere else, keep a low profile. His payoffs were huge. We don't know where he stashed his money, fees and otherwise."

"Otherwise?" Murphy interrupted.

"Sometimes he took things from his targets," Wheeland replied. "In Mexico, it was boxes of cash.

Drug business is mostly cash. In Italy, the wife of the guy was into expensive jewelry. Most of it was gone. It was partly recovered years later, after it had changed hands at least twice.

"We had a lead about some risky investments, once. But there he was just as smart. Risky, but with big payout if he was right. He usually was. Then he took the money and ran. He would travel across the country with smaller cashier's checks. Cash only one in each state he passed through. He may have dealt with 200 banks over the years.

"Not all his victims were targets. Occasionally, some one who hired him would try to take him out. He expected it. I suppose it was, technically, self-defense. Others were when he felt someone was getting too close. Several years after the first one, in New York, two FBI agents were following a vague lead. We found their bodies in Ohio. A local businessman also disappeared. Assumed dead. He was the guy the agents went to see. They thought he knew something. The agent's notes indicated that there was another man in the area who was suspicious – a loner. Avoided most people. Lived in an old farmhouse outside town. This businessman, ran two convenience stores, was the only one who seemed friendly with him. The loner came in once in awhile to get things. He disappeared, too. The house was scrubbed.

"And there was other collateral damage. Businessman had a family. They were devastated and left destitute. I guess the husband, the businessman, was way over extended, barely keeping open. The wife had mental problems all her life. After that, she was a real mess."

Wheeland finally paused. Thank God. He could tell we were getting overwhelmed. He didn't suspect the half of it. We tried again to catch our breath.

Then he went on. "Any strange reports of unusual circumstances surrounding a death, especially near where we might be following a thread, come to us. Christopher's seemingly accidental death would not. But, when we heard about a wired garage, it got our attention. The inspector and I were in Des Moines looking at other things when we were notified. There were some thin things that brought us to Iowa."

"There haven't been any strange murders around here," Murphy said, a little defensively.

"No," Wheeland went on without missing a beat. I think he anticipated Murphy's reaction. "If there had been, and it was Christopher, he would have been gone. This area is mostly quiet. We think he retired. Just a quiet business man alone."

"Retire!" Murphy was getting angry. "Guys like that don't retire. Here or anywhere!"

Wheeland paused looking Murphy in the eye. "There are no guys like that." His voice had a strange tone. It was a cold anger.

In my head, I was thinking, "Thank God there was only one and now he's dead." Then my brain added, "I hope."

Then I noticed something in Wheeland's otherwise stony face. For all his rigid manner, he was in pain that there had ever been even one.

"Alright," Murphy said, still upset but getting more official, "You seem to know something about this ghost. Number one: What's his real name?"

Wheeland and Luciani looked at each other, a little sadly I thought, before getting back to Murphy. "Our best guess is Stevenson."

"Guess!" Murphy exploded. "You've been after this guy forever and all you've got is a guess?"

"We aren't sure," Wheeland said flatly. "Like I said, there are no guys like that. I understand your frustration. He came out of nowhere. He could disappear at will. No pictures. No prints."

"Scuse, signore," Luciani interjected, "There may be pictures. We have pictures of an unknown man, an unaccounted-for man, near two murders."

"Yes," Wheeland confirmed. "Two group pictures that included the victims, one in Frankfort, Germany and one from Rome. Each included a face that had marked similarities. Witnesses confirmed the name in each. No trace of the man could be found afterward."

"We have some pictures of Christopher from plays," I suggested, hopefully.

"We thought of that." Wheeland replied. "We got them from Coppola at the theater and sent them to the lab in D.C."

"Okay," again began the unhappy Murphy, "I'll go

to number two: Who killed Christopher, or Stevenson, or whatever, here and now?"

"We don't know," said Wheeland. He was not as unhappy as Murphy, but it was noticeable. "The case is too new. You know that, Sergeant. And we have no information that would indicate that anyone was tracking him in this area."

"Fine," Murphy spit out. "That's just fine."

"You're frustrated, Sergeant," Wheeland said, as one law officer to another. But you've been frustrated for a few days. I've been on this case for fifteen years. Luciani for eight. We inherited from others who have dealt with it for decades."

Murphy was still unhappy, but he understood where he stood.

"I have word from my director," Wheeland continued, "first, to offer all our resources to help figure this out, and second, to share all the information we have. Anything you want."

For the next two hours, we shared information. Mine came out almost in the form of answers to official interrogation. That was logical. It was in their nature, ingrained after years in a tough profession. Murphy fell right in with the other two.

My own investigative style has always been more subtle. I have no official powers. My links to officialdom are mostly unofficial. To get people to open up, especially if they really are criminals, I have to sneak up on them, to investigate without them knowing they are being investigated. Any attempt on my part to scare them would more likely get a laugh than a shiver.

Information I had to share with these officials was pretty scant. I told them about crossing paths often, but briefly at the theater, and of discovering where he parked. I mentioned my nervousness about his hand in that shoulder bag.

That piqued their interest. No shoulder bag had been recovered.

I also mentioned his off-hand comment about being divorced. I gave no details, and I certainly didn't mention any possible children. As intimidated as I was by these men, including Murphy when he was being very official, I would keep Tony Davenport's presence and pain to myself for a while. Had his mother discovered that her husband and father of her children had been a more than ruthless killer of whole families? If so, I had to keep that from her family.

I was getting very tired. Holding together loose ends is hard work.

— six —

After the three law enforcement officers left, I collapsed back in my chair. I sat in stunned silence as the room darkened. Autumn twilight is gray. Most of the year it is blue. But it was November. When I was in college, I had a friend who was an art major. One painting he had in his senior show was an abstract of gray swirls. It was entitled, "November." It was now the name of my state of being.

Bourbon by the fire wasn't going to cut it. I had two choices: go home, have an early dinner and go to bed; or go somewhere to slam down some Scotch. Scotch is made for it.

No. I didn't have a choice. I had rehearsal at seven.

I fumbled around in my office, trying to put thoughts in order by way of notes. I ended up with a pile of scattered scribbles. I surrendered to the obvious and headed to the theater. I walked up the alleys rather than on Main. I would be very early, but at least it would force me to think of something else. I thought it would be the play. It was not.

I entered by the stage door and went down the hall and into the auditorium without stopping to say anything to Bob. I went up the stairs to the second floor to see Martha Baker, head of costumes. My costume for the play was simple: dark suit; bright tie. I just like talking with Martha, even though that is sometimes difficult. I knew that would make me concentrate on something else.

Martha never quite seems to finish a sentence. She will answer with the same words as anyone else, but her tone, her inflection, always leaves you hanging. Where most people indicate a solid period, Martha puts an ellipsis, as though there is more to say. When you first meet her, you wait for her to catch her breath and finish. It may take two or three seconds, maybe longer, before it dawns on you that she had finished.

"Good evening, Martha," I greeted her through the costume shop door.

"Hello, John," she replied. "It's good to see you...."

"How are the costumes coming along?" I asked.

"Everything is going pretty well...," she answered.

I know her well enough not to wait for another clause. Most expect her to add, "but something." She almost never does.

Martha is a short plump woman in her sixties. She wears her gray/brown hair piled up on her head. Definitely piled. Her round, rosy face always seems happy, even when she's concentrating on a difficult piece.

"Are you ready for another mystery?" she asked. At least you can always tell where the question marks are. But the question surprised me. And after so many in recent hours and days, I didn't want to answer.

She continued anyway. "Aydyn has dispelled one ghost and gotten herself another...."

It was clear that she was about to tell me more, but not with this particular sentence.

Aydyn Littlefield is one of Martha's assistants. She has been with the theater one way or another since she was quite young. She was with the children's group, been in plays and helped with every crew. Now, at twenty-two she prefers working with Martha. She is Martha's granddaughter.

There is no visible family resemblance. Aydyn is a head taller and very slender. Her face is somewhat long, but quite striking. She reminds me of a young Lauren Becall, but where MS. Becall was always cool and calm, Aydyn always seems agitated, happily agitated.

She also has very strange taste in clothes. They are the right size, but still don't seem to fit. I can't quite put my finger on it. I get the idea that she started out the door, realized that she needed to put on clothes and grabbed the first thing handy, which happened to be something her roommate, who's the same size, had discarded. Aydyn doesn't have a roommate.

"We were working late last night...," Martha

recounted at last, with her usual nonpregnant pauses. "Aydyn stayed after…. She decided to sleep in the shop…."

"Yes!" Aydyn came bursting in. "I'll tell him, Grandma. Hi, John."

She smiled and took off her coat and bag. The bag is something more than just a large cloth purse that she usually carries with a cross-body strap. She was wearing blue pants of I don't know what material that seemed to fit her hips well but, overall, were wrong. Her loose-fitting top was neither a sweater nor a shirt. It was neither beige, nor pale yellow. It was all of the above. It was none of the above. Where did she find this stuff?

"I was sleeping on the old couch back in that corner," she began her tale, indicating an old brown lump at the far end. "Just as I woke up to roll over, I heard a noise. It was from upstairs. I thought the refrigerator was acting up. You know what I mean? Like the motor was making way more noise than it should. So, I went up. I thought I might have to unplug it or something.

"When I got of the elevator, I thought I heard another noise – like a door closing. I just stood and listened after the elevator doors closed, but I couldn't hear anything else. I didn't want to go in the kitchen, so I came back down, got my stuff and left."

"What do you think was going on?" the investigator in me asked.

"To tell the truth," Aydyn answered, "Every time

I think about it, I get a different idea. But, one way or another, I think someone was in the kitchen."

"Why do you think that?" I wanted to follow where her thinking would lead Whether that was facts or sleepy imagination would come to light as she spoke it out loud.

"Chicken," she said emphatically. "I'm sure I smelled chicken when I got off the elevator."

That surprised me a lot and confused me not a little.

"The more I think of that," she went on, "the more I'm sure that what I heard was the microwave in the kitchen. And I don't care how much they talk about Laura the ghost, if ghosts eat chicken, they don't nuke it first."

Her logic was fine. She was right. But then anyone's logic about what ghosts do and don't do could be just as right.

Another part of her story made sense as well. The front door of the theater is only unlocked during daylight business hours or when the public is coming to see the show. The back door, the stage door, is unlocked at night for the stage crew or the actors. On three occasions that I know of personally, and a couple of others that Mike has related, someone unauthorized has entered the building. One of those was just a curious teen-ager. Two were adults whose suspicious attitude made us think that their curiosity was not just idle but larcenous. The other two were street people, homeless, looking for a warm place to sleep. Cedar Falls is not a big city, but we have our share of those who need help, too. Those two only spent one night and were discovered. They had slept on a couch in the loft.

The south end of the backstage area has two floors. The lower is the make-up room. There are mirrors and a narrow shelf on the south and east walls. There is a small bathroom in the northwest corner of this room. In the southeast corner is a narrow doorway to a narrow stair way to the upper floor and a similar room above it. This is the loft. On the north end, overlooking the shop, is a half wall. The bathroom here is in the southwest corner. It is a little larger in that it also contains a shower. No one, to my personal knowledge, has ever used this shower. The loft is the women's dressing room.

Both of our overnight guests had come in unnoticed. They made themselves comfortable out of sight. They had used the bathroom, very neatly. They had looked for something to eat in the concession area, the only place open to them, but found nothing. They were discovered the next day. They had pressed their luck hoping for another night under a roof.

Had Aydyn nearly discovered another unregistered guest? One that had brought chicken them? Or had her imagination provided one? Perhaps someone else had warmed up something earlier in the day. What she smelled was just a lingering aroma. The closing door sound? Nothing more than the November wind against the windows.

This was sounding like the way all ghost stories are dispelled. Maybe it's the same way intruder stories are dispelled, too. Aydyn didn't believe in ghosts. She wasn't afraid of shadows. She was afraid, however, of someone in the shadows.

"Aydyn," I asked, "What time did this happen?"

"Well," she replied thoughtfully. "I went straight home. It took about fifteen minutes. The clock in my kitchen said, '2:18' I think."

"So, something woke you up just before two in the morning?" I continued to probe.

"That seems about right," she said simply.

"Do you know how long you had been asleep?"

"Maybe an hour. Probably less."

"Now think carefully," I spoke more softly. "If someone was there, they had to go up in the elevator, or up the stairs. Was the stairway door at the top locked?"

"It usually is," she said, with a hint of confusion. "I sort of automatically took the elevator. I never even looked at the door when I got up there." She was beginning to doubt her own story.

"I'll check it now," I said with a smile, and started for the door. I was sure that I was about to confirm that it had not been what the sleepy young woman had imagined.

"I'll come with you," she said excitedly.

I went out the door turned left, passed the elevator, turned left again toward the restrooms, turn right in front of them and right again at the foot of the stairs. Labyrinth-like.

It is an old staircase more than six feet wide. The steps are not carpeted and painted brown. They go up at just enough steeper an angle as to be noticeable. After twenty steps, there is a landing, then a right turn up eight more steps to the top floor. This flight is narrower and comes to a small space before the doorway. There is a light at this top landing which is seldom on. There are lights on the floor below, but above the stairs themselves there is no lighting, and they can be quite dark even in the daytime.

As soon as we turned at the first landing, there was some light. It could only come from the rehearsal hall. The streetlights below showed through the large windows and then came down the stairs. This could only mean that the stairway door at the top was open.

This door is almost always closed and locked. There is a bar on the inside which opens it for an exit, but unless it is propped open with something, you can't get back in. A broom handle or something is the usual prop of choice for actors who may run down to one of the restrooms below. There is a wooden door stop which is used to open it wide. That it was open now, and probably had been the night before, was most likely careless. Someone forgot to remove the doorstop. It also meant that someone could have come to the top floor without the notice of the sleeping Aydyn. That didn't prove that someone was actually there; it just made it much, much more possible.

The look on Aydyn's face told me that she was somewhat glad to have some confirmation of her story, and a bit frightened to have some confirmation that she had not been alone in the old dark building.

We walked up the last flight more slowly, went through the doorway and stopped by the elevator just on the other side. This is where Aydyn had stood last night. We both listened carefully, even though, logically, that it would be very strange if we heard anything. I was hoping we did. I wanted to hear something that would show that it was not unusual. Something in the building – from the furnace blower or the rattling windows – would account for what she heard. Aside from the traffic noises outside, nothing.

We had just taken our first slow steps when the elevator roared to life. We jumped almost in unison. It didn't really roar, of course, in the usual sense of the term, except in our own hearts and minds. With our ears and concentration focused on the kitchen around the corner, it was a sudden roar.

It was nearly time for rehearsal. Jim Butler and I were scheduled to go through our scene up here, while the principal players used the main stage. Wemyss would be downstairs with them. The assistant director, Lincoln King, would guide us.

Linc is a recent addition. I should say a returning addition. He was active here as a kid and is back now after college. In his early twenties, he seems like a seasoned pro. His vocal range in music is extraordinary. His comic timing is as sharp as a razor. His outgoing personality and open heart make him instantly liked, even loved. He has recently expanded into directing with the same easy talent.

Linc stepped off the elevator, surprised to find us standing in the near darkness.

"Oh, hey," he said with a grin. "You two lost?"

"Hey, Linc," I greeted him. "Just where are the light switches, anyway?"

He laughed his infectious laugh and turned on the lights, which were right next to where we were standing.

"Thanks," I said lightly, "Now, I can investigate."

Linc looked surprised, of course.

"Aydyn is sure someone was up here fooling around late last night," I explained. "I thought I would check it out."

"Another transient?" Linc asked.

"Could be," I said over my shoulder on the way to the kitchen.

"Say," he said, following. "Do you think that could explain all those strange things that have been going on?"

"It could explain some of them," I said, looking around the kitchen. "Imagination explains most of them, I think. If it was all of them, it would mean that someone has been coming and going a lot, or that they've been living here for a couple of months. Both of those seem a long shot."

"I wish you'd said 'impossible' instead of 'long shot,'" he said with a hint of worry.

I looked at him. "I wish I could say that, but I haven't ruled it out completely."

"Well, your honor," Linc said, joking with the title but not the intent, "I hope you make your ruling soon. I spend a lot of late nights here."

I smiled as I opened the microwave door. I definitely smelled chicken. The way these doors are meant to seal could preserve an odor for a few days. But, if not used last night, when?

I closed the door and went to the refrigerator. There were a couple of bottles of wine. The freezer section was stuffed with bags of ice. That was all.

There was nothing unusual in the blower room behind the kitchen. I looked behind the machine, just in case. Someone could duck behind it out of sight in case someone else came into get something, but they really could not hide from someone looking for them.

"Everything seems to be all clear," I said lightly.

"Now," Aydyn said, no so lightly.

The elevator dinged as it reached our floor. Jim Butler got off.

Neither Aydyn nor Linc is a person who scares easily. However, fear of the unknown is part of every human psyche. It's part of our ancient, natural defense mechanism. Most of the time, it is just unrequited curiosity. It doesn't take much to push it to have the same effect on our emotions as outright fear. So, I had an idea that might requite some of that curiosity: a search party.

Linc and Jim would stay in the rehearsal hall. No one could come in without being seen. Aydyn would go back to work with Martha in the costume shop but try to listen for the elevator or anyone in that hallway. I went to the main stage to recruit volunteers.

Wemyss was already talking to the romantic leads: Bonita, Bonnie, Narvaez and Mark Hall.

I suggested that Wemyss stay on the stage to keep an eye on the main entrances to the auditorium, including the ones in the balcony. Bonnie would go up the back stairs to the loft including its bathroom. The other way out of the loft leads to a little hall that goes along the south wall all the way to the balcony. It passes by two theater boxes.

The Oster-Regent has old fashioned boxes on either side of the stage. They angle out not unlike the ones at Ford's Theater in Washington. Lincoln was seated on one such box when he was shot. They are angled so that the occupants can be seen as easily as they can see the play. Wealthy patrons used to pay to sit here for separation from the "masses" but so that those "masses" could see them.

We use the one closest to the stage for an occasional upper-level scene, but mostly they are used for additional lighting. There is one box below these on each side. These usually have speakers from the various microphones.

A curtain separates the boxes from the hallway. Bonnie would look behind the curtains.

Mark and I would check the basement. As we passed through the shop, I stopped to explain things to Bob and Gary. They immediately volunteered. Bob would go out to the auditorium, to the north wall. The curtained arch there near the stage lead to a long hall down the north side of the building and eventually to stairs to the basement. The stairs the rest of us would take come down at the southwest corner. These are the only two ways into the basement, so anyone down there would be between us. We all grabbed flashlights and headed off.

There are a lot of things to hide behind and under in the basement. The overhead lights don't illuminate the corners behind furniture and fake fireplaces and under stairs. More than once we had to get on hands and knees to be sure. When Bob emerged from the north end, Gary joined him so we could move carefully toward the center. By the time we met, there was really only one place left to search: under the front part of the stage.

Our stage has a large apron – the part of the stage in front of the main curtain. The center of that apron is twelve feet in front of the curtain. It then curves to less than half that by the time it gets to the sides. Just to the left of the center of the apron is a trap door. When open, it is a square about two feet on each side. It is used only rarely. We last used it as the opening to the sewer in *Guys and Dolls*, where the famous crap game is going on.

The space under the apron is its own separate room and is really a crawl space. The space is the same size and shape as the apron, but the floor is three and a half feet above the floor of the rest of the basement. With the beams which hold up the stage, it doesn't give you much room to maneuver. And, of course, most of the time it is just used for storage. It took nearly as long to check this crawl space, crawling, as it did the rest of the basement.

We found no one.

We returned to the stage. Wemyss, not happy but understanding the delay, had stayed at his post. He has also enlisted other actors as they arrived to go to the various entrances to watch. All six theater boxes and all hallways had been checked and watched.

"Empty handed, Johnny?" I couldn't tell if Wemyss was happy, disappointed or just teasing.

"Bonnie," I yelled up to her, "Can you go up and check the light booth?"

The light booth is a five by twelve room with a door on each end and windows along the front. It is at the very top and back of the balcony. Bonnie went there, checking behind seats as she did. She went in one end, out the other and waved an all clear.

"Well, that's that," Wemyss said. "Let's get to work."

"You go ahead," I said. "I'm going to take Gary and check one last place.

"Geez, Johnny," Wemyss said, doubtfully. "What's left? The roof?"

I looked up a second or two before answering. "No. I think I'll let that go for tonight," I told him, only a little more than half kidding.

He smiled in return, and called the actors together.

It only seemed remotely possible to me that someone would choose the roof or even be able to get there. On a cold November night, I think they would have given up by now. At least, I hoped I was right about that.

"Gary," I said turning to him, "Bring your flashlight. We'll check the other basement."

Gary had been as excited as a kid looking for Easter eggs. Now, he looked confused.

"What other basement?" he asked.

"I'll explain on the way," Bob said. "I'm coming, too." He explained things to Gary as we left the auditorium and went through the lobby.

Gary was excited again. He laughed and said, "I just realized I've only been in the shop and on the stage. I've never even been in the lobby."

We opened the basement door, turned on the light and went down carefully. Gary kept trying to hurry. I believed, and I think Bob did, that if, in fact, someone was hiding in the theater, this was the only place left. That meant the increasingly fictious tenant, no matter how benign, was now cornered. This stairway, this door, was the only way in or out. How desperate might they be to avoid detection?

At the bottom, we stopped. The first place to look was under the stairs. There were several large boxes of old papers.

Through the doorway into the next little room, we faced divided shelves on the wall. These were actually sort of bins. They held the old eight-inch letters that had once been used on the marquee out front. We have since gone electronic. On the floor were more boxes. In one corner, there were few old wooden folding chairs. We turned left toward the next doorway.

There are two steps down into what almost seems like a concrete bunker. There are two rooms. The first is nearly empty. There are two old tables. The other room holds the main furnace and blower. Except for the machinery, it was empty. It is possible to walk completely around it, so it is not a good hiding place.

The next room runs the length of the other two. Here hang a very large number of uniforms, mostly military, mostly World War Two vintage.

There was now only one space to search. It is the space directly under the main seating in the auditorium above. I call it the cavern. The floor above slopes from the east, where the entrances are, to the west in front of the stage. Therefore, down here, the ceiling does the same. At the beginning, the ceiling is about eight feet. At the other end, it is about half that.

Most of the east end is blocked off by pipes,

wiring and some boxes of Christmas decorations, big decorations, and some Christmas trees. We would be using a lot of these in the coming days. For now, they are stored here. But it means the only real entrance to the cavern is on the far south end.

Two things end at the cavern: the concrete floor and light. The original floor was simply broken rocks and hard packed dirt. A hundred years ago, it was assumed there would be very little need for anyone ever to come down here, so there was no need to make it very smooth. That was the assumption for the lack of lighting. With the darkness, the rocky floor and the declining head room, I think it is obvious why I call it the cavern.

Bob remained back. If someone could get by us in the dark, not unlikely, there was still only one way out. Gary and I began to separate. He stayed toward the south. I went north. We tried to be careful going around support columns and other wires and pipes. We began to crouch before it was really necessary, but it seemed the thing to do. Still, he bumped his head at least four times going in. Only once coming out.

About halfway down, I found a mat. It was one of those heavy, quilted pads that movers use to protect furniture. It was spread out neatly. I'm that someone may have used it as a bed, but not recently. There was a thick coat of dust and dirt on it. I estimated that whoever had done so had done it more than two years previously.

On the far west end, it would be easier to move on hands and knees than in a crouch. On the uneven rubble, even with knee pads, I think it would prove too painful. I still considered it. My back was complaining about this adventure in no uncertain terms. Maybe I could find one spot to kneel so that I could give it some release. I did not give into the temptation.

We reached the wall of the orchestra pit, turned around, and tried to sweep the darkness with our flashlights. They seemed meager in the cavern. Dirt, rocks, a few scattered pieces of litter from earlier explorers or workers perhaps. Certainly, no other person.

We made out way out and reported to Bob. I felt dusty all over. Gary, the kid, had had a ball. I was glad it was over.

Gary and Bob went back to the shop. I went back to the third floor, stopping to tell Aydyn and Martha of the nothing we had found. Aydyn was relieved that no one was found but troubled by what she was sure she had heard.

Somehow, I was not satisfied either.

— seven —

I decided to try one more experiment. After rehearsal, I would stay a while. Maybe I would hear what Aydyn had heard and be able to identify it.

Rehearsal ended at ten. Everyone but me was gone. Lights were turned off and doors were locked as usual. I wanted to be near the third floor. That was a problem. The costume shop, with its old brown couch, was locked, too. So was the third-floor rehearsal hall and kitchen. The only way there was by the elevator. It would make too much noise which I wanted to avoid just in case someone was around to hear it.

My only option appeared to be the balcony in the auditorium. The seats on the north end in the top row next to the light booth would be about directly across from the kitchen, as far as I could determine. Between the back wall of the balcony and the wall of the kitchen would be about four feet of space. The stairway was between them. In an empty building, especially an old one, sound can carry a long way. Still, through two walls, it would have to be pretty loud.

I heard sounds occasionally. Most were from late traffic on First Street. Sometimes, I was pretty sure, it was the wind outside pushing against a window or two.

I was beginning to dose off. Theater seats are not made for dosing, so it happened in fits and starts. Two minutes, then a shift in body position. As long as eight minutes? Then a shift. And always questions. Did I wake up because I was uncomfortable, or was there a noise?

I think there is another set of senses the opposite of the normal ones, sort of like the idea of gravity and anti-gravity. When you are really hungry for tacos, your craving becomes sort of an anti-taste, a particular void that can only be filled by the particular sensation. You don't just want food, you want tacos. Perhaps, silence creates anti-sound, a craving to hear. In the void of the theater was I hearing things, did my ears just crave something? When I would start awake, the silence was like large soft pillows surrounding my head. They disappear when a motorcycle roared away from the intersection outside.

Then, before I could get comfortable, or at least less uncomfortable, I did hear something. It was not outside. I did not know where it came from. I searched the silence. Was that the creak of a stair? Another. Where? It could only be from the back stairs in the near southwest corner of the building, either down from the loft or up from the basement.

I stared intently at the stage. The only source of light was the ghost light.

A dark stage is a dangerous place. Furniture and set pieces disappear. Even empty, in the dark, you cannot be sure where the edge of the stage is. A ghost light, almost always jus a single bulb atop a pole, is put out as a safety measure. There are different theories for the origin of the name. Was it so called to chase the ghosts away, or to keep them company?

The more I stared, the less I saw. The harder I listened, the less I heard. I began to feel that I was under water where vision is blurred and sound all but silenced.

I settled back in the seat. A gentle, warm feeling surrounded me, a good, drowsy feeling. I think I even had the beginning of a dream. My eyelids flitted open now and then, a kind of negative blinking like the negative sights and sounds around me.

During one of these un-blinks, I saw the ghost light flicker. Then my not quite asleep brain said, "Wait!" The light did not flicker. Something had passed in front of it. The warm drowsiness vanished. I was instantly awake, staring at the stage. Again, I saw nothing; I heard nothing.

I realized that in my jumping awake, although I didn't leave the seat, I had made enough noise that someone would have heard. If someone was on the stage, they would have frozen, hidden, so as not to attract my attention. Hiding, for me, was not an option.

I thought for a second of going into the light

booth to turn on as many lights as possible. It might have been a good idea except that I was so unfamiliar with all the switches that by the time I figured out the right ones, whoever might be on the stage could be out the back door and four blocks away. They might be already.

My choice was to search by sound.

The ghost light gave off enough for me to make my way to the other side of the balcony and toward the south aisle. Once I got behind the curtain into the hallway behind the theater boxes, most of the light would be gone.

I moved slowly, listening. Whoever, whatever, I had seen had made no sound that had come to me since I first jolted to attention. I thought, had I been the one spotted, I would duck behind the first thick, black curtain in the wings to wait for my chance to get away. I imagined the mystery shadow being able to move unseen, but not unheard if they moved quickly at all. Their best chance would be when I was in the most darkness. Once passed the boxes, I would be on the walkway above the stage and partly lit up by the faint ghost light.

I inched along listening. I stopped. I heard.

Someone was inching along below me.

I kept thinking, "What would I do next?" I would have moved, too. The walkway is directly above the hallway leading to the stage door to the alley. My choice would have been to run down and out. The one below me did not.

The faint light seemed very bright after the near blackness behind the boxes. I looked down. I could make out the stage floor, the side curtains and a couple of large props ready for their entrance. I could see the stage with its mostly finished set. I could even make out the far stage left wings.

I could hear nothing.

Perhaps the whoever was waiting, hoping I had convinced myself that I had heard and seen nothing. That was entering my mind.

I moved slowly to the west, toward the loft. I did my best to make no sound, but every little shuffle of my foot seemed much too much. I knew that I had to get to the loft and across it to the far side, down the back stairs and through the make-up room to be in the wings. It seemed like miles. Even the Flash might have trouble making the distance before the shadow disappeared from the darkness of the stage to the darkness of the back alley.

I decided not to try. I would continue to creep along, listening. He, she, or it would be long gone before I could catch up, but at least they would be gone. I would hear the door open and close.

I moved as carefully as I could. I tried to float through the doorway into the loft. I glided as best I could across the carpet. Both of those are extreme exaggerations. I was as much interested in hearing noises as in avoiding making them. The biggest challenge was ahead of me. The old, narrow stairway would creak. I could avoid that only by moving at an impossibly slow pace. Lowering myself silently from one step to the next would be exhausting. The best I could hope for would be to pause after each creak to listen for a response noise from the darkness. I also knew that after I reached about the fourth step, I would be between two walls. Any sound would have difficulty reaching me.

I paused at the top, considering my options. I decided to speed up. The whoever out there would hear me no matter what I did. They must know that I was at least near the stairs. My only chance seemed to be surprise. I might be able to get a glimpse if I could catch them off guard, to hope that they expected me to continue slowly.

Still, I hesitated. I held my breath. Running down stairs in the dark is not inviting. I took two slow deep breaths and ran.

It was a mistake.

At the bottom of the stairs, three feet from the last step, is a wall. The door to the make-up room is to the left. It is not difficult to make the turn even when moving quickly – unless you miss the last step. I did. I crashed into the wall. That, too, would not present a problem if not for the full-length mirror. It shattered.

The good news: I'm sure I heard a gasp. It was faint. Sharp and short. My crash had startled someone. I had caught them by surprise. I froze to hear what they would do next. Less than a second after the gasp, there was a sound like a breeze blowing through the leaves of a tree. I could not definitely say it was running feet.

I may have surprised the dark whoever, but they surprised me as well. The sound, the whoosh, was not going down the hall to the stage door and out. It was going into the auditorium. Whoever was not leaving.

In the shock of hitting the wall, and some confusion of the fading sound, I made another mistake. I moved too quickly through the make-up room. I knew the size and shape of the room well. I forgot about the small benches the actors sit on to do hair and make-up. I tripped over three of them on my way through. I felt more like a pratfall circus clown than an investigator. I would have laughed myself, under different circumstances.

Instead of going through the east door directly on to the stage, I turned north, toward the shop. Just inside that doorway is a light switch. It turns on the bright overhead lights of the shop. It was glaring after my clumsy battle with the darkness. I went, limping a little, to the cabinet for a flashlight, and then through the large door to the stage.

The stage was set up for the courtroom scene. That meant I had to go through the fake door of the fake wall just past the real one. The wall also blocked some of the light from the shop, but it was much brighter than what had been with just the ghost light.

I stood at center stage peering into the still shadowy auditorium. I swept under the balcony and through the balcony with the flashlight. I saw only empty seats. They seemed rather eerie as I did that. The flashlight was not made for this kind of search. Most aren't. It is just a standard light, used for getting around backstage during a performance. I made a note in my head to get one with a stronger beam, even though I did not intend to do this again. If I did this again, it would be with every light in the building on. I knew that our earlier search had been nearly like that. But we had missed something, someone. There must be a dark corner we had not penetrated.

I listened as intently as I looked. Nothing. In my stumbling through the make-up room, I had tried to listen, too. I had made enough noise on my own that someone with work boots could have clomped away, but I think I would have heard some door open and close. I had not. Whoever was still here, somewhere.

I moved stage right. I'm sure the gasp and the whooshing sound had come from the back hallway in that direction. Whoever must have gone up the south aisle toward the lobby.

Or did they?

I stopped. It would have taken only a few seconds to go out that way. It would have taken only a second or two longer to turn, pass in front of the stage to the north aisle. The hallway back that way leads to the basement.

Whoever – what a name to attach to someone – could find many places to hide in the basement. I had suspected that before. If I was correct, they had avoided four of us searching there earlier. I did not feel like daring it alone now.

I had almost reached the far-right wings when something caught me attention. I had been glancing occasionally at the empty seats. Something seemed to move at the far stage left, behind me. I turned quickly with my light. Did the curtain move or not? It did not seem to be moving now. Was it the curtain itself, or something near it that had seemed to move? Someone behind it.

I took a deep breath and crossed the stage boldly – or semi-boldly. I was not feeling very bold. I yanked the curtain aside. Against the far wall were chairs and props ready for other scenes. I took another step, looking carefully. I was getting tired of finding nothing.

Then, I heard it again, the whooshing sound. I still could not definitely call it running feet, but almost. It was behind me. But where?

I rushed to center stage again. Another sound, again behind me the opposite of where I was facing. This time I knew it was just the curtain settling back into position. I hoped. It was a strange sound.

It occurred to me that whoever had not left the auditorium. They had only ducked behind some seats. When I walked behind the curtains at stage left, they had taken the chance to move again. Then, another sound and again I turned sharply. This snapping left then right and back again was going to make me dizzy if it kept up. I now thought there might be two whoevers – one stage left, one stage right. Or was my brain so scrambled that all I was going on were guesses and imagination. I'd had a long, emotional day. It was late. I was in an old dark theater. Alone? I wasn't sure anymore.

Another noise. A rattle. Could that have been the stage door being carefully closed? Another speculation. Another hope. Whoever had left the building. I hoped.

Suddenly, I felt relieved. A warm sense of gratitude came over me. Then, I felt another kind of warm running down from my neck to my shirt. As cool as the theater was, I had worked up a sweat in my pursuit, in my running amok. I wiped my neck with my hand. It wasn't sweat. It was blood. I had cut myself when I slammed into the mirror. I hadn't noticed. I think my right shin was bleeding, too.

"Damn," I thought. "I'm a mess."

Then, I thought of the other mess. There had to be broken glass all over one corner of the make-up room.

One mess at a time.

I went back to the shop, scrounged up some paper from the trash can and a pencil from the work bench. I made a large note to say that I would be back in the afternoon to clean up. Then I went into the make-up room to post it. I turned on the lights in there and looked in one of the mirrors. There were several cuts. All but one were just nicks, and the bleeder wasn't very serious. I grabbed a handful of tissues to press on it. Then I turned off the make-up room lights and the shop lights. I decided to keep the flashlight to find my way out without tripping over something else.

I stopped suddenly, and said out loud, "Where the hell did I leave my coat?"

– eight –

The treatment at the emergency room was simple enough. Convincing them that I wasn't a clumsy drunk was more difficult. I quit trying after the third doubtful look.

I got cleaned up and bandaged. It was decided that stitches were not necessary. They offered to call me a cab. I declined. More doubtful looks.

It was nearly one when I finally got to bed. I turned the alarm to a loud setting, just in case. I intended to talk to Frost first thing in the morning. That meant before 6:30 a.m.

At six o'clock in the morning, Frost would be in Island Park just north of the river. The bridge across the river there is the Franklin Street Bridge, three blocks west of Main Street. Frost went there at that time rain, shine, cold, heat or whatever. He did Tai Chi near the river.

I've always been fascinated by the discipline. It appears to be slow motion martial arts combined with slow motion dance. I find it beautiful to watch, but I have yet to give it a try. Maybe it's the discipline part that stops me. I exercise regularly, but not on a schedule. I stretch every day, or nearly, but not at the same time every day. I go to the pool at least three times each week, but not the always the same days of the week. I bike when the mood hits me.

Frost's exact schedule for exercise suits him; it is him. Many of his every day habits are exact, but, at the same time, they don't seem obsessive. When he's not in town, he may do the exercises at the same time, but obviously not in the same place. I've even been aware that he has, because of obstacles, skipped a day here and there. None of that seems to disturb him. Of course, almost nothing disturbs him. I've surprised him occasionally, once or twice on purpose, and he expresses surprise, even good-natured, in-on-the-joke surprise. The expression is mild and soon passes.

Frost's self-control is easy, smooth, graceful, like his mastery of Tai Chi. As I vaguely and over-simply understand it, the way you handle the forces around you, depends on how you handle the forces within you. It's not unlike a skill I learned in canoeing years ago. If you capsize in fast moving water, don't fight the current. Face down stream and lean back like you are in your favorite recliner in your own living room watching TV. Use the current to guide you until you find a good place to plant your feet. Then you just stand up and walk away.

Frost now lived several blocks north of the park in a quiet neighborhood known as North Cedar. With first the Cedar River and then a large tributary, Snag

Creek, and a great deal of marsh land separating it from the rest of Cedar Falls, North Cedar seems almost a village of its own. There are a few local businesses and several dozen modest homes and very little traffic.

Frost had gotten rid of much of the family business in Georgia. Some of it was still tied up in legal tangles concerning his father's conviction. Lawyers were arguing with other lawyers about how much of it, if any, should be forfeited as "ill-gotten gains." It still left Frost with a nice income to live modestly, which he preferred. I had offered to pay him a token salary during what he called his apprenticeship with me. He politely declined, say it would count as his tuition for the education he was receiving.

I have been to his house only once. I had used the excuse of dropping off some forms for him to read. I was really just satisfying my curiosity. He received me most graciously, but with just enough standoffishness to make me realize that he did not receive company. His home was his sanctuary. I have not intruded again.

I drove into the parking lot of the park at 6:20. I had grabbed a quick cup of sort of coffee on the way. I had awakened in pain – everywhere. The cuts on my neck. My skinned shin. Several joints, especially my back. And somewhere in the fog where my brain used to be. The stuff in the Styrofoam cup was not helping.

Frost came from the trees near the river and

across the grass like a fairy emerging from the mist. It still amazes me how lightly he walks. He floats like a balloon who touches the ground or the floor for appearances sake. He came to my car directly rather than his own, a small, dark blue Honda.

I lowered the window as he came near.

"Good morning, John," he greeted me with a smile and his cool southern voice. His eyebrows raised ever so slightly as he noticed my bandages, cuts, and probably sagging expression. I hadn't dared face mirror yet this morning.

"Good morning, Frost," I returned. "I'm going to need you today. A lot. It's very complicated."

"Certainly," he replied. "I can be there rather soon, but I should give you some time to get a bit more together, I suspect."

There are times when I think Frost can read minds. This time, however, the obvious was right in front of him.

"Nine o'clock will do just fine," I said. I would have preferred two in the afternoon, but there was much ground to cover.

Frost smiled and walked to his car.

I went home. I needed better coffee, strong coffee. And I needed a long shower. Soaking in a hot tub beckoned me, especially my back, but a shower, even a hot one would stimulate my mind and senses more. I also needed a good breakfast, my idea of a power breakfast. That would be two eggs, done in the microwave, on special dark wheat toast. Twenty-four grams of protein in one sandwich would be washed down with eight ounces of cranberry juice and two mugs of coffee. I would be as ready for the day as I could be.

I was in my office at 8:45. Frost, of course, came in at almost precisely 9:00.

First, I asked him about his recent trip to Georgia and about his father. His father had adjusted well to prison, or as well as could be expected. They have a good library where he is. He's been catching up on his reading, mostly American classics, especially Mark Twain.

He also filled me in on those I had met when I'd been there. Despite how brief and messy our interaction had been, I considered them friends. I called them now and then. It felt good to do so.

After these pleasantries, we got down to business. Filling in Frost from my scrambled notes and not fully sorted brain took more than an hour. Frost absorbed it in an easy relaxed way. The parts that would disturb most people disturbed him, but you would have to know him well to notice, for the most part.

The stories about the cold-blooded Exterminator of children pushed him farther than I'd seen in the last year. He was on the edge of darkness. Since the murder of his grandfather many years ago, he occasionally would have what his father called, "spells." He would nearly turn into a living iceberg, black ice. I suspect it is a form of PTSD. He did not go that dark now, but I recognized the onset. It passed.

After I brought him up to date on the several directions of the Christopher case, I wasn't sure how to ask him what I needed from him. It was like three or four floating bubbles which were probably connected, but that was not clear in my own mind.

"There are just too many missing pieces," I said finally.

"Christopher was not Christopher," Frost said simply. "But even that is made to appear to be nebulous. We aren't even sure of negatives."

"What was it someone called them," I mused, "the known unknowns and the unknown unknowns."

"It is difficult to look when one does not know what to look for," Frost added.

"There you are, Frost," I sighed. "A shot in the dark no matter which direction you go."

"It is often easy to get distracted by tangents, side issues." Frost was thinking out loud. "I may have to go that way first. Perhaps there is a side door that will allow entry."

"I hope so," I said with some relief. Frost's active mind was already onto something, but I did not know what. As much as I wanted to know what it was, I did not press. Sometimes the more I asked, the less he answered. The world he lived in, in his mind, was his alone. Some of it was beyond his or anyone's ability to describe. Some would just take too long to do so.

We both went out separate ways for several

minutes. We stayed where we were seated but might as well have been in different countries.

My thinking always flows like the ink out of my pen. It forms into words on paper. Sometimes it is like free association: I write down a sentence. The next one seems to connect. Sometimes it doesn't. I may find myself two pages and 500 words later right back where I started.

My wife noticed something about this many years ago. When I write neatly, precisely, it shows concentration, struggle. It is like I am using the pen and ink to force the words, the ideas, to make sense. In reverse, when the ideas are in control and not the ink, my handwriting is legible only to me, and sometimes barely that.

As I looked over my notes of the last few days, the connections were vague. The circular thinking was confusing. There were a dozen question marks. Some of them were on blank lines – no words, just question marks. The penmanship was nearly flawless.

I do not understand the working of Frost's mind. I don't pretend to. I don't try very hard anymore. The closest I can come to it is the word, "murmuration." That word cannot really be defined, only described, and then, it must be seen to be believed.

Starlings travel in huge flocks – thousands at a time. Suddenly, for no apparent reason, they rise up, almost like a single cloud, and begin swirling around. The patterns they make are beautiful and intricate. I've often wondered how they do so without hundreds flying into one another. The patterns may not be just swirls, but discernable pictures. I've seen some on-line that I would have thought to be computer generated images. One, shown in freeze frame, was a nearly perfect geometric cylinder, like a can of soup. Another, again frozen for an instant, was a huge bird in flight made up of thirty thousand birds in flight. Fascinating. It is called "murmuration."

Patterns emerge in Frost's mind out of what most would see as chaos. Facts, seemingly unrelated, swirling around. Frost watches them in his mind like watching starlings in flight, until the patterns form. Then, Frost connects one pattern to another. He can tell you where he started and where he ends. I don't know if even he, himself, can explain, in words, how he got from one to the other. You might have to see it as he does to believe it.

"Well, John," Frost said at last, "you have presented some interesting problems. So many unknowns. So many holes in the clouds."

"I feel like I have a hole in my head," I said, metaphorically.

He picked it up literally. "Several, it would appear. How are your wounds?"

"I'd say more annoying than downright painful." I was glad for the distraction. "Except for my shin. That is a little more than annoying."

"Tell me more about that adventure," he said.

I had only given him a brief description. I told

the story more fully, beginning with Aydyn's experience. I hedged a little on my own mistakes, using the excuses of darkness and drowsiness, especially how easily I had been fooled by things that were not there.

"I wonder," Frost said, a little thoughtfully. For most people, it would appear to be off-hand daydreaming. Any change in Frost's tone of voice meant more than that.

"You think something was there?" I asked, also a little more than daydreaming.

"Most certainly," he said with a slight smile. "Nobody gets fooled by things that are not there. The real question is did they fool you or did you fool yourself?"

I thought for a second.

"There is a third choice," I said.

"Of course," he replied. "Did someone rather than something fool you."

"I am sure of one person in the dark," I said. Now, I was thoughtful.

"Why do you think there may have been another?" he asked.

"The movement stage left when I was moving to the right," I answered. "The sounds I was following were inside the building. It was not wind or traffic outside. Although, it was like the wind in a way. It was a succession of soft sounds, but evenly spaced. It must have been someone's feet, light feet, soft feet, moving quickly but quietly. On the left, I heard nothing, but something changed. Something moved."

"I don't wish to embarrass you," Frost interrupted, "but could it have been your own shadow?"

He had a good point. I laughed. It could have been. The shop lights peeking over and through the set pieces combined with the bare bulb of the ghost light would throw shadows in unusual directions. A slight change in direction would make the shadow appear to jump. With my attention focused more on sound than sight, anything in my peripheral vision would seem strange.

"When you are looking for anything in the midst of nothing your mind makes something," I said.

Frost smiled politely at my belabored word play.

"That is nearly a universal truth," he went on, "although something may have been there. There are times when one cannot be entirely sure."

That last sentence almost seemed directed back toward himself, rather than to me.

"Of all the mysteries," I continued, "the one that bothers me most...." I stopped myself. "That's not accurate. They bother me in very different ways. Ranking them in any way is not likely. But, to finish my thought: How did we miss this person in our search?"

"When did the mysterious incidents begin?" Frost said. We were thinking aloud together.

"You mean things being moved in the theater?" I asked, just to be sure. I didn't wait for a response.

"Three or four months ago, I think. I didn't pay attention at first. Only after they began to pile up."

"Naturally," Frost went on. "A simple mislaid item seldom arouses interest except for the on who wants it. Even two or three."

"I think there has been at least one incident every week since it began," I mused. "Adding in the ones that may have been only imagined."

"From what you have mentioned, the objects, although dissimilar, have one thing in common." Frost had made one of his connections. "They may be things one might gather for everyday living."

"How so?" I asked. I understood, but I wanted to hear him explain it.

"A towel and a screwdriver would seldom be used together, unless something came loose in the shower, perhaps. They are, however, two common and useful items found in nearly every home." Frost's calm, cool voice matched the calm, cool logic. That's why I like to hear him explain.

"In fact, most people have more than one of each such item," I continued his thinking, "Unless they have extremely limited space."

"Or few choices," Frost added.

"Choices?" He had lost me for a moment.

"Necessity," he stated simply. "Sometimes one's needs are immediate, and one must use what is at hand, what the opportunity presents."

"Like using a butter knife for a screwdriver," I said, catching up.

"Yes," he continued without noticeable change. "Some things get borrowed and replaced, perhaps not in the same spot. The questions are, then, 'What gets borrowed and not returned? And for what purpose?'"

"Does one have a continuing need for a screwdriver?" I picked up his manner of speaking. I often do. "If so, as a screwdriver, or for multiple uses?"

"I think that if we look at those things which are still missing, not just moved, that will tell a part of the story. Those things moved, but replaced, would tell another part." Frost showed a glimmer of self-satisfaction. Some things had fallen into place. "And," he went on, "the sequence of the movements, as far as we may be able to discern them, might tie all things together."

"A nest," I burst forth, almost adding an "Aha!"

Frost was startled. Like most of his emotions, it was gone as quickly as it came, but, for one second, it was there.

"Rather than someone coming and going," I explained, "Someone has been living in the theater. Like a mouse, they would gather small things together for a nest, a home base. They venture out at night to scavenge."

"However," Frost joined my train of thought, "not being a mouse, they might clear and clean the nesting area, at first at least, if not continually."

"The cleaning supplies," I said. Of course.

"And perhaps more than one place," Frost went

on. "Perhaps there are two, more or less permanent nests, as we are calling them. Well hidden. The second as a alternate in case of emergency or changing conditions."

"They would also keep close track of many places to hide on short notice," I added, thoughtfully.

"I suspect," Frost said with a slight smile, "that this mouse may have a way of hiding the hiding places."

"What do you mean?" I asked, lost again.

"You were searching for a person," he explained simply. "You hoped to see a body, or at least a hand or a foot. Somehow this body, hands and feet and all, never appeared. All remained concealed. It probably did not occur to you to look more closely in places where a foot did not appear."

I was still stumped. How do you hide a hiding place? When is a dark corner not a dark corner?

"Are you familiar with Poe's 'The Purloined Letter'?" Frost asked.

"Yes!" I said, as the light dawned. The story is considered on of the first detective stories. In it, a compromising letter has been stolen and used for blackmail. The victim lures the blackmailer away while men, hired by a detective, search his house. They even take some furniture apart looking for it. All the time, the letter has been lying in plain sight among other letters on a desk.

I dropped back into the dark. I couldn't make the connection to our search. Frost caught it.

"Perhaps my reference isn't entirely accurate," he said. "I meant only that there is a hiding place or two that did not occur to you. You have been in the theater many times, none, I trust, with the intent of hiding. This person has made it a lifestyle for some time. There may be mouse holes in places you did not consider."

"Rather than looking for a person in hiding," I concluded, "we should be looking for places a person could hide."

"Have you rehearsal tonight?" Frost asked.

"Of course," I answered. "At seven. I'm going early to clean up my mess from last night. Shirley leaves around five, so I'll go before then. No one else should be there before 5:30."

"Would it be alright if I dropped by?" he asked. "I would not get in the way."

"Oh, sure," I said, happy to have him look around. "Would you like to come with me?'

"No. I'm afraid not," he replied. "I have a dinner engagement with a friend. I should be able to come shortly after your rehearsal begins."

I was surprised. Frost is so solitary. He seems not just content but very happy to be alone. For him to refer to his dinner companion as a friend seemed almost extraordinary. I like Frost. I like him very much now that I know him. I must admit, however, that at our first meeting, I was not just put off by his manner. I confess to being a little afraid of him. My observation is that that is how most people feel. I got over it rather quickly through some very unusual circumstances and now, after a year of our working together.

I really wanted to ask, but I chose discretion out of respect for his extreme privacy. But he surprised me again.

"Thank you," he said, coolly, of course. "You are good at your profession because of your driving curiosity. You have often honored me by not pressing me concerning private matters, common things that most share casually. I do keep my life as a closed book."

"You're very welcome," I said, smiling. "I know that you are not a casual person, in the sense you just used the word." I really did feel a warm friendship with this young man.

"John," he began a little more quietly than usual, "Let me get the shock of this out of the way. I know it will surprise you. I have been keeping company with a young lady. I know that is an old-fashioned way to put it, but I really do like the phrase. My dinner date – yes, date – is with Aydyn Littlefield."

Keeping company? Date? Aydyn! I was not shocked. I was tased.

While I sat in something of a stupor (I hoped my mouth wasn't wide open), he explained.

"Aydyn is not a quiet person. Sooner or later, although she will not say anything directly, one of her friends is likely to put things together. That means that some form of a story about our relationship is bound to come forth, probably in a more complex or outrageous form than is the true story. We enjoy each other's company and have dinner from time to time. Most of the time we talk about things we have read. Our interests in reading are very different, but our infatuation with what we read is nearly identical. It is more than pleasant to share such things."

He smiled in a way I hadn't seen before. I tried to smile back and not smile stupidly.

"I have told you virtually the full extent of our relationship to this point," he continued, almost jovial – for him. "I didn't want you to be caught unawares. Anything further, is none of your business."

He was teasing me? Surprise after surprise.

It took me a second or two to form appropriate words. I managed to say, "None of it is any of my business, but I understand why you shared it."

He let me sit in silence for a bit. I felt odd. Frost seemed comfortable. He was only being courteous, both to me and to Aydyn in his revelations. Although in many ways, Frost seems outside the human race, he understands our species almost by instinct.

Just as I was returning to the right side of comfortable, so that my fumbling with things on my desk was more than just nervousness, Sergeant Murphy appeared in the doorway. He was not happy.

Frost noticed his appearing first but deferred to my seniority in greeting.

"Murphy," I said to him, rather coldly, I'm afraid.

"I can tell by the look on your face that you have more bad news for me."

"Thompson," was his flat greeting. "I don't know what to say about your face. What happened to you?"

"I tripped in the dark and ran into a mirror," was the simplest way I could put it. I didn't think he really wanted more of a story. "I've got coffee. Want some?"

He looked at the pot. There was enough for a cup, but it did not look inviting.

"I'll pass," he said, still flatly.

I could tell that he wasn't sure whether to speak in front of Frost.

"I've filled Frost in," I said, "As well as I can with this mess. I thought he could help us find some missing things. You know how good he is at that."

"Another set of eyes is always welcome." Murphy didn't sound convinced. I understood. What could Frost discover any time soon that the FBI had missed, with all their resources, in years of looking.

"Get it over with, Murphy," I urged. "I'm sure there's no easy way into anything concerning this case."

"That's for damn sure," Murphy sighed with resignation. "I'll jump right in. We didn't have as much trouble identifying the body as I thought. The ID he had on him checked out. Well, sort of. The name on the driver's license – New York state – didn't match the name on the credit cards. Both were aliases. But those and the real name were in the FBI files. He had identifying scars and a tattoo, as well."

"What's the real name?" I asked with a sinking feeling. That the FBI had a file on him bothered me.

"The FBI poster lists it as 'Charlie – not Charles – Clearburg.' That's the name he went by, more or less officially. His birth name is Carl Clauburg. He was born in Germany. Naturalized citizen. Came here as a child."

"Didn't Wheeland mention a case with Christopher in Germany?" I asked.

"I thought of that, too," Murphy said quickly. "Someone from the past finally catching up for revenge. Makes sense. Wheeland didn't think so. They have no known connection."

"Okay," I said, still struggling to make sense of it all and to keep my sinking feeling from hitting bottom. "Then what did the FBI want with Clearburg, or Clauburg, or whatever? Another hitman?"

Murphy didn't want to answer. His mouth was twitching in a way that old me he was desperately trying to hold something in.

Sink. Sank. Sunk. I no longer wanted him to answer. I knew he had to.

"It's worse," Murphy final whispered a growl.

"Worse!" my mouth exploded, as well has my brain. "What the hell could be…." I froze. Not just my speech. My whole body. For one instant, in some deep part of my being beyond real words, I understood Frost's spells when the universe must cease all motion. Frost was standing. I don't know how he got there. Then I realized that I was standing, too. I don't know how I got there. We were ice bergs in a frozen sea. Murphy was a volcano on the verge of, not an eruption, but an explosion.

Finally, in a voice that was not my own, I said the one word I did not want to say, "Children."

Murphy did not speak. I don't think he could. If he opened his mouth in the next few minutes lava would shoot forth.

I felt pains. Real physical ones that finally intruded on my emotional ones. Standing stiffly in a frozen awkward position after the strange workout I'd had the night before was more than my body could stand. I welcomed it. I needed it. That cliché of a slap in the face was not only a cliché. It was reality. It was not the reality of evil that Murphy had just imposed, but common, ordinary, everyday reality. I was a human being with a physical body again.

Then a part of my real physical brain began to function, too.

"I think I'll make a fresh pot of coffee," I said, out loud, in my real voice.

Irrelevant. Stupid. Necessary.

I went about it mechanically. Casually. It was a simple routine that I'd done hundreds of times: dump the old grounds, place the paper filter, count out the scoops from the canister, dump the dregs, rinse the pot, fill it to the appropriate line, pour the water in the reservoir, replace the pot, push the button.

In a few seconds, there was gurgling sound. A few seconds more and the brown liquid began to flow into the pot.

I didn't know what to do. Standing there for several minutes staring was ridiculous. Returning to my chair seemed impossible. Had I ever done that? Really? Had I actually sat in that chair? Had I ever been in this room? The whole world seemed unfamiliar. So, I stood, watching, waiting. The mundane brewing was comforting.

The coffee was nearly half done before I did sit. Once again, the painful stiffness of my body intruded. Thank God. Murphy and Frost seemed no more like living people than the pictures on the wall. They, too, were watching the level of the coffee rise slowly. And so, we sat.

– nine –

Frost waited, politely, for the coffee to finish. He declined a cup and excused himself, politely. Wherever he was going physically, I know there was a special place he was going in his mind, perhaps in his spirit. We all have our own ways of repairing injuries, physical or emotional. Those who can "shake it off" or "suck it up" are very few. Personally, I think those who profess to do so are phony. Not intentionally. They think it is the thing to do. Sooner or later, it comes back to haunt you. In some cases, it kills. There is a difference between handling it on your own and just burying it. Some shocks are vampires. Unless you drive a stake through their hearts, they'll be back.

Child sex trafficking. There. I said it. If no one says it out loud, we pretend it doesn't exist. Once it's said, there's no going back to pretending.

Murphy and I had nearly finished our mugs of strong coffee before we actually spoke out loud.

Murphy started. Thank God.

"By the way, Wheeland doesn't think Christopher was mixed up with Clauberg. Not in Clauberg's business."

Murphy nearly choked on the word, "business."

"They're both dead in Cedar Falls, Iowa," I said, with no more emotion than the stapler I was fiddling with. "Both died within yards of each other. Both stabbed with an ice pick."

"Yes," Murphy agreed in the same tone as my own.

Another pause.

"Do you want anymore coffee?" I asked.

"No, thank you. I don't want any more damn coffee," he replied, still without emotion.

What now?

"I don't want to do this," I said, finally.

"I don't either," Murphy agreed.

"So, what do we do?" I asked.

With great effort Murphy began to return to the land of real life.

"I only see one opening," he started. "We have to figure out what Clauberg was doing here."

I didn't want to ask the obvious. Murphy knew.

"Wheeland was surprised, too," he went on. "Clauberg didn't operate in the Midwest. Well, pass through between both coasts. Not enough dirty, old bastards with money." He spit that last part.

I wanted to spit, too. I cannot even describe the taste in my mouth. The coffee alleviated it for a few minutes. When we started talking, it came back.

"Do you think he came looking for Christpher?" I asked.

"No," Murphy said quickly and surely, "He would only look for Christopher for Christopher's business. Christopher didn't operate that way. You didn't find him. He found you."

From what we'd been told, that made sense. But something didn't make sense.

"They didn't just bump into each other by accident," I said. "Clauberg didn't just fall off the train that hit Christopher. Something brought them together then and there."

"That's the missing piece," Murphy said, his voice beginning to rise in frustration. "Right now, it's a gap the size of the Grand Canyon."

"There must be something," I was joining his frustration.

"Yes," Murphy said, through gritted teeth. "It's not just a piece. We are really missing something."

"Missing!" I said as something suddenly came into my head. "Yes! Missing!"

"What the hell is the matter with you?" Murphy looked at me as if I'd lost my mind. But I had just found it.

"Something that's missing!" I shouted. "Murphy did you find Christopher's shoulder bag?"

"Shoulder bag?" he asked, confused of course.

"Yes," I said with excitement. "Christopher always had a brown, leather business bag with him. He came to the theater with it. It had his script and notes and stuff in it. A lot of actors do that. They have a bag, a backpack, briefcase, whatever. What else was in Christopher's I don't know, but I suspect he had a gun."

"A gun?" Now I had Murphy's full attention.

I related to him the story about how I first saw him coming out of the garage, and how he kept his hand in the bag in a strange manner. I told him, also, that when Christopher left the theater that last night, I was sure he had it with him.

"We went over that garage and that car carefully," Murphy was up with me now. "We went over the crime scene on our hands and knees. There was no bag."

"Is there any way it could have gone in the river?" I asked, just to eliminate possibilities.

"I don't see how," Murphy said, shaking his head. "Both bodies were on the far side of the tracks a long way from the bridge. Christopher had to be nearly dead before he stumbled into the train. The bag had to be on that side, too."

"Someone has that bag," I said.

"Someone else was there" Murphy added with confidence.

We had no idea who, but having this much, an unknown someone, was a narrower gap than a vague missing something.

"Christopher was a loner," Murphy continued. "Our missing person was either an accidental witness or was there with Clauberg."

"What accidental witness would have run off with the bag?" I asked.

"Not impossible, I suppose," Murphy said with a hint of worry. Such a scenario would drop us back into the vagueness.

"Wheeland!" I suggested.

"Of course," Murphy agreed. "He would know of possible associates for Clauberg."

Murphy got up with purpose. He handed me his mug.

"Thanks for the coffee," he said with a wink.

"You're welcome," I replied.

Murphy left my office with determined walk.

I needed to get out of this. I'd been drawn in by the police because I knew Christopher, or at least a form of him. The same was partly true concerning Norm and the Davenport family. A strange insurance problem where I happened to know the diseased had turned into dealing with a family terrified of something from the past. The two might be one, but somehow, I had to separate them. More than that, I had to separate myself. I would let Murphy and Wheeland work on their end. I'd try to keep my distance and try to work on the other. I would keep any connections as far away as possible. My search would on insurance matters and only on insurance matters.

It was well past lunch time. My stomach had too much coffee and too much acid from other causes for food. I also knew I couldn't stay in my office any longer. I was parked in front of the building, but I thought a walk around the block in the November cold might feel good. I grabbed my coat and hat and left.

I was right and I was wrong. Cold air forces you to pay attention to it. You pull your hat down a little tighter. You zip your jacket up a little farther. You hunch your shoulders trying to protect your nose. These are conscious actions. While you think about them, the unconscious things begin to settle down like falling leaves. On the ground, they might still be a mess, but it's a mess you can handle. All you need is the right rake.

The wrong part was, once again, my joints. The cold felt good on my neck where I'd been cut and on my scraped shin. Backs are not made for crouching while creeping through a cavern. I thought of going to my gym. They have a very soothing spa. Twenty minutes in the hot water with the jets on my back sounded heavenly.

"Shit," I whispered. Conflicting injuries. I would not be allowed in the public water with fresh open wounds, however minor. I would have to settle for my old heating pad in my recliner.

I had gotten around the block and into my car without speaking to anyone. I hadn't seen them. I kept part of my attention on the cold and my planning on some heat. It was a childish back and forth argument. An eight-year-old me was calling another eight-year-old me a stupid head. "Am not!" "Are, too!"

Cold air. Achy joints. Childish role play. It is amazing

what lengths a mind will go to in its search for healing and peace.

I started off in the car but changed my mind about the direction. I decided to go in search of a newer and larger heating pad. I went around and up to First Street and back to Main. The light was green, so I turned south with hardly a thought. I glanced at the theater on my right and at the coffee shop across from it on my left.

I noticed in front of the coffee shop a strangely dressed man. He was smallish, paunchy and in his forties. He was wearing a forest green jogging suit and smoking a cigarette. It appeared to me that he hadn't jogged in any way, shape or form in years, maybe ever in his life. He was completely out of place. I chuckled to myself. I was two more buildings down when it hit me: he had a brown, leather shoulder bag.

I was extremely glad that the guy behind me was watching me closely and that the breaks of his huge Dodge Ram worked so well.

I couldn't see the strange man in my side mirror. I went ahead. The light was red. I waited for two cars crossing in front of me and turned right. At the stop sign at the nest corner, I had the same traffic and, again, when I finally got back to First Street. By the time I got back to Main, there was no sign of the man in the green jogging suit.

In front of the theater is a space for letting off passengers. I pulled into it and got out of my car. I ran across to the coffee shop. Inside were four or five college kids and one behind the counter. I ran out. I looked as far down the street as I could. There was very little foot traffic. No one was wearing green of any shade.

In the time it had taken me to get back around, the man could have walked a block and turned the corner. He didn't look like any more of a walker than a jogger, but he wouldn't have to be. Or he could have just gotten into his car parked nearby and driven away.

I went back to my car with my head on a swivel. I noticed every person, every movement, every suggestion of green. It was futile.

Instead of going to look for a heating pad, I went to look for Murphy.

The Cedar Falls Public Safety building is only a couple of blocks east of Main. It is a modern design in gray stone that exudes strength, stability. I've been here often on business, mostly seeking little pieces of information about a person who may be in their files. Often a person who tries to get away with something regarding insurance has cut some other corners as well. They bend rules to suit themselves. They annoy me.

We honestly discuss which rules and regulations are unnecessary. I happen to believe that honest studies were done before the city puts up a stop sign. It's safer. I don't see why some people think they are so special that such rules don't apply to them. If you're playing a pick-up game of basketball with some friends and you don't call every foul or every time a toe touches out of bounds, who cares? When you're talking about safety, maybe life or death, screw your head on a little tighter. Is that really so hard?

I spoke briefly with the front desk personnel and some others in the office. Said "hi" to a couple of passing officers. Murphy would be out shortly. I didn't take the offered coffee. They make pretty good coffee there, but I had overindulged.

It was about ten minutes before Murphy came out. He did not look pleased to see me so soon. But he was more puzzled than upset.

"What's going on, Thompson?" he asked. "I thought you'd be home in bed or something. Not here."

"I wish I was home," I said, trying not to sound too disappointed. "Something weird happened."

Now Murphy was annoyed. One more weird thing. "I've written up a memo for the town council to change the name of this place from Cedar Falls to The Twilight Zone." From his tone, I believed him.

"Do you want privacy," he went on, quietly but more officially.

"No," I told him. "It might be nothing, but with things they way they are, I thought I better throw it in."

"Okay," Murphy said, taking a deep breath, "Shoot."

I told him of the strange man I'd seen across from the theater with a shoulder bag. I couldn't say for sure it was Christopher's bag or even how much like it it might have been. It was just too odd a coincidence, if that's what it was. I also told Murphy how I'd lost him.

"You're right," Murphy said. "It might be nothing, but it's too weird to let pass. We need to grab every straw that comes our way. Can you give description to my people?"

"I can try," I said with some doubt. "It was quick, but he was strange looking. Maybe enough stuck in my head."

"Might be easy," he said. "It's the odd ones that stick better then the more ordinary. A hundred guys standing in a group, and you can see how different each is. Pass the same hundred guys on the street and you remember them all as looking alike."

"I think that's right," I sighed. "Well, let's give it a try."

"By the way," Murphy changed directions. "Wheeland thinks we may be right about the extra guy. He's going to have them send information on the six or eight most likely. It'll come with pictures. Maybe we'll get lucky. If the guy you saw matches one of them, we'll turn over every rock in town. Hell. We'll turn over the state to get him."

I spent a good half hour describing and redescribing the man I had seen. I wanted to tweak it more, but the artist stopped me. After the first couple of times, changes are apt to be wrong. Witnesses often talk themselves out of their own memories. They add things, take away things. They can be influenced by the pictures on the wall or a memory from their high school yearbook that they happened to look through the week before. When he was learning his craft, that is the particular one here for the police, he took part in exercises along those lines. Even among other artists, after extreme tweaking, half the final pictures were so different from the original as to be two different people.

I left the building and went straight home. I decided the old heating pad would be good enough, if it worked. There's something wrong with the control. Sometimes it won't go beyond the lowest setting. If it didn't work, well, I wanted the recliner much more than I wanted another side trip.

The heating pad worked but the whole set-up didn't work as I hoped.

The lights were very bright in the shop. Bob was bent over the work bench concentrating on something. Gary was on the floor looking for something. I heard laughter behind me and turned to the make-up room. Jack and Sophie, a couple of high school freshmen in a different play were joking about something.

I turned back to the empty shop. Everything was cleaned up. The work bench was pushed back against a cabinet out of the way. I took a couple of steps toward it when something made me turn around and go into the make-up room. Jack and Sophie were seated on the little benches, leaning back against the mirrors. They were motionless staring blankly at the ceiling. A man stood in the opposite doorway. He had a rather dark complexion with black hair and moustache. He had the strap of a brown, leather bag over his right shoulder. It was Doc.

"Buenos noches, senor," he said to me with a nod. He turned and walked nonchalantly out.

I followed him across the Main Street bridge. I was gaining on him slowly. He kept walking north until he was a few feet beyond the railroad tracks. He turned easily to face me. The moustache was gone. He just looked at me calmly. Then, he lifted his right hand and casually reached into his bag. He disappeared as a train ran between us.

I walked toward Uncle Floyd's house. As I got closer, coming from the east, the little girl I had seen clinging to her mother's leg walked toward the garage. While still several steps away, she reached out her hand as if for the doorknob on the side door. Her grandmother, the one with the blue streak in her white hair, stepped between us, arms folded. She glared at me. The little girl was lying on her back on the ground. The odd-looking man in the green jogging suit came out from behind the garage. He walked toward the little girl and stood looking over her. I was very cold. I turned away.

The darkness of the bare stage was gloomy. The ghost light made it more so. Even as I stared at it, the darkness seemed to engulf it. The bare bulb seemed just as bright, but it had no more effect on the darkness than if it had been painted on velvet. The ghost light was in its usual spot: down right, a few feet from the wings. I was just past center stage. I turned around.

Frost was standing down left, on the apron, just past the steps that led from the audience. He was motionless. He was in one of his dark frozen spells. Aydyn was behind him, at the top of the stairs. She seemed to be swaying happily to the music she heard in her head.

The was a noise behind me in the utter darkness. Where? I looked in every direction. There it was again: soft, running feet. They were in the back hallway running for the stage door. I took a step to follow. No. They were in the upper hallway behind the theater boxes. Going east? No. Going west to the loft.

Suddenly, I had to turn around. All the curtains on the left side of the stage were moving, slowly, as if caught in a swirling breeze. Occasionally, I could see something beyond them like a white mist. It made me feel warm and at ease.

BEEP! BEEP! BEEP! BEEP! BEEP!

The alarm on my phone woke me up with a jolt.

— ten —

My eyes were rested. My back was less stiff. My mind was hash.

Some dreams do that. I still managed to get to the theater before Shirley locked the front door. It was unnecessary; the back door was unlocked. Bob and Gary were there. I also had not anticipated, but was not surprised, that Gary would be nearly finished cleaning up my mess. He'd gotten off work early and come to the theater to see what needed to be done. As soon as he saw my note, he did that.

"You didn't have to do that," I told him.

"Oh, no problem," he said in his usual cheery tone. "Something different to do."

Gary just liked new things, any new thing. I left him to it. He would probably do a better job than I would have done. I went to find Bob.

Bob was on the stage adding some molding around a doorway on the back side of the wall. This flat (that's what sections of scenery are called) could be flipped around and moved becoming a child's bedroom.

"You're just in time," was Bob's greeting. "I could use a hand with this door." He looked at me and added, "If you're able."

"I think I'll live," I replied, "I might even be useful, as long as it doesn't take too much brain work."

I handed him a piece of molding that he pointed to.

"A late night running around in the dark," he began, trying to hide a smile, "especially crashing into things. Yeah. I can see why you might be a little scrambled."

"And then some," I emphasized.

"Of course, how much brains does it take in the first place?" he teased.

"Well," I said, with feigned sorrow, "it seemed like a good idea at the time."

"That should have been your first clue that your brain wasn't working," he said with exaggerated pity.

"Yeah," I chuckled, "sitting in the dark without a good flashlight and no idea where the switch for the house lights: not a good plan."

"I thought the flaw in the plan was looking for someone who wasn't there in the first place," Bob thought he was still teasing.

"There was someone," I informed him. He nearly fell off the ladder.

"What?!" he spurted out.

"I heard footsteps," I explained. "And when I crashed into that mirror, somebody gasped."

Bob climbed down slowly. He looked me in the

eye to be sure I wasn't trying to pull a fast one. "We looked everywhere," he said in a strong voice.

"Evidently not," I responded. "I only stayed because I though maybe I could identify the sound that Aydyn had heard. I was wrong. We missed something and someone."

"That bothers me, John," he said, very seriously. "That really bothers me."

"Me, too," I agreed. "Frost and I are convinced that someone has been living in the theater for three or four months."

"Living here?!" he said, trying hard to understand. "Living here?"

"It explains all those strange things that have been happening," I went on.

"It does," he said with certainty, and some anger. "That makes things worse. I can see getting in and out. It happens. But how do you live here? How do you live?"

"In my mind," I tried to explain to myself as well as Bob, "I can come up with parts of it. There are any number of places to sleep. There are five bathrooms in the building. There's even a kitchen. But where do you keep food?"

Bob thought for a few seconds. Then, he said, "Canned goods. Soup. Spam. Peaches. Cereal bars. A couple of grocery bags full could keep you going for a month."

"Of course," I said, the light dawning. "And they wouldn't need to be all in one place. One or two cans could be put in a hundred places and not noticed."

"Between shows," Bob added, "there could be a whole week when not one person is in the building. But what about now?" he thought out loud. "A cast of twenty. Crews coming and going."

"Shirley's only here during the day," I was trying to analyze, "Mostly just in the front office. Goes upstairs to see Mike if he's in. They'd be easy to avoid. When we're here we stay mostly in the shop. Some one might go down to get some props. They wouldn't be looking around."

"But we searched!" Bob said emphatically.

"Yeah. We thought it would be easy," I said with resignation. "But we thought we were just looking for a vagrant, not some ghostly whoever that has a long time to look around, to plan, to really hide."

"I'm going to get some guys from work," Bob said with determination, "We'll bring work lights. We'll move every splinter in the place."

The look on his face was solid granite.

"Whoa. Slow down, Bob," I said trying to calm him. "Frost and I are going to try a couple of other ideas first. If that doesn't work, we'll go talk to Mike about your plan. He's the manager, you know."

"Of course," Bob agreed. "I just don't like intruders. A homeless guy trying to keep warm for the night? Sure. No problem. But this crosses the line."

"Come on, Bob," I said, more calmly. "Let's get back to work. It'll keep our minds occupied."

He thought that was sound advice for the both of us. When I first got involved with the theater, there was a college student in a play. Theater was her major. She was determined to be a great actress. She's a teacher and a mother, now, doing community theater in Omaha. She had a book that she showed me. It's a classic about acting. The first lesson in it is called, "Concentration." From what he meant, I think the author should have chosen the word "Focus." That is certainly what I wanted now.

For now, I would focus on the set. Later, I would focus on my scene. I would not look beyond what was right in front of me. That might not keep dreams away when I went home, but it would keep them away now.

Bob and I both focused on finishing touches of the set construction. The main parts were all done. What is known as set decoration was left to do: a framed copy of the U.S. Constitution for the courtroom; a small wall lamp suitable for the little girl's bedroom – things like that.

Gary finished cleaning up the make-up room and joined us. Naturally, he wanted to know what happened.

"Before I left," I explained a little vaguely, "I checked something in the loft. Coming down, I missed the last step."

"Not hurt too bad?" he asked, boyishly but sincerely.

"No," I said lightly, "but I thought I should get myself cleaned up first. That's why I didn't clean up the mess last night. Thanks again, by the way."

"No problem," he said again.

"I guess I just got in too big a hurry," I said with a smile. Bob gave me a knowing glance. I had told the truth, but maybe not the whole truth. I knew, and so did Bob, that if I'd told the whole story, Gary would spend the rest of the night crawling around the basement.

"Hey, Bob," Gary changed the subject, to my relief. "We're going to have this all done way ahead of time, aren't we?'

"Well," Bob went on more studiously, like the pro he is, "Everything will be put together. Whether it works or not is another matter."

"What do you mean?" Gary asked.

"There are a lot of moving parts," Bob explained. "This wall ends up in three different places. It has to join up with the others. The bed has to roll out and roll back. You never know about the wheels."

"You remember the trolley car we had we had a few years ago?" I asked Bob.

"Oh, God," he moaned. "Don't remind me!"

"What happened to the trolley car?" Gary asked eagerly.

"The damn wheels wouldn't cooperate!" Bob cried out. He didn't swear much, but I never hear him talk about that show without referring to the "damn wheels."

"All that thing had to do," he continued, "was go straight on and straight off, and that was the one thing those damn wheels could not do."

"Two people could move the thing pretty easy," I added, "but we needed a third one. His job was to keep it straight. He was the biggest guy on the crew and it took all he had to do it."

"Sometimes," Bob spoke to Gary in a fatherly way, "you just don't know what you have until you start moving things. We've moved these around a little, but they weren't completely finished. There's always something that won't cooperate."

"Wow," Gary said as he looked things over, "That could cause a lot of trouble."

"Most of the time it's just nuisance," Bob said with resignation. "We and the actors can just work around it."

"For one show," I laughed, "I was on the stage more than any of the actors."

"What?" Gary was surprised.

"Actually," I said, "I was out of sight. We had a door that absolutely refused to stay closed on opening night. Every time someone went through it, I had to hold it closed. It was a one set show, and that door was used a lot. I had to stand there for almost the whole two hours!"

We all laughed. It felt good to laugh. It felt real.

"We fixed it the next day," Bob said, shaking his head.

We spent most of the next hour and a half telling similar stories. Gary ate it up. Every show has at least one story of something that went wrong. Most of them got us to laughing. We probably didn't laugh at the time, but memories are often more fun than frustrating. There were a couple of stories that were more serious.

One time, the railing around a porch on the front of a house broke. It was a freak weak spot that hadn't been noticed. We fixed it with duct tape between scenes. What we didn't know was that an actor had cut his arm on a nail that had been exposed. He had fixed it with the same duct tape and a towel. His character in the next scene was supposed to remove his suit coat. It was just a bit of extra stage business, not a big deal. The actor left it on, and the scene played out. For the rest of the run of the show he left it on as well. Now, he was covering up the professional bandage over four stitches. It's things like that that get an actor a great accolade: "a real trouper." Among actors it is one of the highest honors.

We kept our stories to our own experiences. That was more than enough. We'd heard a hundred others. Theater lore, backstage stories, is one of the last outposts of the oral tradition. I'm sure someone writes these down, but it's not the same.

I didn't know if Gary had heard the story of the tragic Laura. We didn't tell that one. Not only was it not our own experience, but I also really thought Gary might try to spend the night in an effort to meet her. I can't say for sure that he believed in ghosts. It was more, in my thinking, that he might hope that it was true. In his youthful spirit, every new possibility was a new adventure, a new game, you might say. Ordinarily, I might even encourage him. Right then, I decided not to.

About 5:45, Charles Wemyss arrived, followed shortly by Linc. They were followed by a woman that I did not recognize at first. She was introduced to us as Grace Thurston. She would be in charge of lighting for the play. Then, I remembered her. She had taken a break from the theater for a couple of years, to take care of her ailing mother.

Her mother had resisted going to a long-term care facility. She didn't like the term. She didn't like "nursing home." She didn't like the whole idea. But she was there now, Martha shared with us, and doing beautifully. She had not only adjusted to the idea, she was flourishing. She had been surprised to find such comfortable rooms and caring people. There were several activities that she enjoyed very much. She was most pleased to make new friends, some as much as ten years younger, some ten years older. It was not the "warehouse where you went to wait to die" that had filled her imagination.

Grace, like most lighting designers that I have known, was very exact and solitary in her job. I suppose being at the far back of the theater and physically far above everyone reinforces that. The lighting people are connected to the stage by beams of light. Their focus must be timing – an instant beam here, a slow glow arising there, colors that not only illuminate but also enhance a scene. They have thousands of watts of light to control. I can see why one would want to avoid any distraction when on the job.

Grace is not unfriendly or cold. Quite the contrary. She is a bright, cheerful woman, with one of the warmest smiles. She is so friendly; I would say even loving. She has a wild sense of humor and yet gives the aura of compassion, deep and wonderful. At the cast parties, she could be the life of the party. She knows some songs that could bring down the house on stage. I realized that I had really missed her in the time she had been away.

Tonight's rehearsal would be kind of tough. It would be a "work through." That means we would start at the beginning but make frequent stops. There might be a place where Wemyss would try things a new way, or two new ways. Or there might be a place where an actor just wasn't getting it. Stop and start. Stop and start. It is actually a good learning process, but it can be tedious.

Bob has a good analogy for the process: Let's say you've made a piece of furniture, like a simple table. You are past the stage of putting all the pieces together. Now you have to sand it down before you put on the finish and polish it.

It can take a lot out of an actor, but I remember something Katherine Hepburn once said in an interview. She didn't have much sympathy for young actors who complained about rehearsals being hard work. She said, yes, it could be tiring, but "it's not like we're asked to throw around sacks of feed all day." I may be reading more into it than she intended, but I got the feeling that she thought those "method actors", who got so emotionally tired, were too tired from things outside the production, or maybe just emotionally weak to begin with.

Bob and Gary and I gathered tools and materials and put them away. The work through would be the only work going on, at least on the stage. Grace would be sitting near Wemyss with a script fine tuning her light cues. Some time later, more than once, she would come to test all the lighting instruments (techs never call them "spot lights"). In simple terms, she would make sure they were pointed to the right place and focused correctly.

All the actors were to gather in the audience seats by 7:00. Wemyss would make some general comments and announcements, and then some words of encouragement. He was good at that, even when the encouragement could be taken as warnings.

The one that registered with me most strongly was this: one week from tonight was Thanksgiving!

Thanksgiving!

I had completely blocked it out of my mind. Jack would be in charge of most of the cooking, as he had been for a number of years. He makes even the traditional things seem even better. He has a real gift for that. He and Marta would arrive Tuesday to begin preparations.

Jenni, and maybe Corey, would come Wednesday

night, not quite at the last minute. She always seems to have trouble getting away, but she always plans ahead. There is a woman who does special baking for the holidays. Jenni calls her a month in advance to order a very special dessert. Jack will pick it up as he does everything.

I thought, "At least, that mess will help me block out all these other messes I've gotten myself into."

I estimated that Wemyss' remarks began at 7:03. I assumed that because he began at almost exactly three minutes after Frost appeared. He had said he would come "shortly after your rehearsal begins." That he appeared before told me two things: First, his dinner engagement was cut short if not out right cancelled because of the emotions of the afternoon. And second, that the moment I noticed him coming through the curtain at the far left of the auditorium, it must be seven o'clock. Aydyn came in with him. She looked concerned. Frost look as he always did.

"Let's do it!" Wemyss said cheerily. Everyone went to their places. Mine, for now, was where I was sitting. Frost and Aydyn joined me.

"Hi, Frost," I greeted him, softly. "Good to see you, Aydyn. Did Frost fill you in on some of our morning?"

"Yes, he did," she whispered. That was not like her.

"It's awful. Just awful," she added.

"It is that," I said, quietly. Then I turned to Frost. "How are you?"

He gave a wry smile before saying, "My systems are functioning within acceptable parameters."

I smiled back. We both knew there were some who view him as an alien being or even an android. He took no offense and often found humor in it.

"Do you want me to show you around?" I offered. He was unfamiliar with the theater.

"I'm going to do that," Aydyn said, quickly. "You just concentrate on what you need to be doing. Forget we're here."

"I'll try," I said, trying to assure myself more than her. I knew that Aydyn would be a good guide. She'd been a part of the theater virtually her whole life. Her experience and her natural curiosity had led her into almost every corner.

"Okay," she said, turning to Frost, "we'll start in the basement and work our way up."

He nodded in his old-fashioned gentlemanly way, smiled and followed her back through the same curtain. I sat back in my seat. My small part did not appear until late in the play. It would be interesting to watch the rest of it from out front for a change. I knew the story, of course, but for this production, I had only been in back working on or moving sets.

It turned out to be more than interesting. This was going to be a great show. Paul Gregory as Santa would make a believer out of everyone.

Several minutes after the start of the play, Frost and Aydyn emerged from the curtained archway on the opposite side from where they had started.

They had gone through the basement from south to north (more quickly than I thought they would). Aydyn was pointing and speaking in her usual animated way, but very quietly so as not to disturb the actors. After a minute or so, they continued up the far-right aisle and out of the auditorium. I returned to the play.

The first act went very smoothly, with only a few stops. We weren't changing the scenery, so occasionally an entrance or a chair was not where they would finally be. Some actors, usually younger ones, get a little flustered by such things. Others, sometimes even younger ones, can keep in the scene no matter what. I've seen some here that wouldn't miss a line or a beat if a herd of baboons ran across the stage.

Now and then, I became aware of Frost and Aydyn's explorations. Again, at the far right, but this time in the balcony, I saw them through the doorway that leads behind the theater boxes on that side. I could tell that Frost was taking it all in calmly, but not missing a thing. It isn't only that he sees everything, even things others might miss, but he sees the possibilities in those things. He was calculating every nook and cranny, estimating how someone might hide or elude. He would know their size and their agility of the possibility. Anyone could duck into a broom closet, but only someone small could duck easily and quickly behind a theater seat. I could figure that much out. Frost probably saw ten other ideas.

The couple appeared for a few seconds in the box that was closest to stage left. It's empty. It is used sometimes in plays that call for a short scene that doesn't require a lot of scenery or props – a man making a quick phone call from his office, for example. There is a wooden ladder attached to a backstage wall that goes through the floor just behind the box, so an actor can get in and out unseen. Frost leaned over the rail of the box for a second, looked down at the stage floor, then he and Aydyn disappeared behind the black curtain.

When he did that, it occurred to me that an athletic person could jump from that box to the stage without much difficulty. John Wilkes Booth had attempted a similar jump after shooting Lincoln. In his case, it is believed, he caught either the heel of his boot or a spur on the bunting on the front of the box. He landed awkwardly, breaking his leg. He was still able to get up, hobble quickly off and out the back door to his waiting horse.

I was aware without really hearing or seeing them, that Frost and Aydyn crossed the balcony and went behind the boxes on the south side. I saw the curtains rustle behind the boxes, but the investigators did not appear. I assumed they continued down the walkway to the loft.

It was some time before I saw them again. They emerged as before from the curtain at the southwest corner of the auditorium. Frost gave me one of his polite nods. Aydyn smiled and waved. They walked quickly and quietly up the aisle and out. I did not see them again until rehearsal was over.

Wemyss always tries to end rehearsals by 10:00 p.m. Some of the younger children leave much earlier. With a hard work through, it can be hard to meet that deadline. Tonight, we almost made it. Everyone was pleased.

Most of the cast had headed for their homes before Frost and Aydyn returned to the auditorium. I had returned to the seat where they first saw me. I felt good about having gotten through my scene without having to go back and do it again. I wasn't too surprised to see the couple although I wasn't sure they were still in the building. I thought Frost might wait until the morning to tell me what he might have found.

They came in together. As strange as it had seemed when Frost first told me of their relationship, they seemed so natural together now. The quiet, cool Frost was always so neatly dressed as though he had just come from a tailor. Aydyn, bouncy, excited, always looked as though she had slept in the clothes that were not really her own. Together they really did complement each other. They completed each other.

"John," Frost said as he took the seat beside me, "I wasn't sure you would wait."

"I wasn't sure you were still here," I returned.

Aydyn remained standing in the aisle.

"This is a remarkable old building," Frost said.

There was a flavor of admiration and joy in his voice. "It is quite fascinating."

"It is," I said. "I've always been intrigued by it, even without mysteries."

"Ah, yes. Mysteries," he said calmly.

"What are your thoughts on those?" I asked.

"Aydyn showed me a photograph of the unfortunate Laura," he began. "She was indeed lovely. I can understand why some would hope that she is still present in some form."

"Really?" I said, a bit intrigued by that observation.

He smiled a knowing smile before saying, "Let me say only that I found nothing to disappoint those wishes."

I smiled back.

"Whatever may be one's personal views, it is at least unkind to challenge certain traditions," he observed.

"Absolutely," I readily agreed. "Therefore, let us look at more recent events."

"In that area," he said, "I am quite confident that someone has indeed taken up residence in this theater."

My face did not hide my surprise. I was pretty well convinced myself. My surprise was at the degree of his confidence.

He explained. "There is a great deal of evidence – primarily some, let me say undusty places. The dust was removed by usage in places that would not normally show that much use. And, I must say, as much as I like this building, it is a very dusty place."

Aydyn laughed. "It really is. It would take a cleaning crew a month to dust this place. I guess we just got used to it."

I smiled. They were both right, of course.

"I am also certain," Frost continued, "that I identified at least six places where a person might have eluded your search the other night. One or two rather ingenious."

His admiration showed.

"Well," I said, "what do you think we should do now?"

"Nothing," he said, simply.

"Nothing?" I said, surprised again.

"Nothing yet, I should say," he explained. "There are some interesting things about this situation. It is not as simple as someone looking for rent-free lodging."

My surprise threatened to get the better of me. I controlled myself.

"What do you propose?" I asked.

"I will be spending the night," he said, matter-of-factly. "It is my hope that I can make contact that will not frighten this person. Somehow, I feel that would have most unfortunate consequences, not for me, but for the hidden one."

I had more questions than I could count, but Frost's demeanor and intention convinced me to put those aside.

"I'll be in the office early," I said. I got up and went home.

– eleven –

Frost's composure after his exploration of the theater gave me a more restful night than I had anticipated. The jumbled thoughts and feelings that had given me the strange dreams earlier succumbed to Frost's coolness. Young as he is, most of his life has been spent making sense of such things in his own extraordinary mind. I will not use the word "controlling." He never really controls his thoughts, only his behavior. It's like learning the right way in a storm so you aren't blown over by the wind. And his attitude is contagious.

I opened my office door a little after eight a. m. I did not make coffee. I had overindulged the day before, which is a first for me. I expected Frost at nine, exactly nine. I did not expect a phone call. My cell rang.

"John," came Norman Corrigan's booming voice when I answered. "Good morning!"

To be quite truthful, I had nearly forgotten about him and his part in this strange business. Tony Davenport popped into view now and then, but even that was an afterthought.

"Good morning, Norm," I said casually.

"Say," he went on cheerily, "We're on our way to the airport. I wanted to check in with you before we left."

"Oh, really," I said with surprise. I was trying to refocus on that situation and not let Norm realize I'd forgotten all about him. It is a long way to South Dakota. The family had to get back sooner or later. They couldn't be just filed away until I finally got around to them.

"We've been having a great time," Norm said sincerely. "I wish it could go on longer."

Part of that sounded as though it was intended for Tony's ears rather than mine.

"Listen, Norm," I said seriously. "You won't believe the turns this whole thing has taken. Call me back when you get the chance and can talk freely. In fact, it would be better in person."

"Not much progress yet?" Norm covered beautifully. It was obvious he didn't want someone else to know what I really said. He didn't like what I said, but he would keep it to himself.

"If it helps any, Norm," I told him, "You can tell Tony that I have some evidence that indicates that Geoffrey Christopher was not related to the Davenport family."

"Really?" Norm's tone was hard to read on the phone, but I think he got the message. We both realized that Tony at least suspected that the dead man might have been his father. Any hint, and I had stretched the word "evidence" almost to the breaking point, that would relieve that fear would be welcome. At the same time, if not related by blood, related how? After all, I had stronger evidence that he may have been his father's killer?

"Well, that doesn't solve all the mystery," Norm was speaking for someone else's benefit again. "But it is a step in the right direction. I'll call you when I get back."

"Good," I replied. "Give my best to Tony and his family."

Wheeland had suggested that an unknown loner had killed Tony's father, or, rather, someone's father. The only thing they knew for sure was that they had both disappeared. No bodies were found. That left a lot of inconsistencies and even more questions. Foremost: if Tony's mother's terror, her insanity, were not triggered by her husband, how could they be so strong? If from a stranger, how did she know him? And one more: if the mysterious loner was "the Exterminator," how was it that any of the family was left alive?

A couple more questions would only bring me back to where I started. It was becoming a Mobius stip. That's an idea, a concept, that is illustrated by a strip of ribbon. It is in the shape of an infinity symbol. It has no beginning and no end. No way out.

Frost appeared, as I expected, at nine o'clock. He was dressed as he had been the night before. I assumed that he had come directly from the theater.

Unlike most people, however, no one could tell by looking at him. There was nothing about his appearance to suggest he had been awake all night. His face did not look tired or stressed. His clothes were not wrinkled.

"Good morning, John," he said as he always did. His voice was the first notice of his presence as, of course, I had not heard his approach. I once thought of getting a bell for the outer door, but he probably could still open and close it without a sound.

"Good morning," I greeted him as I always did. "It must have been a long night. Why don't you grab a bottle of water."

He didn't drink coffee and I hadn't thought to make tea for him. He prefers Earl Grey with honey, or a special herbal blend that he has made.

"Yes," he said, "That will do nicely. It was an interesting night."

We got comfortable and he told me all about it.

"Your old theater is even more fascinating in the dark than it had been with the lights on. I can easily understand how tales of hauntings appear in such places. Not only the sights but also the whisperings that appear from nowhere could easily be long lost lines form long ago performances. Whispers that I am sure are more likely echoes of draughts, furnace noises, outside wind and distant traffic, not otherworldly origins. I must admit, however, that some did suggest voices. Intriguing.

"I waited at the top of the south staircase outside

the balcony door until I was sure everyone had gone. Mr. Wemyss was the last. He set the light – what did Aydyn call it? Oh, yes. The ghost light. He set it to the one side of the stage and left by the rear door.

"I waited some time just to be sure. It is not unusual for someone to have reached their car before realizing they had left something behind. I wanted no one else to be there, and I wanted no interruptions. That would have made things impossible.

"I believe nearly a half hour elapsed before I ventured from my station. I was fairly certain that I knew where our little bird had made her nest. I went directly to it."

"Her?" I had to interrupt. It was more than a figure of speech.

"Yes," Frost confirmed. "I have gotten a little ahead of myself in describing events. The person living in the theater is a young woman. I don't mean to keep things from you, but it is a complex tale. I thought one piece at a time the best procedure."

"I am sure you know," I offered, "that I will have a thousand questions. I will try to keep them to myself. I'm sure you'll answer them as you continue."

"Patience, John," he teased a little, "that is what you have been teaching me."

He continued.

"I had narrowed down the possible places for her main, let me call it 'home.' She would, as we speculated, need several hiding places, but there had to be one primary place. The others would only be temporary, in short notice emergencies – a place to use perhaps for only a few minutes. However, there had to be one place more or less permanent where she could sleep night after night. You will pardon me, I hope, if I keep that to myself for the time being.

"I went to that spot and waited. There was a chance that I was mistaken. With your search the other night, she might have resorted to a main back-up option. She had not. There was a slight stirring, a soft sound. As I had done, she was waiting to be sure all had gone. Because of her fear of discovery – you had come very close, you know – she waited longer than I.

"I called out to her. I did not yet know that it was a young girl. She did not respond or stir. Perhaps she believed I was only guessing as I could not actually see her at that moment. So, I explained, slowly, exactly where she was. I also explained that I meant her no harm and that I understood why she was hiding. That is, it was my belief that she was hiding not only from the people of the theater but also from further danger outside those walls. I told her that I wanted to help her.

"There was still silence. I had only one move left to make. I told her that others knew that she was in the building and that it was only a matter of time before she was discovered. I was sure that soon they would notify the authorities.

That left her no choice, if not to trust me, at

least to come forth. She emerged from the darkness, tentatively. There was but faint light, but I was sure she could see me better than I could see her. I backed away, making it obvious that, if she decided to run, she would have the opportunity. She did not.

"She was quite close before I could determine her gender. I introduced myself and aske if I might turn on a light. She assented. Then, I sat down. I hoped that would also show that it was not my intent to capture her in any sense.

"I explained again that it appeared to me that she was living in the theater, not just to have place to live, but as an actual hide-away. That revelation surprised her. I told her she did not have to tell me about the circumstances of hiding, but only how she came to the theater.

"At last, she too sat, although not near me. She was obviously very frightened, but began, slowly, to talk to me.

"She left out the very first part, intentionally, I believe. She said she was helped by a man who knew the building. He got her in and hid her. He came back often. He taught her how and where to hide; how to move around in the building undetected, especially in the dark. He brought her clothes and food and showed her where to hide them. She learned how to use things in the theater that could help her without causing too much suspicion. She had been careless once or twice and that, I think, started the stories of mysterious moving things. She knows nothing of ghosts, of course.

"As she spoke, she became more at ease. I asked about the man.

"She was hesitant and somewhat confused. She said he had saved her life. I thought that an odd admission. However, she said he was not kind. In fact, there were times when she was afraid of him. Yet, he went out of his way to protect her and to teach her. Sometimes, she thought he seemed very sad.

"He would come to the theater very late. Things were always quiet, inside and out. She never heard him enter. He would call to her with a signal that only they would understand. They had other signals that might be used for particular dangers. They practiced them, but never had to use them.

"She paused for some time before saying that she has not seen him for a long time. That bothered her because she thought he was doing something with 'the others who came to play.' That was the phrase she used. She was afraid something had happened to him.

"She seemed confused by the idea of a play, as though it were a completely foreign concept.

"They did not call each other by correct names. He had called her 'Alice.' He said it had about the same meaning as her real name and would be easier to remember. I took that to mean that her given name is not from English. I will leave my speculations as to her heritage for another time.

"I asked what she called him. She said that, at first, that he had had many and that it was not important. She felt she had to refer to him by something, so she started using something she had overheard, from a distance, from one of the others that came to the building. She called him, 'Doctor.'"

"Doctor?!" I erupted. "Doc!"

"Yes," Frost went on. "I believe the late Mr. Christopher was her protector and mentor."

"That will take some processing on my part," I said, trying to calm down. "Go on."

He did: "I did not want to tell her then of what had happened, so I steered the conversation to what I had discovered. I told her that I was a professional investigator with a knack for such things. I hope my stretching that title, under the circumstances, was not going too far."

I smiled.

"I told Alice – I began calling her by that name also – that in discovering her hiding places that I thought some of them were quite special, especially one that I mentioned in particular.

"Yes. I am still keeping some of here secrets from you, John, until she agrees that I might bring you in more fully."

"I understand," I told him. This was a delicate situation. Frost would fill me in when things became clearer. He understood my understanding.

"When I mentioned that I had also found some places where she hid food and other things, she became upset. From her reaction, I surmise that there are other hidden things that she would prefer I did not find.

"I also told her that I knew of her guide – I cannot call him her friend – but did not know him personally. That is when I brought you into the conversation. I told her you were my teacher and friend. I told her that I had only been in town a short time, but that you were a native here and had known 'the doctor' for many years.

"All of this took a great deal of time. Besides being terrible frightened, there are large gaps in her understanding. I believe she does not know what town or even what state we are in. I do not attribute this to a lack of ability, but of knowledge. When I tried it elicit from her how she came to be here and from where, she was very vague. This was not evasion, but, again, a foreign concept, as though she has little understanding of large differences between one place and another. She understands the difference between the building in which she now lives and other structures, but the idea of a different state eludes her.

"Let me be clear, she could not function as she has, living virtually undetected for months, without a great deal of cognitive and creative intelligence. I could glean that from her conversation. However, her whole universe is contained within the walls of the theater. Part of her is like a small child only vaguely aware of a larger world.

"Also, the fear in her comes from the world she lived in before this. That had been a small, contained universe as well, one from which she escaped. That is what she is hiding from more than the denizens of the theater."

He paused. There was something powerful going on within him.

This disturbed me. Frost is not given to broad displays of emotion. This was hardly a broad display as that might be used for others. The slight quaver in his voice was noticeable. The slight change in his expression, would be nearly unnoticeable to those who do not know him well. He cared for and was afraid for this small creature that he had found. That disturbed me.

"Frost," I said quietly. He was staring at the wall. "Frost," I repeated. He turned to look at me.

"I have a speculation," I told him. "It is one that I suspect has crossed your mind. I need you to confirm it."

His analytical mind clicked on. It is not a computer-like kind of analysis. It is more of his murmuration. He smiled.

"The key here is Doc Christopher," I began. "He started by hiding this girl. It is totally out of character. Even if he was just a reclusive retiree, it doesn't fit. And the fact that he was teaching her these tricks shows that he was not that simple person. I'm convince that he is the guy that the F.B.I has been looking for all these years."

"Which begs the question," Frost continued my thinking, "Why was he protecting this girl? According to reports, he killed children younger than she."

There was a tiny catch in his voice.

"He has been virtually alone for ten years," I said, taking my turn. "His only outside interest, as far as I can determine, has been the theater. Role playing. He needed it. It had been his whole life. It became an addiction. He needed it."

"Was he playing a new role?" Frost's turn. "The killings were part of his former roles, the climax of the dramas. What is the climax here?"

"Well, there is a body," I said, my thoughts getting foggy. "Two. Both killed with the same weapon, apparently. It suggests a third person who might be the real killer. But that doesn't add up either. As careful as Christopher was, who could have gotten to him?"

"Age?" Frost suggested. "Had his skills diminished? Was he just out of practice for the physical part of it?"

"Too many questions," I stated. "We're going in the wrong direction. We need to get back Alice. She is our starting point as well as our main concern."

"Agreed," Frost replied. "What do we do about Alice?"

"I have further speculations," I said, "but it seems to me that we need to protect her. To do that, we need to know what we are protecting her from.

Christopher must have known. That is the only way he could have gained so much trust."

"I must talk with her again," Frost said simply. "It may take time. She is a dichotomy: within the world she has made, she is strong, in control; outside of those walls, she is a frightened little girl."

"Would tonight be too soon?" I asked, tentatively.

"Not at all," he smiled. "She has given me a shopping list."

— twelve —

I did not need to be at rehearsal that night. They were only working on some trouble spots. My scene had been adequate enough to let go, for now. Saturday, there would be no rehearsal. Beginning Sunday afternoon, we would have complete run-throughs.

A run-through differs from a work-through in that we will not stop to correct problems. We will just try to push through any that might come up. Only if there was a major foul-up would we back up and try again. I hadn't seen any such major problems. Of course, I'm not the director.

I went to the theater anyway, early. I still considered myself more of the construction crew than the cast. Sunday's run-through would include most of the scene changes. I wanted to help Bob with whatever needed to be done. There was still a lot of painting to be done, most of that would happen Saturday and wouldn't cause problems with moving things. Mostly we'd look at the damn wheels.

"Hi, Bob," I shouted warmly as I came in.

He only nodded in acknowledgement. He was

giving some instructions to Jim Banks and a couple of college kids about what he wanted next. I could tell they had been at it for some time. I felt a little guilty that I hadn't come sooner. I could tell Bob was in a very serious mood.

"Hey, John," he said when he finally could get to me. "I'm glad you're here."

"Sorry I'm so late," I said. "What do you want me to do?"

"Not really anything," he said, cryptically. "It's getting done and you need to think more like an actor than a stage hand."

"I can do both," I said, thinking he was kidding. A lot of the actors, especially those in small parts like me, did both. Most shows couldn't go on if they didn't.

"I know," he said, "That's not really what I mean."

"What's up?" I asked, a little suspiciously.

He paused before answering. "I talked to Mike this morning about the spook living in the building. He was in shock. I told him about my idea to bring in my crew to do a better search. He okayed it." Another pause. "For tomorrow."

Now, I paused. I hadn't realized how much this really upset him.

I put my hand on his shoulder and looked him in the eye.

"Don't," I said, sternly but kindly, friend to friend.

That certainly caught him off guard. He thought I might have reservations about this. He did not expect this.

"Now, look, John," he began. "I know you're an investigator and all that...."

"Bob," I cut him off. "It isn't about that. It isn't about me. This is much more complicated than we thought."

Now, he was just plain stunned.

I decided to talk him into my confidence, a little.

"Bob, Frost and I know who's hiding in the theater. We don't have all the whys and wherefores yet. We're working on it. That person means no harm. Please, trust me on this."

Bob's mind was in a whirl. Intruder. Trespasser. Even spook. That seemed obvious to him. My telling him that wasn't completely true didn't add up."

One of those things from high school you dismiss so easily when you think or even say out loud, "I'll never need to know that," popped up again. It was a line from Shakespeare: "There are more things in heaven and earth, Horatio, than are dreamt of in your philosophy." In my profession, I've proved that over and over, even when my next thought was, "Who the hell was Horatio?"

I didn't say it out loud to Bob.

Bob puzzled over what I had said for a minute before answering.

"I trust you," he said. "It makes no sense to me, really. I don't like mysteries. No matter how harmless this person is, this isn't a homeless shelter or a campground."

"But you'll give us some time and space to work

it out," I said. It wasn't a question. I knew he would. "Thank you."

"I already brought a couple of work lights," he said. "You can use them." Now he was kidding.

"Thanks, again," I said, with a smile. "I'll remember that. Now, let's get this set finished.

We went to work. Bob was still frustrated, but he would not let that interfere and he would not press for more information.

At six o'clock, Gary came bounding in.

"Hey, guys," he shouted. He was excited. "Did you know there's suppose to be a ghost in here?"

Everyone stopped and stared at him.

I spoke first. "Of course, Gary," I said in mock exasperation. "Everyone knows that. Are you just finding out?"

I thought that by teasing him I could steer him away from getting too inquisitive.

"Hey," he said, a bit childishly. "Nobody told me."

We all laughed a little, not unkindly.

"Sorry, Gary," I said. "Every theater in the world has its own ghost or two. It's an old, old tradition. Don't worry about it. They're harmless."

"Unless you go hunting for them," Bob added.

"What?" Gary said, more confused than anything. I was more something else.

"Sure," Bob continued. He seemed dead serious. "They don't bother us. We don't bother them. It's like camping in the woods."

Now, everyone was confused as much as Gary.

Bob continued: "You're just sitting around the campfire having a nice evening, then some fool suggests a snipe hunt. And you know how they are. They hate to be bothered at night."

"But snipe...," Gary started. Then, it hit him. He laughed loud and long. Everyone did.

"Nearly got me on that one, didn't they?" he sputtered, almost through tears.

I had to hand it to Bob. He turned Gary's head around completely. No matter what stories he might hear now, he would not go hunting for snipe or ghosts.

When rehearsal started, at seven, the stage crew and their tools faded away, everyone but me. I wanted to stay until Frost arrived. I would leave him to his own way. I would not even ask for his thoughts unless he volunteered them.

I greeted a few members of the cast and listened to Wemyss getting started before I more or less wandered up to the second floor. The lights were on in the costume shop. Martha was working on a girl's party dress. Aydyn was putting the finishing touches on an elf costume.

"Hello, John...," Martha said with a kind smile.

"Good evening, Martha," I returned. "How are things coming along?"

"We're nearly finished...," she answered.

"I am!" Aydyn exclaimed as she jumped up.

I don't remember ever seeing her just stand up. She always seemed to jump up.

"Are you between scenes?" she asked brightly.

"Only in a manner of speaking," I said. "I'm not working on the play tonight. Since I only have one scene that I did last night and won't do again until Sunday, I'm between."

Aydyn laughed. Martha smiled.

"I did work on the set a little," I said. "I have some other business later."

I said it that way, hoping it was enough for Aydyn to understand.

"Oh, I see," she said. She understood. "Don't worry. I told Grandma all about it."

"All?" I asked, a little worried.

"Yes," she said with lessening of her excitement. "Frost told me all about the girl."

Martha stopped what she was doing.

"You let me know if there is anything I can do...," she said. Her voice was full of concern.

I was concerned, too, for different reasons.

Frost knew first. One. He told me. Two. He told Aydyn. Three. Aydyn told Martha. Four. I told Bob in part. Five. Five people knew at least some. Wait! Bob told something to Mike. What had Bob mentioned to the crew he had planned to bring in? Bob probably would not say anything more, but for how long? Mike, outgoing guy that he is, might have said something off-hand to someone. The lid might come off way too soon.

"I think I have to talk to Mike," I said out loud, but not to anyone directly.

"He's out of town until Monday...," Martha said.

"On theater business?" I asked. If he talked to one of our major donors, he might feel he had to tell of any problems. That would be fair. He would say it would not be good business to say anything to anyone else. Maybe family? And why would they not mention it?

"They went to visit his wife's sister in Dubuque...," Martha explained.

Aydyn had a different concern, too.

"How is Frost?" she asked. There was more than a little worry in her voice.

"He seems to be on top of things," I told her.

"He doesn't always reveal how he really feels, you know," She looked at me searchingly.

"I know," I tried to reassure her. "I've learned to understand the little things he shows."

"I've seen a couple of bigger things," she said, looking to one side as though looking at a different scene.

"Really?" I said without thinking. Then I added quickly, "Sorry. I don't mean to pry."

She smiled a sad smile.

"That's okay," she said. He wouldn't mind. He considers you a very good friend."

"I've known him longer than you have," I said taking her hand. "But I get the feeling he is less...."

I had to pause to find a good word.

I continued. "I think he is less reserved with you than with anyone."

"There are times when he frightens me," she said sadly.

Martha looked up from her work quickly. Aydyn noticed.

"Oh, no, Grandma," she assured her, "I mean I'm frightened for him."

She turned back to me and said, "Sometimes, I think there is a storm brewing in him that will explode. He has powerful emotions. The Tai Chi helps so much. But he has a powerful moral code, too. This child thing…There is a rage in him about hurting innocents. He has to let some of it out somewhere."

Martha and I both looked at her with concern. She smiled and took her grandmother's hand.

"He cried on my shoulder for half an hour," she said to Marth softly.

I was frozen. This was a part of Frost I had never seen, I am sorry to say, never imagined. Everyone must release things now and then, but this? Aydyn had gotten to a place in him I could not reach.

"Aydyn," I said, struggling, "Is there anything I should watch for? Any way I can help him?"

"He told me that the guy who got stabbed," her voice got much less soft, "may have had a partner."

"That is part of our thinking," I said, not know where she was going.

"Promise me something," she said very seriously. "If you find him, don't let Frost near him."

The tone of her voice and the look in her eye

scared the hell out of me. She had no doubt. Frost's inner storms would not be denied.

I didn't speak. I couldn't. I took her hand again. I nodded. She sighed a sigh of relief, some relief. She knew I would try. She could only pray that I would succeed.

After a minute. I changed direction, a little.

"Do you know his plans for tonight?" I asked.

"Yes," she replied, beginning to regain some of her natural energy, not the unnatural kind she'd just shown. "In fact, I may be a part of it."

"How so," I asked, trying to lighten my tone as well.

"Frost thinks Alice should talk to another woman." She laughed a little. "He doesn't know very much about us, you know. Mostly in an academic sense."

Martha stifled a laugh. Well, she didn't try very hard. I was smart enough at least to keep my mouth shut.

"He's going to try to get her to open up some more," she went on. "We know she can't stay here much longer. She doesn't seem to understand that. Any change seems to drive her to hide more. God, how I hope he can reach her."

"That's what we all want," I said. "I feel like her fear has become so ingrained in her that it's almost like a brain tumor. We have to find a way to remove it without doing more damage."

Aydyn looked really surprised.

"That's almost exactly the way Frost put it," she said. "No wonder you two get along so well."

"Thanks," I said. I really liked that. Frost and I often reached the same conclusion, but usually from very different paths. Mine is like following a road map, detours and all. Frost makes his own path. Sometimes the distance is the same for both of us, but his "scenic route" adds information I hadn't seen.

"Something else Frost shared with me," Aydyn said. She hesitated. "I don't want to tell too much. Part of it is private."

"Then it's probably none of my business," I told her.

"Well, it might be," she said. "It's about another girl he knew about many years ago."

She took a breath.

"Okay," she began. "This other girl was also very frightened. When someone tried to help her, she completely shut down. Frost said it was like she blew several circuit breakers. She couldn't talk. It was like she could not see or hear anything outside her own mind, and maybe very little there. He said that, in a strange, way it helped him, but he felt so bad that he couldn't help her. That's why he wants to help this girl so much."

I filled in the blanks about the private things. I think he must have shared with her about being hospitalized as a young teen. She didn't know that I knew that. I had to believe the is where he encountered the other girl. For Frost, closed as he was to most of the world, to open up this much to Aydyn in such a short time was more than remarkable. It was nearly miraculous. God, it was wonderful.

When I could finally speak, I said, "From Frost's report to me, I could tell this was something he wanted to handle very carefully, more so because I think there is a time element. Others know now of her presence. They will not, cannot wait forever."

"Who knows?" Aydyn said with great worry.

"Well, Mike for one," I told her. "He doesn't know half the story, but he's the manager here. Everything here is his responsibility. I will try to explain it to him. He's a good guy. He'll understand, but only up to a point. Sooner or later, Alice will have to be gone. Probably sooner rather than later."

"Oh, my God," Aydyn moaned. Martha stood up and put her arms around her. The party dress dropped to the floor having lost all importance.

"Listen," I said to reassure her, "Frost has already made progress. If he can get her to take the next step, to trust you, that will make a huge difference. It will double the size of her world."

Aydyn's fear turned to hope. Just to say she wore her heart on her sleeve is to damn with faint praise, as the old saying goes. In expressing herself, her emotions, she was Frost's polar opposite.

"Now," I said, a bit over-cheerily, "It's going to be awhile before Frost gets here. Why don't you show me what you're working on?"

Both women were very glad to go along with my game plan. It was time to turn to something else, for now anyway.

Costuming can be a tricky business. It is part of the slight-of-hand magic of theater. The clothes must be appropriate in so many ways. The first part seems to be the easiest: matching the time period. "Miracle" takes place in the late 1940's. It can be updated only a little. Not just fashion but society itself began to make drastic changes after 1960. So, keeping it right takes a good eye. Martha has a good eye and extensive knowledge of the history of clothing.

Another part of the costume has to do with the characters. The costumes tell part of the story. Rigid character would wear rigid clothes. Two characters that clash in the story might wear clothes that clash in style and color. Changes in attitude throughout the story might also be expressed in changes of costume.

In the original movie, Maureen O'Hara (one of my all-time favorites, by the way) wears clothes that shows she means business. A 1947 businesswoman had to do that with ease. Martha and I talked about how most viewers don't even notice the subtle changes in what she wears that reflect her changing attitudes. Magic.

Little Susan's party dress, the one Martha was working on, shows subtle changes in the child's attitude. Martha used a dress almost identical to the first one she wears: a simple, tan dress. But late in the play, this one has pink buttons instead of brown ones. There are bows on the sleeves that help change her from her mother's "mini me" into a ten-year old like other ten-year-old's. Also, for the Christmas party, a brown belt has been replaced with one that has red and white candy cane stripes.

I loved every bit of it.

The elf costume that Aydyn had just finished had a different kid of subtleness. The actor who would wear it, in two brief appearances at Macy's, would look uncomfortable. It didn't fit, on purpose. The costume had to appear to be something Macy's kept stored away until Christmas season, when it would be given so some unlucky seasonal worker. It looked like a combination of costumes from two other people neither of whom was the size of the one wearing it.

We had a wonderful time talking about these and costumes from other shows. Like Bob's stories of the sets, Martha had a treasure trove of tales of costume lore, everything from when one actor had to leave the show and her replacement was a very different size to embarrassing "costume malfunctions." We laughed a lot and lost track of time, which was our aim.

"What a happy looking group," Frost said from the doorway.

We jumped at his silent appearance and laughed some more. I looked at my watch. It was 9:30.

Frost noticed and said, "Rehearsals do not

always follow a strict schedule for ending. I did not wish to be locked out. In fact, as I came by the stage, it would seem that I am not overly early."

"Then, we should be on our way as well," I said to Martha.

She turned to Aydyn. "Good night, dear...." This time, I think her trailing off left the unspoken, "and be careful." She picked up her things.

I turned to Frost. "Is there anything you need from me?"

"No," he smiled holding up a bag. "I have everything I need and everything Alice said that she needed."

"Good," I said, "And Aydyn?"

"Oh," she jumped up. "I stay right here. I'll crash on the old sofa again. I won't sleep, but I'll try not to make any noise."

She giggled a little. It was little-girlish, and very nervous.

"I'll be at home," I told Frost, "Come by as early as you need to. Good night."

I hope my "Good night" also carried a "be careful."

– thirteen –

On my way home, I decided I had fooled myself that morning. Frost might have waited until nine to come to the office, but I am sure he must have left the theater much earlier. He would have been risky to be seen leaving in the daylight. The persona he presented to the world was as well rehearsed as any actor's role. It was who he needed to be. We all do that to greater or lesser degrees.

Everyone has different characters they portray depending on the circumstances. Think of all the people we see in their working roles every day. Servers in a restaurant often dress alike. It is like a uniform even if it is more casual. Most big-box stores have their employees dress alike. Many of those are even more uniform-like. Out of uniform, they are sometimes very different characters. I once ran into my doctor on a bike trail. I didn't recognize him at first. He wasn't in uniform.

Most people also dress more formally for certain situations. There are still men who would not think of going to church without a necktie, even if they never wear one any other time.

Except for the gi he wore when exercising, Frost is almost always more formal than most. His choice is what is known as business casual: sport coat over a dress shirt, no tie. He prefers shades of gray. The way he wears his clothes reminds me, not of business, but of even more formal occasions. He wears it the way Gary Grant wore a tuxedo. Or, maybe, Grant wore a tuxedo seem like business casual.

I was now sure that Frost had gone home, changed, gone to the river like he did almost every morning, and then back home to change again before coming to the office. My mind, guided by his persona, concocted the notion that he had overcome time, space, weariness and even wrinkled clothing.

That notion did not present itself when Frost appeared at the side door of my house – at 3:00 a.m.

When I had finally heard him at the door, I stumble there with only parts of my mind and body working. I had been deep asleep. At first, it was just someone, anyone, at my door. Halfway there, I began to think of Frost, certain that morning had come. By the time I reached the door, I knew he had stopped by early to give me an update before going home and going about his routine. I even half expected Aydyn to be with him.

He looked as haggard as any other young man might look who'd been awake so long. His hair was mussed. His clothes were wrinkled. He was not Frost.

When I saw him, I was instantly fully awake.

What woke me up the most was not his weariness or his wrinkle, it was the fear in his eyes.

"Oh, my God, Frost," I exclaimed. "Get in here!"

I ushered him to the nearest chair.

"Sit here," I told him, as calmly as I could manage.

"No," he said. "I had better remain on my feet for a time. A collapse would be...dangerous."

I blinked a little, trying to grasp the whole situation. It dawned on me that the fear in him was personal, from the inside out. The danger was to his mind, maybe, to his very soul. He was struggling for control. His expression, and even some of his movements, reminded me of two evenly matched college wrestlers locked together with neither having a clear advantage. Frost's opponent was unseen by anyone but himself. It was himself.

"What can I do?" I asked, trying not to sound as desperate as I felt.

"I do not yet know," he said, slowly, apparently calmly, but not.

He took a few steps and then back again. I wouldn't call it pacing. It was just moving so as not to freeze in place.

"Tai Chi," I said, from out of somewhere. He was on the edge of some kind of hysteria. So was I, I think.

Frost looked at me with confusion.

"Tai Chi," I repeated, a bit louder. "Move. Move the forces."

I really didn't know what the hell I was talking about, but it sounded right.

It must have been enough right to register. He looked at me for a couple of long seconds, then pulled himself into a beginning pose, or stance, or whatever it is called. Slowly, he began to move, pulling and pushing unseen energy, blocking others, dancing with some.

I watched for a few minutes. Then, I said, "I'm going to make tea."

He did not answer. I went to the kitchen.

Again, I didn't know what I was doing, this time from two perspectives. First, I'm not much of a tea drinker. When I have made it, sometime in the misty past, it was just a bag in a cup of hot water. I had no tea bags.

A few months before, Frost had given me a gift. It was a can of his special herbal blend. It came with an egg.

By egg, I mean an egg-sized, egg-shaped metal container full of holes. It twists open in the middle. You're suppose to fill the bottom half with tea and replace the top. There is a small chain with a hook on one end that attaches to the top. You hook to the cup rim or handle, place the egg in the cup, and pour boiling water over it.

That's all in theory for me. I'm sorry to say, I had never tried it. I had thanked Frost, sincerely, for the gift and put it away in a cupboard. I honestly intended to try it. I just never got around to it.

Going through the motions of this unfamiliar task helped me clear up, a little, of my other problem.

Frost's arrival, looking as he looked, had shocked me awake. At the same time, that shock pushed me into a different kind of cloud.

What the hell could have pushed him to this extreme?

I put a glass measuring cup of water in the microwave. I've got a teapot around here somewhere. I haven't seen it since my Sarah died. She drank tea more than I did. The egg was filled, I guess. I put a cup on the kitchen table. I didn't know how long I would have to wait, so I started the coffee maker. It was already set up. I do that before going to bed and set a timer.

The microwave beeped. The water was boiling. I left it. I didn't want to make the tea before Frost was ready for it. Just as the coffee finished, he appeared at the kitchen door.

"John," he said calmly. He was himself again.

"Have a seat," I offered. "I'll check the water."

I hit the microwave for another minute. When the water started bubbling, I stopped it, took the cup and poured the water over the egg.'

"Do you need anything else with your tea," I asked. I hoped I wasn't sounding too mothering.

"I find this particular blend perks up with just a little lemon juice, if you have any," he replied.

I did. I keep a little on hand for my friend and neighbor Alan. There are a couple of cocktails that he likes that call for it.

I handed the small bottle to Frost. He shook it

and poured about a teaspoonful of it into his cup. As he did that, I got him a teaspoon, to stir with, and the saucer I should have gotten when I got the cup. Then, I filled my mug with coffee.

"I thank you, John," Frost said, as though it were a coffee break at three in the afternoon. "I will let this steep for just a few more minutes. I must ask you for two further indulgences."

"Whatever I can do," I said. I was still struggling to maintain steadiness.

"First, I know you must have a report, the story of the preceding hours," he said. "I must ask you to wait for just a bit longer. I will take some strength to relate it. I am not yet recovered to that point."

"I know," I told him sincerely. "Your recovery is first, however long it takes."

"I know you understand that," he said, just as sincerely. "The other task is a bit more delicate."

I sat down. The way he put it made me believe I might need to sit.

"I was in such a state," he said, chagrinned, "that I left the theater and came here directly. I'm afraid I left dear Aydyn completely in the dark, both literally and figuratively."

I had forgotten all about her, too. I couldn't imagine what state she might be in.

"Would you do us both the kindness of calling her?" he asked. "I'm not sure I am up to it, and I think her presence here would aid me greatly. I hope she will agree."

"I'm sure she will," I said.

He took his phone from his jacket pocket. He called up her number and handed it to me. I hit the phone icon. Halfway through the second ring, she answered.

"Frost," she said with a tightness in her voice, both from tiredness and worry. She was anxious but trying to sound calm.

"It's John Thompson," I said, in a straight-forward manner. "Frost is with me."

I hoped by saying it that way it wouldn't add to her worry.

"With you?" Her confusion was doing as I had hoped.

"He's fine," I said quickly, "He needed to see me immediately. He didn't want to leave you behind, but it seemed for the best at the time."

That sounded lame, but it was the best I could do at the time. Maybe the lameness would also make things seem better than they were. Aydyn didn't speak, and I could not understand the strange sounds I was hearing through the phone.

"Frost would like you to come here," I continued, "We're at my house. Do you now the address?"

"I'm not...sure," she stammered.

I told her not to worry. I gave her the address and told her the best route to get to it from the theater. She said she'd be there right away.

During the exchange, I had watched Frost. He seemed pleased with the way I had handled it. He pulled the egg from his cup, let it drip for a few seconds and placed it on the saucer. He brought the cup to his nose first, inhaled deeply, smiled and took a sip.

"Ooh," he said. "It's still a little too warm."

"Worth waiting for, I hope," I said, rather inanely.

"Yes," he said, simply. "I must ask, 'Have you actually tried it?'"

He knew I hadn't. I was torn between sheepishly confessing and giving a sigh of relief that he had recovered enough to tease me.

An occasional word here, a sip there – we passed the few minutes until the excited Aydyn came to the door.

She looked worse than Frost. She is always just this side of disheveled. A few hours of tossing and turning on and old couch had done her no favors – not that anyone there cared about that.

I opened the door and stepped out of the way. She didn't think and didn't need to greet me. There are times when traditional courtesies are necessary. This was not one of them.

I pointed to where Frost was now standing. She ran past and threw her arms around his chest. He had raised his arms in anticipation. He put his arms around her gently. She was trying to fold him in two backwards.

"It's alright," he told her coolly. "I have had a hard time, but now...it is alright."

"Please sit down," I suggested. "Would you like some coffee or herb tea?"

"Oh," she said looking up but not letting go, "I don't know. I...I don't know." There was no better description of the word "befuddled."

"How about just a glass of water?" I offered.

"Yes," she sighed. "Yes. I think that would be best."

She sat and I got it for her.

Frost returned to his tea. I refilled my mug.

After a few minutes of mostly silence, Frost was mostly ready. He took Aydyn's hand and looked at me.

"I am sorry for all this drama," he began. "I will try to tell the story without more, but I cannot fully promise that.

"I will not tell all the details. I cannot. It would be too much of a strain. As much as I can tell you should be sufficient for you to understand what I am leaving out.

"John, first of all, I thank you again. Your suggestions and care have been exactly what I needed to regain myself. I have not had a spell, my father's word, of that intensity for several years."

"Oh, Frost," Aydyn interrupted. The fear she had indicated to me earlier was glaring in her voice. "Maybe you shouldn't...." It was a Martha-like pause, but in Aydyn's case, she simply did not know how to finish the sentence.

"It will be alright," Frost smiled. "Alright, still."

"If it gets to be too much," she warned, "you just stop. You hear me? You just stop!"

"I will," he said calmly. "I promise you. With you and good friend John here, I will have ample support. And, if you suspect that it is getting away from me, just pinch me. Okay?"

Aydyn smiled and, I think, blushed. My reaction must have seemed like I had been pinched, but I did not pursue it.

Frost began again, in a steady voice. It was almost mechanical at first.

"Alice revealed to me more than she said in words. It was not just my reading between the lines, as they say. Conclusions were rather obvious. At first, I was only guessing, but it all became clear. I know the source of her fears and pain. It is worse than we imagined.

"I went to her as before. This time she came out of hiding more readily, but still with caution. Again, I asked before turning on the light. She, again, consented. I put the bag of items she had asked for where she could reach it, backed away, and sat.

"I started the conversation casually, just to get her in the mood of answering questions. Easy questions first and then a step further when it seemed good to do so. This is the way you taught me, John.

"I asked her how she was feeling physically, emotionally. I had to put the questions simply. Her vocabulary is limited. From the way she spoke, I concluded that she is remarkably uneducated. If I had used the word 'emotionally,' I don't think she would have understood. She seems to be able to distinguish the labels on the things I brought, but more from the pictures than the words. Those items which she has had before may not have pictures, but the words are more like familiar pictures than words.

"I doubt she has been to school in any way that we might recognize. This accounts for some of her childlike understanding. She has been isolated from most of the world.

"I am reminded of those stories of children, who were 'raised by wolves,' as they say, coupling the lost child with the Roman myth of Romulus and Remus. Those children, when discovered, shocked those who found them, and were in turn shocked by the society.

"Alice was raised by wolves."

He hesitated. The darkness started in him. Aydyn squeezed his hand with both of hers. The light returned.

"Alice is, I believe, something of a natural genius. I don't say that simply because of how she has survived in the theater. I say it for how she as survived long enough to escape her old world and come to the theater. She did not tell me these things directly. The clues in her conversation led me there.

"As we talked, I asked her about her food. Was it enough? Was there some special treat she might want? That disturbed her.

"I assumed that treats may have been used in the past to control her – positive reinforcement, as they call it. The truth was more terrible. 'Treat' was entirely twisted. It was something she did not want but would be forced upon her. She would have to accept it with a smile or be punished."

Aydyn gasped. I think, I did, too, just not as noticeably.

Frost paused again. It was difficult for him. I could tell there was much more that he was not saying, that he could not say. Aydyn pulled his hand closer looking into his face. She was searching for any sign that it was time to end this.

He continued.

"I changed direction again. Or so I thought. I told her I was very happy to help her, but I thought I knew someone who could help in better ways. Her fear and confusion returned. I told her not to worry. I would bring no one in if she was not ready. I don't think she fully believed me. I am sure she has been fooled many times in the past. I told her my friend, Aydyn, was loving and kind, that she wanted to help, too.

"Then Alice asked me something very strange. She wanted to know if Aydyn was a 'Mama,' too."

For Aydyn and me, "surprise" is not the right word, but there is no other.

"The way she said it," Frost voice indicated that he was still trying to figure it out, "was so odd. I take her to be in her middle teens, or she looks much younger than she really is. That does not make motherhood impossible for her, but somehow, I do not believe she was referring to having given birth.

Especially when she when she added, 'I don't want to do that anymore."

"She began to retreat into a shell, so I changed directions again. Every time I circled back to things that might concern personal things, her past intervened. Almost everything reminded her of some kind of pain. That is another reason she only wants to live in the immediate, today, maybe tomorrow. She sees no further. That is where she feels safe. Other possibilities carry the threat of putting her back where she was.

"I tried to get her to talk about 'Doctor.' I still haven't mentioned his death, only that he is unable to come now. I mentioned, again, that I had a friend, John, who knew him better.

"That bothered her but she accepted it.

"I asked how it was that he had come to help her. This is what she told me:

"'He found me. I was sick. 'He was weird. He walked away first, and then came back. He didn't want me, but he said he'd help me. He brought me here. It took a long time to unlock the door. I guess it was stuck. He had funny keys. He stayed with me that night. Far away, like you do. I fell asleep. I was real tired. Then he showed me where to hide. He went to get food.'

"Well, so it went, one piece at a time. She filled in some blanks. I filled in others. I wanted to stop, but I forced myself to go on.

She began to speak a little more freely. "I will

leave out most of the rest of the story. There are a lot of very hard details."

Frost leaned toward me a little. "John, if you would be so kind as to heat more water. Another cup of tea will help me with the strength I need to finish."

I did that. I asked if anyone wanted any breakfast. No one did. I knew that as the words came out of my mouth. Aydyn did ask for coffee. I gave her most of the rest in the pot and started a fresh one. As it brewed, Frost settled back with his tea. It looked like he was meditating, a motionless round of Tai Chi.

Aydyn was still pulled in two directions. She knew Frost needed to tell this story. She knew it was hurting him, terribly. It was hurting her, too. Me, too.

He began again.

"It will be better at this point if I go quickly toward the endings – of her story and my conclusions. When I do that, you will be able to fill in many of the details that I have omitted.

"Alice is hiding a box. She is hiding it from a man she called, 'Master Charlie.' Doc knew about the box and about Charlie. He told Alice he would take care of both. Master Charlie and others were very bad men doing very bad things. Doc would take of them, too.

"I surmised that Doc was going back to his old business. He was going to kill people. Alice did not really understand that. Like many things death is too abstract for her to grasp.

"I must...." He froze, but only for a second, and not much differently than someone else would in that situation. Still, it made us uneasy for that second.

"I must finish."

"Master Charlie was Charlie Clearburg. Carl Clauberg.

"Alice has been his property for at least ten years."

— fourteen —

Frost's years of practice in self-control served him well. It allowed him to finish his story without dropping back into that place where he had been when he first came to my door. He was aided, unintentionally, by Aydyn.

She was damned near hysterical.

The secret of Alice's past was worse than she had imagined. Her mind and body already tired from lack of sleep and the strain of her fear for Frost had left her no reserves for the terrible revelation. She jumped up gasping for breath.

Frost reached out for her hand so quickly I barely saw it move. He pulled her to him, on to his lap, and engulfed her in an embrace like a small child. Her need for someone matched his need to help someone. They became one.

Having no one to hug, I found, unintentionally, help in a different, physical shock that allowed the raging of the flash flood to settle into a deep, muddy, but manageable mess. In other words, I spilled hot coffee on my leg.

Despite my yelping and jumping, neither Frost

nor Aydyn changed their positions. Nor did they seem to notice when I left the kitchen to seek first aid and dry clothes.

By the time I got to my bedroom, the pain was nearly gone. The coffee had not been hot enough to do much damage. As I moved around, time slowed. The amount of time it took to do each small thing took longer and longer. I had on my jeans and picked up my sweatshirt. It seemed to take a full minute to raise it from the bed to my chest. Then everything stopped.

There is a feeling that comes over you that accompanies the misnamed ailment called the stomach flu. There is an aura first, almost as though you can feel the light touching your skin. Then, your body temperature rises as you feel chills. There are strange muscle twitchings in your abdomen, deep. You know what's coming. Or do you? It fades. Then, suddenly, it's back, stronger. You are torn between hoping it won't come at all and praying that it gets over with.

This wasn't nausea. This was and wasn't physical. This was deeper.

I hoped it wouldn't happen. I prayed to get it over with.

I grabbed a pillow and shoved my face into it. I screamed. I tried to hold the pillow tighter. I screamed. I screamed.

I pushed and pulled tighter until I could not scream. I could not breathe. Just short of falling over, I let the pillow fall to the floor. I stood wobbling for five minutes. I put on the sweatshirt and walked into the bathroom. I combed my hair with my hands and returned to the kitchen.

I didn't know how long I'd been gone. Aydyn had returned to her chair and was fiddling calmly with her water glass. Frost was calmly finishing his tea. My coffee cup was in the sink. The spill that had made it to the tile was wiped up.

"I need some orange juice," I announced. "Anyone else?"

"I would like some," Aydyn said. The voice was barely her own.

"None for me, thank you," Frost said, coolly. "Are you alright?"

"Yes," I answered as I got two juice glasses from the cupboard. I went to the refrigerator. "The coffee wasn't too hot. Enough to startle me, but not enough to require treatment."

As I poured the juice, Frost's cool smile told me that he had not asked about the injury from the coffee. We both knew it.

I handed one glass to Aydyn and sat down. The cold and slight sharpness of the juice tasted and felt good.

I took a very deep breath.

"It is time for an investigation," I said, in a business-like manner. "It is time for me to go to work. Frost, you have had a very hard time. We will go in different directions. I will deal with the official end.

I'm going to talk to Murphy first. There is a tricky situation ahead. We will need the F.B.I and their reach, but I will not tell them about Alice. They will want her and her secrets. We can't allow that at this time."

I had Frost's full attention. I could feel his mind working on that. Aydyn was looking back and forth between us. This was not her realm. This was foreign to her.

"Frost," I said, low and slow, "I need you to protect Alice. The best way to do that is to keep visiting her. Don't press her on the past. We have enough of that for now. You must become Doc's replacement, and more. If it is at all possible, you have to become her friend. I don't know if she understands the idea, but it is necessary that we try.

"It may be possible," Frost said, flatly.

"The play is going to ramp up: full rehearsals every night. It isn't that long until we open. I'm guessing Alice arrived at the end of the last one and has gotten settled in between. Now, more and more people will be there every night. I'm also guessing we'll sell out every performance. Full house.

"Alice's movements will be more and more limited. If she has no plans for that, you will have to make some."

"Of course," he replied. "I have already considered that and have some ideas. I will find out from her."

"Can you?" I asked, a bit sternly.

"Yes, John," he said. "The initial shock was quite

strong. Aftershocks will follow. They will not be as unexpected, and I will be prepared."

"Good," I said, satisfied. "Are you also up to a little predawn speculating?"

"Yes," he said. "I believe I am."

"Do you need for me to leave?" Aydyn asked, obviously afraid that the answer would be "yes."

"No," I said, quickly. Then, I looked at Frost as I continued talking to Aydyn. "I, for one, need you to stay."

That surprised and delighted her.

"I think there are at least two roles in this for you," I explained. "First, support Frost. Whatever he needs. That's an easy one."

They both smiled.

"I might have a way for you to gain Alice's trust," I went on. "I don't know how soon she will need any other food or whatever. I want Frost to send you for them. She may not see you or hear you at first, but she will know that someone else is helping."

"Ah, yes," Frost inserted. "Like making deliveries to the back door."

Aydyn laughed a little. her excitement and real self returning.

"You also need to be a kind of back up," I said thoughtfully. "I don't have a good feeling about this. There is a person missing from the equation. I don't know his plans or his exact connection. Unknowns are always a problem."

"I don't know," Aydyn hesitated, "I've never investigated before."

"You won't be investigating," I assured her. "You'll be a look-out."

"A what?" she gasped.

"We have a lot of assumptions here," Frost said, taking her hand. "We are fairly certain that a third party was at the scene of the crime. It is most likely that person was an associate of Clauberg. From what I just learned, I believe we must also assume that person is searching for Alice."

"Oh, my," she gasped again.

"Your part in this won't be as bad as you might think," I said quickly. "Whenever Frost goes to talk to Alice, you be there, somewhere. The theater should be empty except for the three of you. If you see or hear anyone else, you warn Frost."

"Oh, I see," she said excitedly. Then, she sighed, "I can do that."

"Frost," I said, turning back to him, "You need to tell Alice, in some way, that 'Doctor' is gone. He can't help anymore. I don't know if his death would be to traumatic for her. I don't know how she might react to anything."

"I understand," Frost said. "I am not entirely sure myself. How do you tell a small child anything? That is, how I approach her. It is the only way."

"Yes," I said, simply. I knew he would find a way. "When you have done that, you need to establish codes. Find out how Doc did it, what kind of dangers they had prepared for, and what responses were expected from Alice. We don't know what surprises may come. We need to anticipate them."

"Will I need some special signals, too" Aydyn asked.

"I think not," Frost replied. "Not any but what I might use with Alice. We will work it all out."

"Good," she said, with another sigh of relief.

"I saw a man across from the theater yesterday afternoon," I told them. "He had a bag like the one Doc carried. I only saw him for a second. It might be nothing. But, at this point, I'm going to assume worse case scenarios."

"Worse case?" Aydyn was frightened again. That heart on her sleeve was getting a workout.

"I'll assume, again," I explained, quietly to calm her. "I assume this unknown man is the missing associate. He has Doc's bag. Among other things, he would have found things connecting Doc to the theater. This guy wasn't across the street buying coffee. He was casing the theater."

"He's been watching us?" Aydyn exclaimed.

I was getting it. Aydyn handled things out loud. I scribbled on paper. Frost sorted out swirling patterns in his mind. Aydyn examined things out loud through her emotions. Very out loud.

Frost noticed the look of understanding on my face and smiled.

"Sometimes she sings," he said. "Thinking aloud through show tunes. Sometimes I find it quite insightful."

I smiled with him. Aydyn blushed.

"I gave the police a description of the man, and

we worked out a sketch," I related to them, "They are circulating it and have contacted the F.B.I about it. They are supposed to send pictures. I'll find out where that stands. I'll try to get them to you so you can look out for him."

"It would be helpful to have something more concrete to watch for," Frost said.

"It will also be secret," I said seriously. "I want to give you all the help I can without revealing to the police that you're involved in anything that has very much to do with the investigation."

"Sergeant Murphy is already aware of some of my involvement," Frost reminded me.

"Only to a point," I said. "When I talk to him, I'll try to convince him that you are only doing research, background information."

Frost smiled again. Some knew of his wizardry with computers. It would not be difficult to get them to believe that Frost was at home plugged into his laptop.

"All that is well and good," Frost said, "but where does Alice really fit in?"

"You said that Alice is hiding a box. What do you conclude about that?" I probed.

"It is something she brought with her when she escaped her past life," Frost explained. "It is nothing personal. She has a disoriented sense of self. The word, 'personal' would have no meaning to her. What she values of her person is safety and the safety of the things she needs most, like food."

He paused, thinking. He didn't want to go off in bad direction.

He went on with composure. "The box must have belonged to her captor. It may contain some kind of evidence of the monstrous that was her former life."

He waited for me to catch my breath, realizing that I needed to proceed, but I did not want to think in terms of details. The broad idea of incriminating evidence would be enough.

"That is my conclusion, as well," I offered. "It may give me another opening. I think her childishness is a direct result of her captivity. However, in some part of her mind, her psyche, whatever, there was at least the idea of freedom, release, escape. She knew she had to get out. That, in itself, was amazing."

"Indeed," Frost agreed.

"However," I went on cautiously, "she took a box. She hid a box. Why?"

"That is just another germ of an idea," Frost said, a bit worried. "Her sense of right and wrong has been twisted. I cannot imagine what she was thinking."

"I, or you," I conjectured, "Anyone with the common notion of right and wrong, might take it as protection, leverage or even a kind of blackmail. I don't think she could."

"She could not," Frost said, with certainty. "It must have value of some kind to her. What?"

I had come to a dead end. The swirls in Frost's mind were abstract patterns.

Aydyn shouted with excitement: "Protection!"

She was thinking out loud, again. Very loud.

"We've already eliminated that," I said, rather condescendingly, I'm afraid. "She wouldn't have an idea about that."

"No, no, no!" she exclaimed, jumping up. "Why are we doing what we're doing?"

"We're trying to get answers and make plans," I said.

"No, John," Frost interjected. "She means, what are we doing about Alice?"

"Yes!" She was still shouting, and continuing to jump, like a little girl who just guessed a riddle. "We are trying to protect Alice."

"Yes!" My turn to shout. I didn't jump up, literally anyway.

"I was trying to think," Aydyn explained, "why people do things that are out of character. If Alice can't think of herself, beyond survival, maybe she is thinking about someone else."

"She did it to protect someone else," I said. This could be major. But then I had a downturn in my emotions. "That can only mean someone she left behind."

Aydyn stopped jumping and clamped a hand over her mouth. Frost stood up, icily.

He spoke with difficulty, "In our effort to put her past out of the picture, for now, we were fooling ourselves. It is who she is."

"I'm still going to speculate," I said, also with

difficulty. "I think Alice is only vaguely aware of what she has. I think Christopher knew exactly what it meant. He got word to Clauburg. I don't know how. I don't care. I have no doubt now that he intended to kill him. His M.O. was not one. Maybe he wanted to wipe out Clauburg's whole stinking business."

"There are two things wrong with that theory, John," Frost said, sitting back down. "Clauburg came here. His business was somewhere else. And, most importantly, Christopher has been a different kind of evil, but evil still. I do not shy away from that word. What was his pay-off?"

"I've been trying to sort that out, too," I answered. "I'm going to go farther out on the limb. I'll answer the easy part first: In his own way, Clauburg has eluded authorities, just as Christopher did. That means he was very careful. He may have insisted on a first meeting to feel Christopher out in person. Christopher would have played the role necessary. North of downtown, just past the tracks, in a small Iowa city. Just isolated enough to make everything seem safe.

"As for the second: I realized this is the greatest leap of all – remorse."

"As you say," Frost responded, shaking his head, "a great leap. It implies a conscience. There has been no sign of that in the past."

"The Davenport family," I said, looking at Frost closely.

It was more than one of his very subtle responses. He was startled.

"Why are they his beneficiaries?" I pressed. "Is he really their father? Does that mean anything to him? Anything close to what it means to others? He left them behind in chaos. Was he forced to make that choice? Had he retired once before, only to have it blow up?"

Aydyn collapsed in her chair, her mouth wide open.

"Yes," Frost said, in a whisper. "One small chance, one small part of redemption, and at hand, not distantly through anonymous checks."

We were silent.

"Something went wrong," Frost said, at last. "Clauburg would not have tried anything without access to the box. Christopher would not have had the box with him. A first, meeting to size things up for both of them."

"The unknown person," I said. "But why? We always come back to that."

"Naturally," Frost said, completely himself now. "Means and opportunity we have. Motive is next."

"Not entirely means," I corrected. "How could he have surprised Christopher? What went wrong?"

"I cannot think that another party would be at the meeting," Frost went on, "without Christopher's knowledge. Even if he didn't arrange it, I think he would have been on the lookout for a trap."

"If that other person had played his role

perfectly," I added, "he might not have been seen as a threat. Clauburg was also surprised. His associate was just a flunky. Of no concern for either."

"Someone," Frost's turn. "I believe, who saw his opportunity to do something he'd been thinking about for some time. He wants to be head man."

"That makes sense in many ways," I confirmed. "I think the box supports this, too. This third person isn't as concerned as Clauburg was, or he would not have struck that night. It may not directly implicate him."

"Still," Frost added, "he remains. He still wants the box. Perhaps, it is details that could keep the operation intact or provide leverage against others."

"All this is still just speculation, guesses built on assumptions," I said, looking at Frost carefully.

"I know little about such things," Frost said cryptically, "But do you know anyone who would bet against what we have laid forth?"

"I do," I smiled, "but he loves long shots."

Frost smiled in return. Aydyn was coming around, too.

"Say," I said, "We did a lot of work tonight. I've got some genuine Vermont Maple syrup and I make great pancakes. Who's in?"

"I am!" Aydyn cried, jumping up, of course. "I want to help."

"Delighted," I told her, as I got up.

"That does sound good," Frost said, but remained

seated. "However, I must ask you again, John – Are you sure you are alright?"

I looked at him, stumped. "I think so," I said. "Why do you ask?"

He smiled, and said, "You have on only one sock and your sweatshirt is on backwards."

— fifteen —

Frost and Aydyn ate rather heartily. I'm the one who nibbled absent-mindedly. I had made a double batch of batter. It was nearly gone. The early dawn light was beginning to show. Third week in November – that meant it must be nearly seven. It was time for me to bring out my father voice.

"You two children need to go home," I said, with exaggerated seriousness. Then, more normally, I added, "You may not be able to sleep well, but get what rest you can."

Aydyn protested. She wanted to finish clean-up. I told her she had done enough and emphasized that Frost would need her to be sharp later. She agreed.

We said our short good-byes. They got in their separate vehicles and left.

I was not as tired as I thought I would be. The determination I had for what had to be done added to my energy. After a long hot shower and fresh clothes – complete and worn correctly – I was off to the office.

I was already forming my game plan. I'm sure Murphy would be on board, after a little persuasion.

Anything official would be the result of the "anonymous tip" I was concocting. The FBI might not buy it. I didn't know if Wheeland would be directly involved. His case was Christopher. Someone else might head up Clauburg. It is my experience that any official with a long case, particularly one of years, becomes obsessed. If they are sure of their case, but don't have enough hard evidence for conviction, it can be especially frustrating.

On the way to the office, my mind went in a very different direction. I remembered reading, once upon a time, about the language of original natives of Alaska. They have more than twenty different words for snow. Differences in texture, size and conditions determined the word to use.

The sky was clear, dark sky blue. The sun was out. There was little breeze. There were tiny crystals floating through the air. I really wondered what the word for that was.

At the street level door leading to the offices stood Old Mr. Young. I liked saying that. He loved to hear it.

Warren Young, now in his eighties, was the founder of the accounting firm with offices down the hall from mine. He seldom comes. He usually just drops in to say, "Hi." It's not that he can't do the work. Far from it. And he handles the old stairs better than his son, Young Mr. Young, who is now senior partner. So, it was odd to see him there.

"Hello, John Thompson," he greeted me, brightly.

He always called me that as a way of returning what I called him.

"Old Mr. Young," I returned, also brightly. "Hello. What brings you out on a cold Saturday morning?"

"Attempted break-in," he responded, "Or so I'm told. Police got a call about someone trying to get in this door. They called Billy. He called me this morning."

Billy was William Young, the son.

"He came down last night," Old Mr. Young continued, "Sometime after midnight. Didn't find anything amiss, but I thought I'd see for myself."

"Really?" I said. "No one called me."

"They called us first," he explained. "Guess they thought we keep money up there. Or maybe we needed to check the new fancy computers. They checked the doors and are sure they hadn't been messed with. Also, the kids that called the police are pretty sure they scared the guy away. Didn't see any reason to get you out of bed."

"Well, I appreciate that," I said. "I'll check things out when I get up there. Might have been some kids fooling around. Friday night. You know how it is."

"I thought that, too," he said with a chuckle. "But I guess it was an older guy. Seemed old to the kids, I suppose. Thin guy in his thirties, they said. Nervous. That's what made them suspicious."

"I see," I replied, filing the information away. "Still, he couldn't have been much of a thief. This isn't exactly a bank door."

"That's for sure," he laughed again. "That's for sure."

He opened the door. I followed him in and up. At the top, we went our separate ways. There was no sign of tampering with my door. I went in. All was as it should be.

I spent the first hour straightening my desk and the notes on the various parts of the various cases. The notes I'd done before had gone off in several directions, mostly dead ends. Now, I had a different perspective. Alice, no longer a separate mystery, had become the link to the others. I had to start with her. That was the key and the problem.

Alice was a fragile little girl. Above all else, I wanted to protect her. At the same time, I knew that if she was to get real help, to become the whole person she could be, she needed professionals. Some people, after years of abuse, become like the girl Frost had known, lost. Despite all best efforts, some never come all the way back.

Alice had a certain kind of strength. She proved that. But she was living in a cocoon. Like the cocoons of some insects, it could withstand a great deal of natural stress. It was unexpected, unnatural things that were most dangerous, especially people. A curious and unknowledgeable, or unthinking person might probe to see what's inside. Some uncaring or even mean person might crush it just because they can. Right now, I did not know how to prevent either one.

Officialdom often has no face. In fact, often, people see it as a wall. It's the building where official things happen. They know where official things happen. They may know some of what happens. They have little understanding of how, and even less about who.

It really annoys me when politicians use that for votes. They blame bureaucrats, turning hardworking people into nothing more than file cabinets stuffed with paper. The politicians ignore the fact that they, or their predecessors, are the ones who created the bureaus and continue to dump papers on the desks.

I deal with a lot of those real people. Like the rest of the world, they are a mix of different kinds of wonderful with an occasional klunker. Each office that I deal with has the face of a real person.

The most immediate face of officialdom that I needed right now was police Sergeant Sean Murphy.

I needed to show him the chart I had made. It was my third attempt. In the center were the words "the box." Alice might be the link, but I would not use her even in my drawing. Arrows connected the box to Clauburg and to Christopher. Other arrows connected them to each other. Arrows led from the dead men to the FBI., with Wheeland in parentheses. Murphy and I were on one side, connected to things by dotted lines, indicating that we may not have as much to do with things as we wanted.

At the bottom of the page, I had three circles with numbers only: Frost, Aydyn, and the Davenport family. Something else I would keep to myself for a while.

Other circles held just question marks. There were a lot of unknown people and possibilities.

I stared at it for several minutes. I had to make a decision about how much of this I would share with Murphy. Then, I called him.

"Murphy here," he answered, very officially when I was transferred to him.

"Hi, Murphy," I replied. "John Thompson, here. I really need to see you today."

"You can come over right now," he said, a little less officially.

"No," I said. "It would be better if you came to my office." I paused. "It's very important and very tricky."

There was a longer pause.

"You sound worried," he said, concerned but suspicious.

"I am," I told him simply. "I have some important information, but it can only be partly official."

Another pause.

"Okay," he said. "When?"

"When it's good for you," I replied. "I'm just staying right here until you can make it."

"I really don't like the sound of this," he said. I could hear his anger rising. "I'll try to be there in a few minutes."

I made coffee. I paced.

I'm not a pacer. Usually, I'm a doodler, or scribbler.

After two trips around the office, I walked down the hall to check on Old Mr. Young. He had gone home long ago. The younger Young, Bill, was there. We said, "Hello." We exchanged, "Nothing missing." "Cold day." "Happy Thanksgiving." He probably thought I was nuts.

It was two more trips around the office before Murphy arrived.

"Well, here I am, Mr. Thompson," he announced, rather roughly.

"Thank you for coming, Sergeant Murphy," I returned. If he was going to start out formally, so was I.

"Please, close the doors," I said, a little more normally.

It was anything but normal, and Murphy knew it. The other day when Wheeland and Lucianni were here was the first time Murphy had ever been in my office with the door closed, official business or not. He closed both doors and stood just inside the second, staring at me, trying to judge my mood.

"I brought the report from last night," he said, calmly. "That's one of the official reasons I'm here."

"One?" I asked.

"Yes," he continued as before. "I also brought the pictures from the FBI. Do you want to look at those first?"

"Sure," I said. God, this was awkward. I still didn't know what to say to him or how. Maybe looking at the report and pictures would give me time to form the words.

"Sit down here next to my desk," I offered. "I'll get you some coffee."

"Thanks," he said, and sat. He still hadn't taken his eyes off me.

I put the mugs between us on the desk.

Murphy passed me two folders, looking only at my face.

I looked back at him and opened the top folder, only looking at it enough to know it was the incident report. I assumed there wouldn't be much in it that I hadn't already been told.

"Don't think it was just some drunk, huh?" I asked, absently.

"Nope," Murphy replied, flatly.

"Probably nothing," I said.

"Probably," he echoed.

I closed the folder and pushed it toward him.

I opened the second, again, rather absently.

"That's him!" I shouted, slamming down my finger on the face on the page.

That changed Murphy's demeanor.

"Clayton Sheridan," he said coldly. "Believed to be very close to Clauburg. Lives in Connecticut. Works in Brooklyn. Import/export. Probably involves shipping young girls. A middleman among middlemen. Hard to get to from either end. Layers of protection. And that scum is here in our town."

We stared at each other again, but with a difference. This was the area that could get Murphy unhinged. He never told me any stories, but a word here and there had led me to believe there was something personal in his past that made him lose it in such cases.

"Murphy," I began in the calmest voice I could manage, "What I asked you here for concerns that guy. I wasn't sure until I saw that picture. Now, I am. I think I know why he's in Cedar Falls."

"Be careful, John," he warned, for more than one reason.

"We need the FBI without the FBI knowing why we need them," I said. I knew my saying that would make him even madder but was confusing enough to keep his attention.

"What?" he growled through gritted teeth.

After a second or two, he realized what I was doing.

"This better be good, Thompson," he said. "This better be very good."

"I hope so," I said, "although I don't want to use the word 'good' for any of it. It's something you want. Take a breath."

He did. I did. Then I told him the story of Alice, most of it. I started vaguely – a girl ran away from Clauburg. She has a box. I was sure that box is what brought Clauburg and Sheridan to Cedar Falls even more than the girl. Christopher had become the go-between. I was convinced that Sheridan had killed the other two and now he wants that box.

I could see it in Murphy's face: A box. Hard evidence against the kind of guys he hated. I had to continue to be very careful.

"Right now, there is no way of getting the box without maybe destroying the girl," I told him.

I know he didn't completely understand that.

I explained who she was, how she was, what kind of life she had escaped from that had made it a danger to push her too hard.

As I had been early that morning, Murphy was torn between rage and nausea.

When he calmed down a little, I laid out the rest of what I knew, what I was guessing, and how I thought we might proceed. At different points, I would pause to allow it to sink in and settle. At other, points I was still evasive. I never mentioned where she was hiding. I never mentioned Frost.

"Murphy," I said in a low, careful voice, "this girl is more fragile than I think she could possible understand. If there is any way to protect her, I'm going to do it. I'm sure Sheridan is after her. That's one. I'm afraid if we bring in the FBI too far too soon, it will have the same effect."

"John," Murphy said, with a tight voice. "I want Sheridan. I want the whole rotten bunch. I don't know what's in that box any more than you do, but if it can save some other children, I want it. I want it bad."

"I honestly don't know where it is," I told him. "The girl won't say. I won't push her. In some ways, she's a frightened toddler. She doesn't even know what it is she frightened of. I told you. This is a real mess."

"How the hell am I supposed to proceed?" he shouted at me. "Wait for you to toss me one crumb at a time?"

He was standing, leaning on the desk – right in my face. In all the years I'd known him, I knew he was tough, but this was the first time I was afraid of him, really afraid.

"An anonymous tip," I said, nearly in a whisper.

Murphy froze in place to let me explain.

"The tipster was a witness. Afraid to come forward. He saw the killing. He heard the three men arguing about a box."

Murphy sat back down.

"Can you use that, Murphy," I asked with a sigh. "Can you sell that to Wheeland? Maybe they'll have some guesses at what's in that box and why Sheridan wants it so bad that he's still around here."

"Yes," Muphy said, more to himself than to me. "I can do that." Then, to me directly. "What's in that box must have something to do with the operation. It might have details of how they operate, but most import: it might point to who. Who!"

"If we can do this, and do it right," I said, "we can take out...." I stopped. I was getting too far ahead of things. I was only guessing, hoping, what was in the box.

"If we can save one more," Murphy whispered, breathing as hard as I was.

We looked at each other for a minute, then, I picked up my chart.

Murphy agreed that the box, not the girl, should be in the center. I still hadn't given her a name, but I suspected that Murphy suspected that I had one. He understood that. He was not as pleased that the circles at the bottom had no names.

"Look, Murphy," I told him, "I need to be certain in my own mind about what's next. Circle one will be clear soon enough. The other two are mostly irrelevant. I put them there for my own thoughts. I don't want any collateral damage. Okay?"

"I'll let it go," he grumbled, "for now."

"Thank you," I responded. "Now help me with the question marks. What am I missing?"

"Let's be clear about target number one – Sheridan," he said. Why is he carrying around Christopher's bag across the street from the theater?"

He already knew the answer.

"Christopher's script and rehearsal schedule were probably in it," I replied. "The killings took place two blocks north of the theater. I know I'd check it out."

"As far as we know," Murphy added, "Sheridan did not know anything about Christopher other than what's in that bag. Christopher's pattern would have tried to cover up as much as possible. If Sheridan wants what's in the box, it's his only lead."

"Yes," I agreed. "That worries me. Somehow, he'll want to get in there."

"Is it really that hard?" Murphy asked, again knowing the answer.

"No," I said with resignation. "But it wouldn't do him any good. The box can't be very big, or the girl couldn't have gotten away with it. There are ten thousand places in the theater to hide it. Christopher would have chosen a good one. It might take years to find it."

"That leads to two conclusions," Murphy leaned in. "One: the box must be in there. Two: only the girl knows."

He leaned back studying me.

"Thompson," he said, "I trust you. I know what you can do. I know what you are trying to do here. I respect that, but I have to know things. I can't help you in the dark."

He paused.

"The girl's in the theater, isn't she?" he asked point blank.

I paused.

"Even if I tell you everything I know," I told him, "There are gaps. I don't know if you would believe that I don't know some things, but I don't."

He looked at me. He looked at the chart. He reached out and tapped number one without speaking.

I nodded. He knew there must be a go-between. He almost certainly knew it must be Frost. The tap and the nod were enough.

"We're good," he said. "Now, we can go ahead."

We spent another half hour comparing ideas, plans for moving ahead. He threw in a couple I hadn't thought of. They were good ones. I felt good.

Primarily, our interest was Sheridan. There had

been no sign of him. Murphy would step up the search. For now, he would not involve media – no newspaper, no TV. He would focus on motels and restaurants. Sheridan had to eat and sleep somewhere.

Then, it was my turn to put Murphy on the spot.

"There's something you haven't shared with me, too," I said suddenly. "To be fair, I haven't asked, but I thought you would let me know."

He froze, suspicious.

"Christopher's house," I said, point blank.

"Oh, yeah," he said, as if just reminded. "Believe it or not, this is what I don't know much about. Wheeland took the lead. I went with him the first time. So did Jakes. It was an easy entry. Preliminary search didn't find anything. In fact, it seemed too easy and too much nothing. I thought there must be things hidden somewhere, like the car. I didn't see it. I wasn't invited back. Wheeland said he'd fill me in after they finished. He didn't say how long after. I haven't heard anything else."

"Damn," I said. "I was afraid they might freeze us out sooner or later. Maybe your 'anonymous tip' and my ID of Sheridan will shake something loose."

"Maybe," he said, with a wry chuckle. "I'm sure we'll get all the details when someone writes a book about 'the Exterminator' in ten or fifteen years."

"Think they'll spell our names right?" I joined his cynical attitude.

"Oh, hell," he went on, "I'll be surprised if we're even mentioned in Wheeland's reports."

"What are you doing next?" I asked, moving on.

"Going back to the office," he said. "I'll call Wheeland and wait. I've got two other break-ins and a couple of nuisance reports to look at. What about you?"

"As far as I can tell," I replied, "almost nothing. I've got an insurance thing I'm looking into. No big deal. Mix-up in names it looks like. Probably a clerical error."

Again, I wasn't going to mention the Davenports to him.

"Sounds about as interesting as most nuisance reports," he said with a smile. "Good luck."

He left. I picked up the coffee mugs. They were full and cold. We hadn't touched them.

— sixteen —

There was more nothing to do than I thought.
Norm left me a message that he had been called out of town on a family matter. He didn't give details. He said it would be after Thanksgiving before he would get back to me.

Some places close down for the entire holiday weekend, in spite of "Black Friday." Some people close down sooner. They may still come to work or social gatherings, but their hearts and minds are in a different mood and mode.

I have to admit that I have been like that for most of my life. For me, holiday breaks from school began a full week ahead of actual dismissal. Ask any of my former teachers. It continued into adulthood. It expanded when I became a father. "The Twelve Days of Christmas" at our house sometimes tripled.

Then things changed. The kids grow up. Empty nest starts long before they move out. It starts when they move on. Many of the attachments one has with parents become attached to others. Some of the remaining bonds become stronger, to be sure, but there are all those empty spaces.

Then Sarah died.

The pain does not leave. It only becomes less intrusive, mostly.

At holidays, it often manifests itself as lostness. There are times, sometimes days, around holidays when I have this nagging feeling that there is something I am supposed to be doing but am not doing. Then, I realize that there is something we are supposed to be doing. There is no we.

That lostness was amplified for the next two days. I tried to focus on the case, but there was no case. Only Frost could connect with Alice. He would report any new things. Murphy was coming up empty. No sign of Sheridan. I speculated that maybe even creeps took holidays off. Wheeland had taken Murphy's reports. He offered nothing in return.

I was left with two options: rehearsals and fixing up the house a little for the kids' arrival.

Our family has always made a bigger deal out of Thanksgiving than most. In fact, it seems to me to be a forgotten holiday. It is ignored until Halloween is well over and is immediately swallowed up by Christmas. If it wasn't for a parade or two and a football game or two, most people wouldn't pay any more attention to it than they do Flag Day.

Not at our house. There is a cornstalk sheaf display in the front yard with pumpkins. I have decorations in every room, even yellow, orange, and brown quilts on every bed, and similar lap robes and throws everywhere.

Our meal is very traditional – stuffed turkey, candied yams, cranberry sauce, the works. Jack, who is a whiz with all the latest combinations and presentations expected in upscale restaurants, relishes in recreating the traditions. Modern businesswoman Jenni would tear up if any part was left out.

For years we had a cheesy turkey decoration: one of those paste board things that folds back with a paper accordion breast. It finally became irreparable. I think Jenni wanted to have a ceremony and bury it in the back yard like an old family pet that had passed away.

And we give thanks. Sometimes it's old-fashioned corny. Sometimes it's awkwardly lame. Sometimes it gets silly. Always, it's sincere.

Everything I could do was done before Monday night rehearsal. Jack and Marta would be in town by noon, Tuesday. Jenni and Corey were scheduled to land at Waterloo airport twenty-four hours later. I was already feeling thankful.

Rehearsals were a different matter. I talked to Bob. There were two new stagehands. I knew them. Together we worked out where they needed to be and what they needed to do. They were fast learners. For this show, I was now out of the stage crew entirely.

I spent most of my time at the theater trying not to think about Alice. She was out of sight, but not out of mind. In the two-hour show, I'm on stage for about five minutes. After rehearsal Sunday afternoon, Wemyss told me he thought it was ridiculous for me to just hang around.

"Johnny," he said, "You're doing fine. Monday and Tuesday, anyway, why don't you make your call 7:30 instead of 7:00. If there's anything you need to know from the notes, I let you know. And after your scene, I don't see why you can't just take off if you want to. You go on home."

"Thanks," I said, relieved. "Don't tell anyone, but I really don't like theater seats."

He laughed, loud. "You're not alone, Johnny. Believe me!"

Frost's first report, Monday about 7:00 a.m., had a couple of interesting items, and a couple of troubling ones.

Alice was less reluctant to show herself, showing familiarity if not real trust. Frost's task was to explain what was going on in the theater and what changes were coming. Alice had some childish ideas about pretending. That, too, had been perverted by her former life. Everything had been twisted into bizarre shapes. Alice was able to grasp the general idea. Her emotions were mixed. She seemed to understand that what was happening was supposed to be fun, but her idea of fun was also different.

Frost's greatest difficulty came in trying to explain the story of the play. Alice did not know who Santa Claus was. It took some time for that to sink in when he told me. As far as she was concerned, he might as well have mentioned some obscure Siberian myth.

She had never celebrated holidays. The names of many had been mentioned in her presence over the years, but her only connection to them was as twisted as everything else. She was aware that others had something called "birthdays." She did not. Her isolation from the world had been nearly total.

I don't know how Frost held it together. I barely did when he told me all this. We wear our culture, the real and the imaginary, like a second skin. We take it for granted.

Andy Griffith, in his early stand-up career, told a story of a guy "from the hills" who accidently gets swept up in a crowd and finds himself watching a football game. He's never seen it or heard of it. He can't figure out why all those big guys are fighting over "a funny, li'l punkin'." We laugh at his mistaken ideas about things we take for granted. But honestly, how would you explain it to someone who has never heard of it?

That was our problem: how do we bring Alice into a world she's never heard of?

Frost had an idea: pizza. Alice knew pizza. They used to eat it a lot, "back there." We didn't know who "they" were or where "back there" was exactly. It was a thin connection between that world and this one.

Frost had been asking Alice about her necessities. Her food was adequate, if uninteresting. Most things could be eaten directly from the cans, boxes, or bags. Christopher had tried to get some variety, but that was difficult. Occasionally, there were some things that could be warmed up in a microwave. The chicken Aydyn had noticed that night was from chicken soup. Aside from juice boxes, Alice drank water.

She missed pizza, hamburgers, fries, and root beer. She liked to drink the root beer in big gulps. That made her burp. That made her laugh. That made us smile. We wanted to hear her laugh.

Her clothes were also adequate, but uninteresting. They were mostly black or dark gray so she could not be easily seen if she was not in hiding. They were also well suited for quick, easy movements. Frost mentioned that what little movement he had seen from her was athletic and graceful. "Like his own," I thought, "and probably as silent."

The next subject got tricky: hygiene.

"I'm always clean," she had said, proudly but obediently, it seemed to Frost. "Doctor" had insisted on that. So had "Master Charlie."

It must be hard to do in the dusty, old theater, but she did what she could. It also explained her use of things from the janitor's closet.

"Technically," Frost said, "I haven't seen her 'nest,' as we have called it. I'd venture to say, however, that it is one of the cleanest places apart from the public areas."

I agreed, smiling. Frost stopped smiling.

"As we proceeded along those lines," he said tightly, "she revealed another aspect of her past."

He saw the worried look on my face.

"It was unintentional on my part," he said. "I was endeavoring to avoid it. She jumped ahead to another area that I had intended to broach delicately."

"Her period?" I asked, indelicately.

"Yes," he said. "I was afraid my rather old-fashioned manner would hamper any such discussion. She pushed ahead without hesitation. She is well supplied for now."

"How does that bring up her past?" I asked, afraid to ask.

"I will try," he said with a struggle. "In the terrible life before, when a girl grows up – menses – she is too old…." He trailed off for a minute. "Someone takes those girls away. Alice has no idea where or what becomes of them. Once in a while, one is kept. She becomes a caregiver to the youngest ones, a surrogate mother. That is what Alice meant the other night when she said she had been a 'mama.'"

I was beginning to feel the aura of nausea and rage.

"John," Frost said to me suddenly with a tone I had never heard from him before. "I feel helpless. More than helpless. I don't want to feel helpless. I feel as though I were tied to a tree watching Alice drift away toward Niagara Falls."

We stared at each other.

"John," he said in almost a whisper, "Please. Please, tell me this is not so."

I took him by both shoulders and looked as deep into his eyes as I could.

"This is not so," I said slowly, solidly. "The river is there. The falls are there. You are free. You can act. Alice is not in the river now. And you are not alone. You and I will do whatever it takes to set her free as well."

He closed his eyes, put his hand on my arm, and bowed his head. A second went by. Ten. Fifteen. He took a deep breath and raised his head. He was Frost, again.

"Let's talk about pizza, again," I said. "Do you have a plan?"

"Rather simple," he replied. "I order one. I pick it up. I bring it to her."

"That's good," I said, "but have you considered having Aydyn bring it?"

"I have," he answered, "but our change in subject matter did not give me the opportunity to speak to Alice about it."

"Does she know that Aydyn is helping you?"

"Not by name. I told her I have a special friend who lets me into the building. That confused her a little. I take it that in her experience someone who has keys has been someone in control. I remembered that she said Christopher had 'funny keys.' I took that to mean he had picked the lock to get in. Still, he was the one with keys and, therefore, the one in control. It confuses her that I seem to have control, but do not have keys."

"We are moving in a strange environment," I interjected. "We're in an old, haunted mansion with long corridors, mostly locked doors, and secret passageways."

"Nor do we know when ghosts might appear," Frost added.

"Perhaps you should order garlic bread with the pizza," I joked, sort of.

"Garlic is for vampires," he corrected me.

"I see some progress here," I said hopefully. "She has known only control imposed. It has only begun to dawn on her that she might have some control over her own person. Her running away must seem like some kind of dream. Christopher found her a safe place, but one in which he seemed in control. In a sense, that gave her a feeling of the familiar and, therefore, safety. It is still a closed habitat."

"Yes. I see," Frost said. "Her encounter with Christopher saved her from Clauburg, and also from those who would only have seen lost child and not understood."

"In some ways, I see that my life is partly closed off as well," I said pensively. "I knew such evil existed, but it never invaded my world before."

"And we are still on the fringes," Frost added.

"These shocks and shadows keep distracting us!" I said, a bit loudly. "We must focus on the immediate. What does Alice need most from us right now?"

I shook myself physically, to get back to where I needed to be. Frost, I think, did so internally.

"Alice needs a pizza party," I said emphatically. "Pizza and root beer."

"Excellent!" Frost agreed.

"Let me lay out a plan," I said. "You tell me what you think."

He nodded.

"Have the pizza at a table in the rehearsal hall. Sit on chairs. Use forks and napkins. Make it as close to normal as possible. I'm sure that most of her meals have been in dark corners or deep in hiding. This will bring her out into a larger world. And eating with someone else, with you, will add to that."

"That is a sensible step," Frost said, "but we will still need to stay in the dark. Bright lights would be seen from outside and disturb Alice."

"Of course," I agreed. "The light from the kitchen should be enough. Can Aydyn bring the pizza up in the elevator, but no get off the elevator?"

"Very good," he said. "I will prepare Alice for that. Aydyn could wait for me in the costume shop. That would also be a good look out position in case someone comes by."

"Another thought," I went on. "We have a holiday break – no rehearsals after tomorrow night until the next Monday. Do you have any plans?"

"Aydyn invited me to her family gathering," he explained, "but not seriously. Only as a polite gesture. She gets her exuberant nature from her father's family. She knows that a crowd of such, as she puts it 'craziness' is not to my liking. I told her I could survive. She said I would be welcome, but if I wanted to take it in smaller doses at another time, she would understand."

"That sounds like a sensible step," I joked.

He had a cool, quiet laugh.

"This might surprise you," he added, "Aydyn has a brother and a sister. Among the siblings, she is considered 'the quiet one.'"

I would have laughed if not stunned by the concept.

"We're doing the traditional thing," I managed to say. You are welcome to join us. I assure you it will be quieter."

"Thank you," he said. "I know that, too, is a polite gesture, and I appreciate it. I am formulating a plan to see Alice that day, during daylight hours."

"That seems like a big step," I said, a bit worried.

"I think not," he said with assurance. "The theater should be entirely empty. I want to explore with Alice when lights would not be noticed. To check her contingencies without much chance of discovery. I think she will understand and accept that."

"A good idea," I said, "It should also expand your understanding of how she sees things."

"My thought exactly," he smiled.

"You don't need to check in with me every day," I told him, "unless there is some real breakthrough or real problem, but even on the holiday I am available."

We said our good-byes.

My next plan was to tie up a few loose ends.

There were many, but the main one was Mike Coppola.

Bob had told him of the intruder. I have a close relationship with Bob, so it was easier to leave him partly in the dark. Mike's responsibilities to the theater as a whole made things more complicated. For him, the friendliest of intruders was still an intruder and could not be tolerated. It could make him very sad to do it but do it he must. I could not tell him we were protecting someone without telling him the whole story, and even then, I could see no other option for him. I could not hedge my bets; I could not tell a story with large omissions. I was going to have to lie to him flat out.

When I arrived at the theater for a ten o'clock appointment with Mike, Murphy was in the lobby waiting for me. My response was depressed frustration which could only be expressed, as, "O shit. Now what?" I didn't say it, but Murphy read it on my face.

"Hang on, John," he said. "We may have caught a break."

"A break?" At least my mood turned a corner.

"C'mon," Murphy said, "We'll go see Coppola together."

We went up to Mike's second floor office. Technically, the northeast section of the second floor is all one room and an extension of the costume shop. Mike's desk area is a separate entity. It seems so different from the rest of the room you have the impression that you are looking at it through a glass wall. It is neat and well ordered. It is also well lit. Much of the rest of the room is in semi-darkness unless some major costuming work is taking place.

Mike's round, beaming face also lights up the room, any room. Even though he couldn't have a clue about a joint visit from a bit actor and a police sergeant, he still beamed and greeted us warmly.

"I'll get right to it," Murphy began, after we were seated, sounding official, "so you two can get on with things."

He opened the folder he was carrying and showed it to Mike. It had Sheridan's picture in it.

"Have you seen this man?" Murphy asked.

"Yes," Mike answered, startled by the picture. "I've run into him a couple of times when I got coffee across the street. What's it all about?"

"It's rather routine," Murphy said, "As we say, 'he's a person of interest.' That doesn't always have the ominous meaning you get when you hear it on the news. He just may have some information about an on-going case."

I like the way Murphy explained this without really explaining it.

"Someone saw him across the street," Murphy went on without implicating me directly. "One of the kids over there said he saw you talking to him the other day."

"That's right," Mike responded. "He asked me about the play. He saw our sign out front and saw me come out of the theater."

"Oh, I see," Murphy said casually.

"Yeah," Mike continued, "he said he was new in town. Comes from a small town in New York state west of the city. Loves community theater. Not that he does it. He just loves to go to the productions."

Mike loves to talk. Murphy let him.

"He said he was divorced. Kids are grown and scattered. He has a cousin that he's always been close to who moved here several years ago. The cousin raved about this area, so this guy — said his name was Tyler, Jim Tyler — decided to check it out. He's ready to retire. Shipping business of some kind. I'm guessing trucking or something like that."

Mike didn't exactly stop, but there was enough of a pause for Murphy to jump in.

"That fits with the things I've been told. You see, we were notified by authorities back east that this guy, Tyler, may be a witness to some things."

"What kind of things," Mike asked, a bit worried.

"I'm afraid I'm not informed of all the details," Murphy said, a bit annoyed. "I can't even tell you how they knew to get in touch with us."

"Maybe they knew about the cousin," Mike suggested. "He seems like a friendly, open guy. Liked to talk. I'm sure those who know him back east knew about the cousin."

I like it when people fill in gaps of a story with things that fit but lead them away from what the story is really all about. Mike was doing it very neatly, which is what Murphy wanted him to do.

"O sure," Murphy said. "I guess something came up recently. He wasn't at home in New York, so they checked around. Problem is, for me anyway, they never mentioned any cousin. Did Tyler mention his name?"

"No. No, he didn't," Mike said a bit sadly. "All he said was that he was staying with him until he could get his own place."

"Did he give you any idea where?" Murphy tried not to sound too much like a cop interrogating someone.

"I'm afraid not," Mike responded. "He said something about a big, old farmhouse. But that could be anywhere."

"Yes, it could," Murphy chuckled a little. "There's still a lot about this we don't know, so I have to ask you something a little odd. If you see this guy again, please give me a call, but don't mention to him that I talked to you. I don't want him to get all worried when it might be nothing. It would be better if it came directly from me."

"Of course," Mike was happy to agree.

I was thinking of suggesting to Murphy about trying out for one of our plays. He certainly played this part perfectly.

"By the way," Mike jumped in again, "I didn't get a chance to tell you. I know he'll be back."

Murphy's expression got more serious. Mine, too, I suspect.

"I gave him two passes to our first Sunday

matinee," Mike said, beaming once again. "For him and his cousin."

"When is that?" Murphy asked, all casualness gone.

"The second Sunday after Thanksgiving," Mike said. "Three weeks from yesterday."

Murphy wrote that down. Then he turned to Mike, all smiles again. "It may be all settled by then, but it's good to know, just in case. Thank you for your help."

Murphy started to leave, but I stopped him.

"Hang on, Sergeant," I told him. "I'll walk out with you."

I turned to Mike.

"Mike," I said. "That problem that Bob told you about?" I spoke softly as though I didn't want Murphy to hear too much. "It wasn't what he thought it was. We've got it all taken care of. I'll fill you in sometime."

"Oh, good," he replied. "You'd think after all my years in theater, I could have figured it out. But then, after all my years in theater, almost nothing surprises me anymore."

He laughed. I laughed with him.

Murphy and I left together. We'd gotten to the bottom of the stairs when Mike shouted down to us.

"Sergeant Murphy. I just remembered something. After talking to Tyler, I came back to the theater. When I looked out the window, I saw him get into a beat up, old, blue Ford. I think the driver must have been his cousin."

"Really?" Murphy asked. "What did he look like?"

"I only got a glimpse of him. Skinny guy. Thirty-five, maybe," Mike said. "He was very fidgety. Always looking around."

Murphy and I looked at each other.

— seventeen —

I was uneasy the rest of the day. Sheridan had an accomplice. That man was hiding him. That man matched the description of the man who tried to get into the building where I have my office.

Why?

I'm involved with the theater. At the time of Christopher's death, I can't imagine there would be any mention of me in the things in Christopher's bag.

Was Sheridan checking out everyone? The cast list may have been in the bag. That was easy. He seemed to be watching the theater. Would he have seen me coming and going? Many times, I walked to the theater from my office down the street. It wouldn't be hard to make that connection.

Had he seen me with Murphy? Maybe at the garage? Maybe at the crime scene? Either of those would make a stronger connection.

What else?

A beat-up, old, blue Ford. A thin, thirty-five-year-old man. Not a lot to go on. Murphy was checking. He didn't want to press Mike for more details unless it became necessary.

New information. New clues. We couldn't really call it a step forward. It was more sideways.

Wheeland wasn't much help. He had remained in Iowa, attached to the Des Moines office. The words he relayed to Murphy from Washington usually consisted of, "Thank you for the information."

"Relay" was the key word here. Wheeland spoke to his superior in Washington who in turn talked to someone else: sometimes the agents assigned to the Clauburg case, sometimes to a division head. Wheeland called Chief Moorman in Cedar Falls who then talked to Murphy. No matter how smooth and efficient a chain of command operates, being at the far end seems far indeed. You can't help but wonder who left out what. My being outside the chain made it seem like I was in a galaxy far, far away.

The only bit of information we received that we liked much at all wasn't a great deal of help. The investigation into Clauburg was at a standstill, and not just because of his death. His whole operation seemed to be at a standstill, too. Nothing seemed to be happening. We were glad of that.

It increased speculation that the Box held more important information than we thought. Perhaps things could not happen without it. That also increased our fear that the FBI. might come crashing in demanding the Box. Murphy may not be able to hide behind the anonymous tip story much longer.

We decided that the best course of action was to proceed as if that would not happen soon. Murphy would continue to look for Sheridan and the thin man. I would continue to monitor Alice's progress through Frost. Other than that, we were concerned with family and Thanksgiving.

Jack and Marta arrived just as expected. It's a five-hour drive from Chicago. They'd started the night before. They'd been in town for a couple of hours before coming to the house. Jack was already getting ready for our feast.

We hugged and kissed and grabbed bags. We hugged and laughed and grabbed more bags, mostly grocery bags. Like me, Jack tends to pack to lightly. He had another pair of jeans, besides the ones he was wearing, and three shirts for the next five days. No one worried. He would probably be wearing something of mine before the day was over. He always did.

He did pack four aprons. Watching him in the kitchen is always a lot of fun. He enjoys being watched almost as much as doing the work. He takes it very seriously, too. Of course, I have all that fatherly pride knowing he has found the career he wants and does it so well. He is a professional.

Marta is not a pro in the kitchen. She works at a Home Depot. She's a pro with hardware. However, she makes a perfect assistant for Jack. They are partners in several senses of the word.

We spent most of the time just getting caught up and fussing about the house. Marta loves Thanksgiving as much as we do. She even brought the perfect gift: a rather cheesy, pasteboard turkey that folds out with a paper accordion breast. She'd heard the story of the one we lost.

The afternoon disappeared in a hurry – laughing all the way.

Through e-mails, they already knew that I had a rehearsal that night. I had until 7:30 to get there, but I still wanted to eat light. Jack had anticipated that and all the meals for the week. For this first night, he put together a genuine chef's salad. Most of the ones I'd had in my life were chef's salads in name only.

Rehearsal was too uneventful. Everyone was happy off-stage, flat on stage. It was obvious that almost everyone was in a holiday mood. Only the real pros among us were on their game. Some of us hacks didn't even notice. Wemyss noticed and let us know he noticed. I was only partly aware that I "was not in the scene." I'll dare to use that actor's phrase. I said all the words correctly. I moved and gestured just as I was supposed to do. It seemed lifeless and even meaningless. I was glad when it was over, but a little contrite that I had done so poorly. I think most were.

Another part of my brain was also preoccupied: tonight was pizza night. Frost and Aydyn had it all set up. Rehearsal was to be over at ten. The way it was going, I'm sure no one was going to hang around. The restaurant where the pizza was ordered is just down the street. It closes at eleven. Aydyn would pick up the order at 10:30 and take it directly to the theater. Frost would already be there.

By turning on the kitchen light before rehearsal was over, it would seem perfectly normal to anyone who might notice. The neighbors in the apartments across the street are used to seeing late night lights. Because each floor of the theater has unusually high ceilings, the theater's third floor is significantly above the buildings on the other side of Main. Unless someone was on the roof over there (unlikely in November), they could see very little in the rehearsal hall. Frost and Alice could have a private late supper.

Frost would fill me in the next day. And over the next two weeks "wait," I thought, would be an often used and descriptive word.

Frost's report was very interesting.

He came to my house at about nine the next morning. He found us in a lounging mood. Frost, in his usual attire, seemed quite formal. He usually does no matter what the situation.

Jack and Marta greeted him warmly. They had only met briefly once before. They treated him as if he too were wearing lounge pants and a t-shirt and had been all morning. (I'm not sure he even owns either of those items.) They refer to him as my "assistant from Georgia." I had never told them the whole story of how we had met. They knew it had something to do with an investigation, but that was all.

The kids were curious about Frost's family and

Thanksgiving plans. Frost rarely volunteers any personal information and is adept at turning the conversation when it tends deeper than he cares to go.

"There is only my father," he said, cordially. "I visited him a short time ago. I will be spending time with a new friend."

"Maybe you and your friend would come by later in the day for some pumpkin pie?" Marta asked, with some enthusiasm.

"Thank you," Frost replied, politely. "I may come, but I'm afraid my friend has a commitment."

I liked his use of the word "commitment."

"Another day?" Marta offered, hopefully. "We'll be here until Saturday."

"Thank you, again," Frost replied, again politely. "As this is a new friend, I hesitate to impose. I, myself, am rather slow with friendships and reflect that feeling on others."

"Oh, I'm sorry," Marta said quickly. "I didn't mean to be pushy."

"Do not fret," Frost returned. "I felt no offense or push."

He turned to Jack.

"I must say I am fascinated by your profession," he said with obvious admiration.

"Thanks," Jack replied. "I'm fascinated by it myself.

We all laughed.

"Do you know the story of how Edison failed a

thousand times before perfecting the light bulb?" Jack asked, with a smile.

Frost looked at him with interest.

"It's often the same in the kitchen," Jack said, with a laugh. "I hate wasting any food, but there are times when I have spent more time trying to salvage a bad experiment than in preparing a meal."

"I had never considered that," Frost remarked.

"I've changed many fine cuts of beef into ground beef," Jack laughed again. "Fortunately, Tomas and Steven, the head chefs where I work, allow me to donate that to a shelter nearby. They have some of the finest chili in Chicago."

Now, we all laughed, again.

"I understand that your sister is due to arrive today," Frost changed the subject, "so I will conclude my business with your father and be on my way."

Jack and Marta excused themselves and went upstairs.

"Would you like some tea?" I asked as we headed to my home conference room, the kitchen.

"Thank you. No," he answered.

"Did it go well?" I asked, a bit anxiously.

"Very well indeed," Frost said. "I hadn't asked Alice if she had a favorite, so we went with plain cheese to be safe. That appeared to be just fine. We were already in the rehearsal hall when Aydyn brought it up in the elevator.

"When we heard the elevator start up, Alice went to hide. We had decided that ahead of time. If it turned out to be anyone other than Aydyn, I would tell them that I was waiting for Aydyn. That we were having a private Thanksgiving supper as we would not be together on that day. If the unexpected person lingered, Alice could escape in more than one way. Two ways I had already determined, but she hinted at a third. I hope she will share that with me.

"Fortunately, it was Aydyn. I asked her to wait in the open elevator while I took the pizza to the table and called for Alice. Alice was reluctant when she saw the light from the elevator. I explained that my friend, Aydyn, had brought the pizza and was only waiting to be sure all was well.

"Then I took a rather daring chance: I asked Alice if Aydyn could say 'hello.'"

Alice was obviously frightened. She took my hand, squeezing it rather hard, and nodded. I called to Aydyn who stepped out of the elevator but did not approach.

"'Hello, Alice,' Aydyn said. Alice moved behind me and did not reply.

"'I'll go back down now,' Aydyn said. 'I hope you enjoy your pizza.'

"She did as she had said."

"That's great!" I interjected. "I see two wonderful things about that: First, Alice sees you as a protector, not a captor, or she would not have clung to you. And second, she did not run from Aydyn. She has taken a major step!"

"I certainly saw and felt that as well," Frost said,

"and there was a third point. Alice's apprehension disappeared very quickly. She relaxed and enjoyed our little party.

"I kept the conversation away from anything troubling. We talked about the pizza – next time she would like sausage and pepperoni. We talked of other foods. In addition to burgers and fries, she is fond of spaghetti. I assume part of that is the childish way. Spaghetti can be fun to play with."

"Frost," I said, with genuine admiration, "I think you were marvelous. I know it is still just opening the door a crack, but what a wonderful beginning."

"If I may continue your metaphor," he added, "it is a clear sign that the door is not locked and bolted."

"That is surely wonderfully true," I echoed.

"Oh, yes," Frost said coolly smiling, "There was one more wonder. "The root beer did make her burp. It made her laugh. It is a delightful laugh."

I laughed. It was indeed delightful, even if I did not hear it.

We enjoyed that joy for a few minutes before I turned to a more serious matter.

"Sheridan is not working alone," I told him.

I explained about Mike having met a Mr. Tyler and the man referred to as a cousin. I told him also about the near break-in at the office by a man who matched the description of the supposed cousin. Frost understood the meaning of it all.

"The way I see it," I continued, "this adds to my belief that Sheridan wants to get in the theater. He could get in easily enough. I wouldn't be surprised if he already has. He could only have gotten a cursory look, but that may have been enough for him to know some of the complexities. Before we knew about Alice specifically, there were some who suspected something. They've been more careful about watching the doors.

"Either way, I think Sheridan wants to be very careful. Mike gave him tickets to a Sunday matinee. I think he'll use them."

"He expects to get lost in the crowd," Frost inserted. "But that would only be in coming or going. Won't we know what seats Mike gave him?"

"I've been thinking about that," I said. "He's too careful for that. Maybe he'll give them to the 'cousin.' He may not know we have a description of that guy. I'm thinking that one may wait until the play is over and everyone is gone. He'll try to hide somewhere and then let Sheridan in. Or he may try to find Alice alone."

"Can't the authorities simply arrest whoever takes those seats?" Frost asked.

"Maybe," I said. "But it would be tricky. A large holiday crowd. A lot of kids. It would be risky. In addition, if it's not Sheridan, Sheridan could get away. He's been almost untouchable so far. They'd have to catch him red-handed."

"I do not like any of these possibilities," Frost said, with obvious concern.

"I know," I agreed. "My immediate concern is the next few days," I told him seriously.

Frost showed even more attention.

"They must know that the theater will be empty," I explained. "There is nothing scheduled for five days."

"I, too, have considered that," Frost replied.

"The good news is," I continued, "that this other man does not seem to have any real burglary skills, or he could have gotten into the office."

"That is a good point," Frost said. "His nervousness would preclude any attempts during the day, and at night, only in the alley, at the stage door."

Frost thought for a second, and then smiled.

"A booby trap," he said simply. "Nothing dangerous, just noisy. I have noticed many metal objects in the theater that might be stacked precariously near that door."

"Very nice," I said. "Alice would have plenty of time to hide, and the nervous guy would probably take off on a run. The only person who might come in that way this week would be Bob. I'll give him a heads-up. What other plans do you have?"

"I've already explained about tomorrow," Frost said. "In addition to understanding her own plans, I wish to work with Alice about some new ones. I do not know if Christopher had instructed her on entry to locked places, but now that I have access to keys, perhaps we can find new places. Afterall, rehearsals will intensify – full cast and crew. The chance of accidental discovery will be higher than intentional."

"That's true," I said nodding. "I will be here at

home, but everyone will certainly understand if you need to come by for anything."

"Good," he said. "I will come only in case of something extraordinary."

"There is hardly anything ordinary in this mess," I said cynically. "I am sorry to spoil your holiday."

"It is not spoiled," he replied. "Holidays in my home were always rather subdued, not without meaning and warmth, but with little ceremony. Even before my mother's passing, they were quiet times at home. Mother was almost as reserved as I. Now, I am finding a good deal of pleasure in observing how others celebrate. It is intriguing. I believe sharing my own new observations with Alice will benefit us both."

I was taken aback a little. First, Frost had never mentioned his mother. I would like to know more, but, of course, in his own good time. And second, I now had a new dimension of how good it was that Frost was the catalyst for bringing Alice into a new world.

We wished each other a good Thanksgiving. Mine would be very traditional. Frost's would be unique.

I was very reflective after Frost left. Jack and Marta noticed. All I told them was that it was a very touchy case and had to be handled with great care. Though I shared no details (I rarely did with my work), they both understood. I think they also understood Frost better than most people.

My mood altered soon enough.

Jenni and Corey arrived in a flurry of noise and excitement. They had both had some busy weeks but were now free of obligations and ready for an uninterrupted holiday.

The joy really jumped when Jenni opened one of her suitcases. She grabbed a package and held it high in triumph. It was a pasteboard turkey with a paper accordion breast.

Jack and Marta nearly fell over laughing. When Marta pointed to the turkey she had brought and set up in the dining room, Jenni paused for a second and collapse in a chair with a happy squeal.

I walked to the china cabinet shaking my head at these silly, sentimental children. I opened a drawer and turned around holding a pasteboard turkey with a paper accordion breast.

– eighteen –

It was definitely an overstuffed Thanksgiving. Yes. We overindulged on the food. We were more than filled with the happiness of each other. Everyone.

The only slight damper on anything was Jenni. God bless her, she tried, but she has never understood the excitement of football.

Marta does. She even played one year in middle school, but she stopped growing. Desire only goes so far when the next smallest player still has twenty pounds on you.

Corey was the most expert among us. His playing days also ended some time ago. In his case, his freshman year in college. He blew out a knee. The idea of probably multiple surgeries was more than he wanted to pay. He did stay with the team as a manager and even an assistant coach. He has a couple of pros (not big names) among his clients. He is a financial manager.

Jack had never had a desire to play. He is, however, as dedicated a fan as you could want.

Jenni had attended several games in high school

and college. She went for the social aspects. It is, after all, usually a fun thing to do. She was only vaguely aware that there was some sort of game going on. That was true when she joined us in front of the television.

Our family traditions for the holiday extend through the following day.

Jack remains in charge of food, naturally. We eat much lighter. I admit that I can't imagine how we could have eaten more heavily. Jack uses the day and the leftovers to experiment. Like many others, I suspect, one of the main parts of the day-after menu is turkey sandwiches. Whatever Jack actually did, my turkey sandwich was unlike any I had eaten before. It was very, very good.

Jenni is in charge of entertainment. One of her lifelong passions has been old movies. Each year since we turned it over to her (her reward for enduring hours of football the day before), she has selected DVDs of a theme. Only once has that proved off. I love film noir, but they are hardly holiday fare. She realized that too late. It wasn't really that bad. They were good movies.

This year was a wonderful surprise: three films from the writer/director Preston Sturges. I knew the name, but I had never seen any of his work. I discovered that not only was Mr. Sturges brilliant, but also, he used the same actors in almost all his films. I now believe that the old actor, William Demerest, was one of the funniest men who ever lived.

Saturday was a day of good-byes. No one had any real commitments until Monday, but they all wanted to get home and let their minds and bodies get back into the usual mode. That's relative, of course. The time between Thanksgiving and Christmas can be anything but usual. For some, it is busier than ever, for others just the opposite.

I had nothing.

We laughed, talked, and hugged all the way to the cars. I waved until they disappeared. Then, I just stood until the cold forced me into the large, empty house. I felt small, diminished.

During a total solar eclipse, a definite edge appears between the black moon in front of the sun. That line is called the "penumbra," the line between the darkness and the rim of light. It can be translated as "next thing to a shadow."

That's where I felt I was. The brightness of the holiday seemed to surround the darkness of my house. Since Sarah died, I always felt this whenever the kids left. This year especially.

The bright lights and joy of Christmas would soon be on the stage at the Oster-Regent Theater. The auditorium would be filled with excited children and their parents and grandparents, many of whom would be in childlike wonder. At the same time, maybe in some very dark hole in that same theater, was a wounded, frightened child who believed the darkness she lived in now and the different darkness she came from was the way the world always is.

When and how does the total eclipse of the soul become a bright, new day?

Such thoughts did not just intrude on me in the next few days, sometimes they exploded into my mind no matter what else I might be doing.

On Sunday, we had a special day at church, one of the few times I rarely missed. It was "the hanging of the greens," the decorating for Christmas. For me, it meant the real start of the Christmas season.

It was an all-day thing – it's a big church. Occasionally, we would stop for blessings for different parts of the process and sing a Christmas carol. Then we'd go back to work. My main role was carrying boxes. Actual decorating was left to someone with a better eye for those things.

At least twice during the day, I sat down by myself as if to catch my breath. That was only partly true. I was fighting the darkness. Was Alice still alright? Was Frost?

Twice, Pastor Joan Cotton noticed. I told her it was just the recoil from the kids leaving after a wonderful visit. The first time, she accepted it. The second, I'm sure she did not, but she left me to work it out. It helped just to know I had someone who would listen.

On Monday morning, Frost came to the office. His report added some new lights of hope.

He had spent most of Thursday afternoon with Alice. He had already explained to her that he wanted to see things in the light when they would not be noticed by someone outside the building. She had said that "Doctor" had done the same thing.

They went over her special hiding places and escape routes. Frost was quite impressed with the plans for several reasons.

He had already noticed some of the places where she could hide. Two of these were very difficult to access, but Alice showed him how she could do it. That impressed him. She showed him two other places he had not considered. These were temporary, for emergencies, but still impressive.

She also had several escape routes, some obvious, some not so, but logical. She also had routes that would boggle the imagination.

Some of the escapes would involve leaving the building. Those would be as a last resort. Anything outside had multiple dangers. Two inside escapes were physically dangerous. I had already guessed one of those: the leap from the theater box to the stage. Alice wanted to demonstrate. Frost told her it was not necessary. He was sure she could do it.

After this, Frost carefully explained about the upcoming problems. For the next three weeks perhaps, Alice would need a new home base. Frost now had easier access to places Alice had not.

The doors into the theater are unlocked only for business hours or when something is going on. Even during rehearsals, the only door opened is the stage door. Inside, there are two places that are almost always locked: the costume shop, which also contains

Mike's office, and the costume storage rooms. Through Aydyn, Frost now had the lock code for the shop and the key to storage.

Frost was not as surprised as I when Alice told him she had been in both areas. Christopher's knack with locks had gotten them in. These places were also refuges of last resort. Alice had not been taught the art of picking locks, but she had been instructed on how to sneak in unobserved. Once in, she would have to hide until the door was closed and locked again.

At this stage of the production, all the costumes that would be needed were hanging on racks in the costume shop. Soon, they would be in the dressing rooms. There would be no need to go to storage, except in case of emergency, until the show was over. This would become Alice's new "nest."

She understood why this was necessary, and she understood about propping the door open if she left, to use the restroom for example. She and Frost worked out contingencies: to hide if someone did come in; to flee if the wrong person came in. This was a more confined space than where she had been. Escape was more limited and more dangerous. Escaping through a window on the second floor of a building must be done with great care. There were ways, but it scared me to think about.

All the things Frost told me were practical, logical, solid. I felt some relief. Alice would be safe from the theater people. The smaller space would make it easier to watch. However, I couldn't help but think that protective custody is still custody. I felt a little like we were locking her up.

Frost felt this as well, but still had some other progress for Alice.

"Alice likes the daylight," he told me. "She has been out and about, so to speak, during the day, but only for short periods. Once or twice, she explored with Christopher as she did with me. He was a stickler for double checking and more for every detail.

"Now, with me, I think she feels more at ease. Remember, she said Christopher scared her sometimes. He was helping her, but I think he was extremely cold, unfeeling. Evidently, even I seem warmer.

"We did not entirely avoid the windows but did not get very close. The rehearsal hall does have quite a vista of the river and the parks beyond. She was drawn to them. I told her that someday, I hoped soon, I would take her there. Her reaction was as I expected, a blend of childlike hope and joy but with apprehension. The idea of going somewhere so different is difficult for her to understand. A stroll in the park may seem mundane to us; to her it would be like being transported to the land of Oz."

"Unfortunately," I interrupted, darkly, "it still contains a wicked witch and flying monkeys."

"An apt analogy, I'm afraid," he agreed.

"Next Sunday," I continued, perhaps not quite as darkly, "I'm convinced that's when Sheridan will make his move."

"You may be right," Frost said, with a bit of an edge in his voice, "I do not trust that entirely. Evil has its own twisted logic and makes plans accordingly. It feeds on the normal. It lies even to those who would help it. It looks for opportunities to deceive."

I was caught off guard by the depth of his feeling. He was right. Until Sheridan, his partner, and several others were behind bars it would be foolish to take anything for granted. We had to be alert to everything.

Frost's idea along these lines was also practical and logical: the theater would have two residents. Alice would be living in costume storage; Frost would be just down the hall in the costume shop. Aydyn would be a frequent visitor. She would use the excuse of always working on some last-minute problem. She would do her best to keep Martha away. Alice would not be completely alone in the building.

— nineteen —

I had a lot to do but not a lot of ideas. All of what I wanted to happen could not work unless I told it all – all – to Murphy and to Mike Coppola. I didn't know how Mike would take it, but he had to know. There was too much going on and too much at stake.

I called him. He would come to my office in about an hour.

I called Murphy. I told him my plans.

"Frost is right," I said. "There is no way to be sure of Sheridan's plans. We need to prepare for the worst every day until we nail him."

"Until I nail him," Murphy said, sternly.

We both wanted that guy, but I had no authority.

"Okay," I conceded, "But the theater is the only target. Everything Sheridan wants is in there. None of it is coming to him. He will have to get in."

"I know," Murphy continued in his official tone. "We've been watching pretty closely. We keep track of anyone coming or going."

He didn't say it, but I knew that he knew Frost was coming and going.

"Do you have any other ideas?" I asked. "I want all I can get."

"I think if we push too hard, watch too close," Murphy explained, "Sheridan will spot it. We have pictures of everyone who is supposed to be there. Anyone else we spot, we will assume should not be. I understand about being ready for anything, but I think Sheridan can only come in with a crowd. I'm guessing he won't use the tickets Coppola gave him. Different seats, probably different day."

"It's still more than a week until opening night," I said, cautiously. "He may not wait that long."

"I know, John," he said, more kindly than I expected. "Patience is not one of my strong points. But traps don't work if the rats stay in their holes."

"Do you always have to be such a damn good cop?" I said with only partly mocked frustration.

"I have my moments," he said, a bit sadly. "If I wasn't at the station, I'd tell you about it."

"Frost is going to camp out in the theater," I told him. "I think that means I have to tell Mike the whole story."

"How do you think he'll react?"

"He'll probably freak out. At first, anyway. I think I can bring him around."

"Would it help if I made it an official request?"

"Thanks," I said, sincerely. I was hoping he'd offer. "It might not be necessary, but at this stage, I don't want to take any chances."

"One other thing may help," Murphy added, "if

it doesn't make things worse. The FBI is coming back to town."

"What?" I nearly shouted. "They could blow it all up!"

"Settle down," Murphy said. "I've been expecting it. It is their case, after all. I don't think it will be a problem. Wheeland called. He won't be here. It will be a new team. Faces and names that Sheridan won't know."

"Don't tell me it's a bunch of rookies," I said with real concern.

"Oh, no," he replied. "They think they may be closer to closing this than they've ever been. So, they put together a team from other divisions. They've been studying all the Bureau has on it. They'll be here by the end of the week for me to fill them in on where things stand."

"That's some relief," I said.

There was one of those pauses that meant Murphy was getting ready to get very official again.

"I will have to tell them everything I know," he stated. "You will, too. If there is anything else, now would be the time for you to tell me."

It was my turn to pause. It was much longer.

"Thompson," he said, strongly. "Are you still there?"

"I am," I said finally. "It's hard to know where to begin."

His guessing so far about what I had not told him had been pretty accurate so far. He probably had some other things that he had not told me that were just as accurate. I knew he needed to hear it all to confirm most of it, and any details that I had avoided.

"What time are you meeting with Coppola?" he asked.

"In about an hour," I answered. "Maybe less."

"You know that new place on First? The one that just has carry-out soup?"

"Yes. I've been by it. Has a Serbian name."

"That's right. I'll bring the soup and all three of us will have a nice talk."

Murphy and Mike arrived together. It wasn't planned. Just coincidence.

Murphy had three kinds of soup. We'd each choose; he'd take the third.

I chose tomato-basil. It was very good. Mike chose the chicken noodle. He was a little nervous. He thought that would settle rather than further disturb his stomach. Murphy didn't mention his, but it looked like vegetable.

Murphy spoke first. He explained that he had not been entirely open when they had spoken before. The man Mike knew as Tyler was wanted by the FBI. He apologized, but it was a delicate case and the fewer people who knew, the better.

Mike was mostly okay with that part. He had suspected there was more and understood the caution. He was sorry he had not been more help. He had not seen the man again.

Then it was my turn.

"I also had a sin of omission," I began as calmly as I could. "It is true that the situation in the theater was not what Bob suspected, but there has been someone living in the theater for about three months."

The gasp and the expression on Mike's face confirmed that he had made the right choice of the soups.

"Take a deep breath," I told him. "It gets worse."

Mike was speechless. He fumbled with some sounds. They could not be called words or even syllables. Finally, he took my advice and took some deep breaths. When I thought he was ready, I continued.

"Our guest," I said slowly, "is a probable witness against the man Sergeant Murphy asked you about."

Mike couldn't have been more shocked if I'd jumped up and stomped on his toes.

"We think Tyler, as you know him," Murphy added, "has been watching the theater looking for an opportunity."

"Jesus H. Christ!" Mike exploded. He had no place to go after that, but at least he got it out of his system.

"I'm sorry, Mike," I said sincerely. "I've been trying to work this out, but it has gotten...." I trailed off. "Complicated" was not nearly enough of a word.

"Okay," I said, taking a breath. "There are no short cuts. I'll have to go back to the beginning."

Mike braced himself. Murphy settled in.

I started with Doc saving the girl and getting

killed. I left out his past life for now. If I had added that, Mike would have needed a sedative. I brought him up to the present day with most of the twists and turns, but, again, leaving out some things.

By the time I had finished, both Mike and Murphy knew as much about Alice, including the name, as I did. I only hinted at her past life. It was still enough that now I thought it was Murphy who would need a sedative.

On the other hand, Mike was more surprised by Frost's part in all this. He had only been vaguely aware of Frost's existence. Neither he nor Murphy knew what to make of the relationship with Aydyn.

Throughout my narrative, I emphasized that Alice, despite her resourcefulness, was in as much danger from those who might want to help her as those who wished her harm.

Murphy certainly wanted to protect her, but he also wanted to lead a cavalry charge to wipe out those who had done this to her. I understood that, too.

Mike surprised me. He seemed to grasp the whole picture. He calmed down from his initial shock. In fact, he laughed.

"Some manager I am!" he smirked. "I thought I knew everything about the theater. We've been a sanctuary, a home for a wounded girl, and I had no clue. She's been hiding someplace I can't even imagine. And who found her? Some guy who just strolled through one night."

"Don't be too hard on yourself," I told him. "You

weren't looking for her. I missed her when I and six others were trying."

"Alright," Murphy brought us back to the present. "Old news. The question is 'Now, what?'"

"Now, we wait," I said. "Like you said, Muphy, it's the rats' move."

"Yeah, I know," he said with resignation. "I was just hoping."

We went our separate ways for a while.

The Sunday night of the last week before we opened, there was a party at my house. Two old friends that I hadn't seen in years dropped by along with three of their children: two young women and one young man. A third man arrived later with pizza and soft drinks.

That was the story.

The five people were agents of the FBI. The man with the pizza was Sergeant Murphy.

The lead agent was Robert Remington. He had come out of retirement for this special assignment. His specialty had been drug traffic. He understood how criminals moved from one part of the country to another. His experience gave some new ideas of this case. We now had some suggestions of where to look for Sheridan that we had not considered.

Another of his specialties was identification. Within the Bureau, according to the younger agents, he was almost legendary. He never forgot a face. A lot of people say that, but with Remington it went to a whole new level, almost mystic. Even through disguises, even through some plastic surgery, he could spot the person he was looking for. He had been studying every picture and even one pretty good video of Sheridan that the Bureau had.

The main purpose of the meeting was to coordinate all our efforts.

Remington would be playing a role at the theater, not on stage, in the lobby. He would be one of the ushers. Mike would go over his procedure so he wouldn't seem out of place. Since our ushers are volunteers and mostly older, he would fit right in. And, because everyone came in the same door, he would see everyone.

The other agents would be taking turns as audience members. They would have two tickets, one for the main floor, and one for the balcony. They would come at the last minute. Which ticket they used would be up to Remington. He would not only show them to their seat but also tell them who to keep an eye on.

Murphy had four officers watching as well: two inside; two out. The two inside were the two new stagehands: officers Jakes and Sebetka. They would always be the last to leave.

The outside officers were hardy souls. They were on rooftops in the cold December night. One was atop the tire place where Gary worked watching the stage door. The other was across Main watching the front. Both had to be frozen in place on purpose, hoping they didn't literally freeze accidentally.

I and two police officers were on the stage. We couldn't see much, but it seemed impossible for someone to get in the back. Two FBI agents were out front. Again, impossible? If not, it seemed remote. Frost was in the same room as Alice. Aydyn was down the hall. Our side of the trap, if that's what it was, seemed sound.

Seemed. Not positive. There was still the unknown. That unknown was the quarry himself. We had no idea where Sheridan was or who exactly he was working with or what he had planned. All we could do was play our roles as well as we could.

— twenty —

It had been a struggle for me to get through the last rehearsals. No matter what I told myself, I kept listening for any possible commotion; I kept looking for a wrong face to appear in a wrong place. I had to talk to one of the stage crew to help me. When the curtain closed, just before my scene, she would make sure I was ready to go on, even if she had to shake me to get my attention.

By the time we got to the last rehearsal, I was better. I had tried to focus my frustration with the case into the frustration of the campaign manager. Apparently, that's what I was supposed to do. Wemyss said I was doing great.

Murphy kept me updated on the search for Sheridan. It was an easy report: nothing. The FBI had no information on any associates or clients of Sheridan or Clauburg in the area, or in Iowa for that matter. Yet, there must be an associate. Someone was hiding him. Someone was helping him.

Frost's reports were more hopeful.

First: Aydyn was no longer just an accepted outsider. She joined them for meals, which was a regular occurrence. She had even taught Alice a couple of children's songs and had shown her three or four picture books. Alice was smiling and laughing at more than root beer burps.

These were the first of what Frost called "person lessons." Frost realized that Alice had been treated as little more than an object, a toy for the use of twisted individuals. He further realized that, as an object, she could not become part of a larger society. She needed a sense of self, a sense of being a person.

One of Frost's most intriguing lessons was teaching her to say "no." She'd been told "no" for most of her life, so much so that she felt she had no right to use the word in a personal way.

Frost and Aydyn has set up a little play. They'd brought burgers and fries for supper. Frost's order didn't include fries. As they ate and talked, Frost reached across the table "to steal" a French fry from Aydyn.

"No!" Aydyn said firmly. "That's mine. You said you didn't want any. If you want one, you will have to ask. You can't just take it."

Frost pulled back his hand. Alice was enthralled but confused.

Frost looked for a minute at Alice's fries. Alice looked at Aydyn, then back at Frost. He started to move his hand slowly across the table.

"No-o," she stammered, and added, almost in a whisper. "That's mine."

Frost quickly pulled back his hand.

"You are right, Alice," he said. "I was wrong. I cannot take anything from you. I'm sorry."

Alice was torn between a strange feeling of satisfaction she'd never felt before and her continuing confusion. She had never really been in charge of anything, not French fries, not anything of her own.

Aydyn strained to maintain her role. She wanted to sing and dance, but she went on to scene two.

"Would you like one of my fries?" she asked Frost.

"Thank you," he replied. "That is very kind of you."

Aydyn gave him a French fry and turned to Alice. "I can give him anything I want, but he can't just take it. That would be wrong."

Alice was a little stunned and more than a little fascinated. She understood that they were also applying this to her. She reached out her hand toward Frost with a French fry.

"Do you want one of mine?" she asked softly.

"Only if it's alright with you," he said. "You don't have to give me one just because Aydyn did."

"Can I keep it?" she asked.

"Of course, you can," Frost assured her. "It's yours."

Alice looked confused again. She was going ahead of them, making a jump.

"But you gave it to me, first," she said, a little nervously.

"Yes," Frost stated firmly. "I gave it to you. That makes it yours. No one can take it from you, not even me, unless you want to give it."

Alice quickly popped it into her mouth and stared at Frost.

He laughed. Aydyn laughed. Alice laughed.

Then Aydyn did sing and dance, and Alice laughed some more.

They carefully added to the lesson by trying to explain the difference between giving something and loaning something. Alice grasped it easily, so they added the idea of a trade. She got that, too.

Another part of the report concerned Alice's new "home." Most of the costume rooms were overstuffed with things. The front room was much larger so there was some room to spread out. The main difference was that this room had windows. Alice loved looking at the outside world. The holiday crowds she watched excited her, even from her perch above them, even though she had no real idea why they seemed so happy.

It snowed. Alice had seen the snow through a window before, but this time she was free to watch it as long as she liked.

Free to look out a window! How much we take for granted.

Alice also enjoyed some of the costumes, hats mostly. Aydyn, actress and costumer, encouraged her, played games with her. Expanding her imagination also expanded her world and her person.

Aydyn did notice that some of the costumes seem to disturb Alice. A cloud would come across her face. Aydyn assumed, rightly I'm afraid, that they reminded her of something in her past. Aydyn quickly turned to something else.

Aydyn and Frost saw Alice more and more during the day. Her new room was brighter and that made everyone's mood brighter, as well. Occasionally, there would be an unexpected noise from the theater. Some technical elements needed fine tuning. Mike still needed to get to his office. He had always come up the stairs, which are heavily carpeted. One can come up them without making a sound. Now, he took the elevator, knowing that sound would alert them to his presence.

Frost also continued his study of Alice's theater world. The use of the "undusty" places he had discovered were, for the most part, pretty obvious. Some were storage: two cans of food here; three, there. Some were hiding places. Doctor had insisted that Alice practice getting into them on a regular basis. In case of emergency, she could not afford to be slow or clumsy. She demonstrated for Frost, particularly one that looked especially difficult. Frost described it "as smooth, as quick and as quiet as a mouse disappearing behind a bookcase."

After that tour, Frost suggested that Alice practice similar things in her new environment. In this more closed space, her options were very limited. She had to be quick and agile here, too. He also installed a couple of simple devices. By pulling a string, something would move, making sounds. An intruder, it was hoped, would go in that direction while Alice went in another.

"It is not unlike watching a dancer or a gymnast," Frost told me, with obvious admiration.

The final dress rehearsal, Thursday night, was our "Invited Dress." Each member of the cast and crew is given two passes to give to friends or family. In this way, we had our first audience. It is not a full house, and the people are certainly biased in our favor, but it does help by having real time responses.

My passes went to Murphy and his wife.

The show was a hit. The rave reviews that I overheard afterward were more than just what might have been said by friends and family.

"I think you did a damn good job, Thompson," was Murphy's review, as he shook my hand.

"I'm glad you thought so," I replied.

Jane, his wife, laughed. That caused me to pause with raised eyebrows.

"It's about the only part he paid any attention to," she said. "He kept looking around everywhere else."

"Now, wait minute...," he started to protest. He gave it up when he looked at Jane.

In his job, Murphy plays a lot of roles himself. He can be tough or caring, hard or understanding, or half a dozen other adjectives, each of which precedes "cop." It is useless for him to try them with

Jane. They all may apply, from time to time, but none of them would end with "cop."

Jane is a woman of average height and size, but gives off an aura of strength, more of self-confidence than physical. Her hair is dark brown and so were her eyes. I think they could be quite piercing if she was angry, but with her bright face and smile, they were warm.

I'm sure that being a cop's wife must be very difficult, anxious, even in a town the size of Cedar Falls. We don't have a high violent crime rate, but then, it only takes one time.

Jane can handle it. She raised three kids. The two boys are in college; the daughter is a junior in high school. Jane is a counselor at a middle school.

I'm sure Murphy had to let her in on what was happening. The case had him so stirred up, he couldn't have hidden it from her. How much and how detailed, I didn't know, but I suspected she knew a lot. Then, she gave me a hint.

"John," she said, lowering her voice, "when this is all over, come see me. I know some people who can help."

I had considered that already. I hadn't mentioned it to Murphy. Alice was going to need more than Frost and Aydyn could do for her in a dark, old theater.

I looked at Murphy. He nodded. He knew.

Mr. and Mrs. Murphy went home. Jakes and Sebetka and I did a quick walk-through of the theater, then they left as well. Remington had been in the front office, just to get familiar with some faces. His role as usher was unnecessary for this night. He left shortly after the last guest.

After walking around, I ended up in the front lobby, alone. Very alone. It's strange, but in the dim light there, mostly from the outside lights, the lobby seemed emptier than the much darker auditorium when I entered it. Maybe it was the lingering chill from the December night after the last patrons had left. It didn't seem, however, that that was all there was to it.

As I walked down the aisle toward the stage, I felt better – not as anxious, not as cold, not as alone. I had a passing thought that the theater ghosts were more than solitary figures in the dark. Perhaps they haunt the stage because the remnants of an audience are waiting for them. I could feel the warmth that I had gotten from the applause and an almost-echo of the laughter. All the seats were empty. Or were they?

A solitary figure moved faintly, silently on the stage. I wasn't afraid or startled even before I realized that it was Frost.

"Well, John," he said, "it seemed to go very well tonight."

"Did you watch?" I inquired.

"No," he answered. "I only listened. I was watching the hallway upstairs."

"Of course," I stated, matter-of-factly. "I'm afraid that will be your view until this is over."

"I may never leave," he said, with his cool smile. "This is becoming quite homey. Getting to know Alice, to watch her grow, along with the delightful Aydyn, has been fascinating."

"That's good," I said, returning his smile, although I'm not sure he could see that. He was near the ghost light, and, so, very visible to me. I was on the far side of the orchestra pit, mostly in the dark.

"I do know," he continued, "that the only thing more satisfying will be to walk out of this building with her."

"Yes," I said firmly. "When Sheridan and that whole bunch are locked away. I hope it will be a small, dark cell. It will please me to know they would be there while Alice walks around free and in the light."

"Yes," he replied. There was something dark in his tone. He wasn't thinking of Alice. I remembered Aydyn's warning about keeping him away from Sheridan. I think the dark hole he had in mind was six feet deep.

Frost casually glanced to his left. I started and looked where he did. I saw only darkness. Had someone hidden there?

He looked back to me. His darkness had passed. He smiled again. I was relieved for two reasons.

"I think, John," he said, "that it is time to call it a night. Because of the unusual crowd, Aydyn will be spending the night with Alice. I will return to my usual place. I'm getting quite used to the lumps in that couch."

"Will that be your plan for other nights as well?" I asked.

"Very likely," he replied. "But with the full audiences, we will be even more vigilant."

"So will we," I confirmed. "Jakes and Sebetka will make their usual sweep afterward and then hunker down for about an hour. So will I."

"I could suggest some excellent hiding places," he stated, almost seriously.

"That won't be necessary," I said, seriously. "Sebetka will be in the bathroom in the loft. Jakes will be in the one in the makeup room. I'll take a seat near the light booth."

"And the federal agents?" he asked.

"They won't be staying as long," I answered. "It would be too many people. No way to do it smoothly. If Sheridan and his friend are spotted, it will be over quickly. If they manage to stick around somewhere, I think we'll know it soon enough."

Frost went on coolly, "The only way they could get their way would take careful planning. They are skilled at that, it would seem."

"That's very true," I agreed, "We must plan for the worst. I already assume they have examined the theater some. How much on the inside, I don't know, but I don't see how they could have made a deep study of it without our spotting them."

"We will take nothing for granted," Frost warned.

"Good night, then," I said. "Tonight, or tomorrow at least, try to get as much rest as you can. Opening night, you know."

"Take your own advice," he said, a bit wryly. "Opening night, you know."

— twenty-one —

It is hard to follow any advice, even your own, when the voices and images in your head are playing tag. I don't think I was really afraid of another nightmare. I don't think I was afraid of failure. The theater may be complex but Sheridan's target, Alice, was now isolated. That made his goal specific and more easily identified.

I think what bothered me was the Box. Sheridan was going to a lot of trouble to get it, taking big risks. Every day that passed increased the risk. That meant the probable value of the Box had to increase in our estimation. He wanted it bad.

In my thoughts or imagination or nightmare, whatever, I'd see the Box. At first, it was the size of a shoe box. I'd reach for it, and it would shrink and then disappear in the darkness.

It was not a restful night. It was not a restful day.

I didn't want to stay in the house. I stayed in the house. I didn't want to fix a meal. I ate all day, in pieces. I had a sandwich in stages. I had a slice of bread. Later, I had a slice of ham. Finally, I had some cheese. I ate a pickle. At least I didn't just eat mustard from the jar.

I moved a chair in the living room – twice. The second time was to put it back where it had been.

The actors' call for hair and make-up was six o'clock. I showed up at the stage door at five. It was still locked.

I intended to walk around the block and do some window shopping. When I got to the corner of First and Main, I turned north instead of south. I found myself north of the river by the railroad tracks. There was a dusting of snow here and there near where the real nightmare had started. Twenty feet from where I stood the quiet man I called "Doc" was hit by a train. It was a strange thing. I wished it had remained only that.

I stared at the empty spot between the tracks and the trees for some time.

When I returned to the stage door, it was unlocked. I was still very early, especially so for my character. I had no real make-up to do. In fact, it was better if I just stayed out of the way. Some of the actors, especially some of the women and girls had to appear in hair-dos and make-up of the 1940's. Some even had to have lines drawn on the back of their legs to represent the seams of the stockings of that period.

For the next hour, I mostly just wandered around. I'm sure it looked like wandering or nervous pacing to the others. I was searching the basement again. I was trying to see what Frost had seen and I had not.

I did find one of the special hiding places. I knew

I had to think differently. If I hadn't, I would have missed it. It was perfect for a small person and involved a make-shift door that didn't look like a door. I would have to tell Bob that I found his missing piece of underlayment.

The few "undusty" places that I noticed produced nothing. They were probably just some places that people brushed by in passing. Frost's discerning eye and mind could see the minute differences between one kind of dust and another. I could not.

I wanted to look in other places, but time grew short. Patrons were beginning to arrive. When the house "opened," that is, when the ticket holders were allowed to take their seats, all the actors had to be out of sight. The basement and backstage were all that were open to me.

I was nervous as hell about the play, too. This was my first time in front of an audience with dialogue, not just "a man with a briefcase" walking through. As I had been doing, I tried to focus my nervous energy into what my character was supposed to be feeling. It almost worked.

In my last line, I'm supposed to say to the judge, "You can count on just two votes: yours and the District Attorney's." Instead, I said, "You can vote on just two counts...." I froze. Jim Butler just stared at me, caught off guard.

"You know what I mean!" I shouted and stomped out the door. It got a big laugh.

Everyone got a standing ovation. When Santa,

Paul Gregory, came out for his bow, I fully understood the old saying, "He brought down the house." It was very exciting and wonderful.

I was slow getting out of costume afterward. Everyone was. The afterglow of joy slowed down every process. I imagined that Doc would have been gone long before everyone else even began to think that way.

The play had ended at about 9:15. It was after 10:30 before the last of the cast and crew were gone – all but four.

Remington met with us backstage. Jakes and Sebetka had made their usual sweep. Except for the ghost light and the shop lights, all the lights in the building were off.

"There were some suspicious occurrences," he began, all business. "There were two men who left before the end. One was a thin, nervous man that we'd been watching closely. He went to the Men's room. When he didn't come back my way, I looked for him. The Men's room was empty.

"The other was a big man, muscular, with a hard face. He went out for a smoke. He walked away to the north and didn't return.

"There was some activity with the elevator. Only a couple of people had used it to get to their seats in the balcony. They were still there. I had Agent Smith check out the third floor. She didn't find anyone."

"What do you make of all that?" I asked, trying to match his tone.

"I'm thinking that your opening night was their final rehearsal," he answered.

"Do you think that means tomorrow night?" I asked, this time not quite so business-like.

"That seems most likely," he replied. "But we might head them off. I think we have a break."

"What do you have," I asked, making no effort to maintain my calm.

"I got a message," he went on. "We may have found where Sheridan has been hiding. I'm going directly to the station to coordinate that."

I was really excited, but Jakes cut me off before I could speak again.

"Should Sebetka and I go with you," he asked.

"No," Remington replied quickly. "These bastards are slick. It might prove to be nothing or even a red herring. You need to act in the same manner you have until you hear otherwise."

Jakes nodded.

Remington went on. "If our lead is wrong and the two men come back tonight, any time, they will not get a seat."

I had an uneasy feeling after Remington left. There were certainly indications that the bad guys had left. Remington was a complete professional, but there was something more than just covering all the bases in his instructions. There was something in his tone, call it my hunch that he had a hunch, too.

Jakes and Sebetka turned off the shop lights and went to their stations. I thought about their dedication, too: stuck in a small restroom in the dark for an hour or more. I made my way to the balcony. Frost was waiting for me.

"I heard the applause," he said. "I'm glad it was so well received. Congratulations."

"I was very nervous," I told him. I didn't mention my near disaster.

"Anything of interest from Agent Remington?" he inquired calmly.

I gave him a full report, including my uneasy feeling. He was concerned about the two men and the elevator business and intrigued about the lead to finding Sheridan.

"From what Agent Remington said," Frost was thinking out loud, "he did not see the thin man leave the building or the large man return. It does not mean that neither occurred."

"What do you make of it?" I asked, trying not to sound anxious.

"First, if the thin man did not leave," he explained, calmly, "he must have hidden. If so, I believe there is only one place that could be."

"The east basement," I said, with a little excitement as it occurred to me.

The door to that area is right next to the Men's room door. He could have slipped through it quickly without being seen.

"Yes," Frost continued. "As for the other man, it is more complex. Going out to smoke so near the end is suspicious. Getting back in without being seen would be tricky, but not impossible and might require assistance."

"How do you mean?"

"The most likely way would be through the door on the northeast corner of the building. It is what I supposed to be an emergency exit. Someone would have to open it from the inside."

"Wait," I interrupted. "That is on the front of the building. Murphy's officer across the street would have seen that."

"Not necessarily," Frost went on, still cool and calm. "The focus would be on the main doors. If the man walked around the corner, the associate could ease the door open just enough to unlock it. Then, the other could return and duck through very quickly, especially if he waited for the crowd to be leaving."

"That would require the thin man to have gotten there beforehand," I added logically.

"Either that, or there is a third person," Frost stated.

A third. That did not help my uneasy mind. What he added next made it worse.

"There is also the possibility that no one is watching from the roof," he said.

"That seems the least likely of all," I said, almost sure. "But back to the door. How would that happen?"

"The elevator," Frost replied. If I didn't know him and he wasn't so logical, his extreme cool and calm could get on my nerves.

"Access to those stairs is only possible on the second and third floors of the building," he continued. "One could get to the elevator from the Men's room or basement without being noticed by Remington."

"Jakes and Sebetka walked through the rehearsal hall," I said, nervously, "but I don't think they would have looked in that stairwell."

"I will check it now," he said and walked away.

He was so sure and quick that he was gone before I remembered Aydyn's plea: "If you find him, don't let Frost near him."

I started to go after him when I heard giggling from the south entrance to the balcony. One voice was Aydyn's; the other, I did not know. It was soft, melodic, childlike. It had to be Alice.

They appeared and continued down the aisle that would soon lead to the hallway behind the upper theater boxes. They were completely unaware of me. They were like two schoolgirls in the park.

What the hell was Aydyn thinking?

Aydyn stopped suddenly and almost screamed, "Alice!"

I jerked my head to the right. On the opposite end of the balcony was a man with a flashlight – Sheridan!

I shouted: "Sheridan! Stay where you are!"

He threw the light in my face. I was blinded for a second. He turned and ran back out the north exit, more quickly than I thought he could. That leads only to the stairs to the lobby. Perhaps I could still catch him if I could get down the south stairs fast enough.

Aydyn was still frozen in place, open-mouthed. As I moved that way, another movement caught my eye. Alice appeared in the box closest to the stage. She was over the rail and made the eight-foot drop with no more trouble than someone might jump the last two steps on a stairway.

She landed right next to the ghost light. As she did, Jakes appeared through the door of the set. Frightened by the unknown dark figure, she ran down the stage steps, crossed in front of the orchestra pit and disappeared through the curtain on the north end. Behind that is the hallway that eventually leads to the basement.

Through all of that, I stood still as slack-jawed as Aydyn. Just as I collected myself enough to do something, other commotions erupted.

First, Sebetka emerged from the doorway on my end of the balcony. Aydyn's scream had brought her there down the hallway from the loft, just as it had brought Jakes out onto the stage. That's why Alice had taken her leap – to avoid whoever was coming that way.

Then, Alice reappeared. A thin, wiry man of about thirty-five was holding her firmly by the wrist.

Finally, I moved. I ran out of the balcony and down the stairs. I knew Sheridan was gone. I was going to head off the thin man before he could get to the lobby.

Just as I reached the bottom of the stairs, I was hit by a truck.

I was slammed into by a huge force which in turn slammed me against the wall. The irresistible force did not meet the immovable object. I was between them. Through my nearly glazed over eyes, I saw the shadowy, blurry figure of a very large hulk. It walked away paying no more attention to me than a fly he had swatted and brushed away.

I had to follow. I couldn't. Every move I made, I every breath I took, sent stabbing pains through me.

I managed to get to my knees with the assistance of the chair nearby. Then a strong, gentle hand helped to sit. It was Frost.

"Sit, John," he said. "You are injured. Rest. We will have them."

He walked away as casually as a stroll down the lane.

Between each breath of agony, I tried to think clearly. The only thought I had was, "Alice. Alice." Then Aydyn was with me, crying, near hysteria, again.

"Aydyn!" I managed to sound firm, but my obvious pain was bringing her around.

"We need you," I gasped. "Frost needs you. Alice."

That did it. She was conscious.

"Telephone," I whispered. "Police. Now!"

"I don't...," she stammered. "My phone is...."

Maybe she wasn't fully with it yet.

"Front desk," I said. "Hurry!"

It registered. She ran for the phone.

With more will power than strength, I got to my feet and staggered for the auditorium entrance. Just inside the nearest one, to the right, is the control table for the sound system. I stumble into the chair there. My hand hit something. It was a flashlight. I looked at the stage.

A new performance was taking place. It was a struggle between Jakes and the dark hulk. Jakes training and agility were matched against the big man's sheer power.

Jakes was able to dodge most of the haymakers that were thrown at him. The ones that did land were blocked or just glancing blows. Even so, they were enough nearly to knock him off his feet. In turn, Jakes punches didn't seem to register. He might as well have sparrred with a heavy bag at the gym.

I wanted to help but it was dawning on me that I had at least one cracked, if not broken, rib. One punch from the mountain could be fatal.

Suddenly, the big guy managed to get a hold on Jakes. He picked him up and threw the police officer halfway across the stage like a sack of potatoes. Jakes landed awkwardly but got to his feet. He was favoring his left leg. He staggered back to catch his breath.

Just before his opponent could attack, Frost appeared from the wings at stage left. He was still as casual as a spring day.

"I advise you to surrender, now," he said calmly.

"No!" came the sudden cry from someone beside me. "You're the one that's through."

There was a man standing in the aisle with a gun pointed at Frost. He was a thin man, but not the same one I'd seen grabbing Alice.

"C'mon, Humpy," he shouted to the man on the stage. "Let's get out of here."

Humpy. The name sounded familiar.

Humpy hesitated. Even in the faint light and from my distance, I could see he wanted to finish off the two on stage first. I also realized that the man in the aisle had not noticed me in the dark.

Using all my remaining strength, or all my adrenaline, probably, I made a sudden swing with the flashlight. I connected with his wrist. The gun fell to the floor. The man yelped. I swung again. I hit him squarely across the bridge of his nose. He fell between the seats across the aisle.

I dropped the flashlight and managed, just barely to fall into my chair. I was done.

The spectacle on the stage increased.

When he discovered that he no longer had help, the big man made a charge at Frost. Frost simply slid to one side and gave the monster a slight push as he passed. Humpy crashed into the proscenium. When he stepped back, his lip was bleeding. By then, Jakes had come back across the stage. He gave the man a sharp punch in the throat. That staggered him at last.

The man was moving backward toward Frost. Once again, Frost stepped aside and gave the man a small push. He stumbled back and fell into the orchestra pit. The crash was accompanied by a sickening thud.

I gasped and nearly stood. The pain would not allow it.

Frost stood at the edge of the stage looking down, expressionless. Jakes stared at Frost for a time before starting down the steps to the fallen man.

"He is alive," Frost said, almost casually. "I believe he will survive.

Jakes checked the man, briefly, and turned to Frost.

"Where is the girl?" Frost asked, coldly. I didn't just hear the cold; I felt it.

"She ran away," Jakes responded. "I jumped the guy that had her. She ran up the aisle, then turned back. I didn't really see. I was occupied. The skinny guy slipped away. When I started chasing him, I ran into this one."

Officer Sebetka entered from stage right.

"Myra," Jakes yelled. "A guy ran that way. Did you see him?"

"Yes," she said, smiling. "He's caught."

"Where?" Jakes asked.

"I came down the back stairs to check the hallway to the alley," she related. "He tried to get out that way. When he saw me, he ran up the back stairs. I pursued. Then, he panicked. He went up that ladder up there. It goes to the roof."

"Did you follow?" Jakes went on as though receiving an official report.

"Yes," she said smiling again. "But only to lock the door behind him. There's no way off that roof. It's twenty degrees and windy outside. He didn't have a coat. He won't be any trouble in an hour or so."

Now I knew why she was smiling.

Frost was not smiling.

"That's three," he stated firmly. "There is one more and the girl to account for."

Just as he said that Aydyn appeared next to me.

"Aydyn," I said weakly. "Did you get the police?"

"Yes," she said, still upset. "I'm sorry to be such a mess. I was so frightened."

"You're not as much of a mess as I am," I told her. "I think I have a broken rib."

"Aydyn," Frost projected from the stage, "Please, stay with John. Keep him from moving. He has done quite enough. The officers will look for Sheridan. I will go to Alice."

In seconds, the stage was empty.

"Is there anything you need?" Aydyn asked, softly.

"Nothing for now," I assured her. "Don't be startled if I say 'ouch' from time to time."

"I won't," she replied.

"I may say some things a bit stronger than that," I tried to joke. It was no joke in any way. Aydyn smiled anyway.

I decided I had better stop talking. I knew it would be a while before I got any more help. If an ambulance came with the police, and I would be surprised if Aydyn had mentioned it, they would be doing other things first. When the ambulance did arrive, the man in the pit would be their first priority. I would probably be third after the unconscious man across the aisle. The most comforting thought I had was that Aydyn hadn't seen Frost's cold push that could easily have sent a man – a bad man, to be sure, but a man – to his death.

Aydyn was trying to catch her breath, too, but from a very different perspective.

There was a movement on the stage. A figure appeared from the wings, stage right. Sheridan!

Aydyn clapped a hand over her mouth to keep from crying out. Still, it was enough of a sound for Sheridan to notice, but only for a moment. Another figure appeared from the archway at stage left. Alice!

She didn't see him. He moved a step or two forward and turned on his flashlight directly in Alice's face. She stopped, staring in terror.

"Alright, little bitch," Sheridan snarled. "It's Master Clayton. It's over. You do what you're told and maybe I won't punish you. You know what that means."

Alice was trembling.

"First, you're going to show me where to hide," Sheridan spit out. "They'll think we got away. Then, when everyone is gone, you're going to get me that red box. Then, we'll go back."

"No!" Aydyn jumped up. "No, Alice, no!"

Sheridan turned his light on Aydyn.

"You just shut up, or I'll take care of you, too," he growled. He turned back to Alice. "Let's go, little bitch!"

"No!" Alice said firmly.

Sheridan was stunned. "What?" he stammered.

"No!" Alice said with a little more force.

"You can't say that to me!" Sheridan tried to sound in charge again.

"No!" Alice said in a roar that echoed throughout the building.

Frost appeared from the shadow behind Alice.

Sheridan, shaking visibly, started to turn away. Jakes was standing behind him.

Sheridan backed away, and then started for the stage steps. Sebetka was there. He was surrounded.

He stared from one person to the next and dropped his flashlight. His shaking increased. He dropped to his knees.

"Please," he begged. "Please, don't hurt me."

He started to cry, repeating "please" over and over.

Alice advanced toward him, raising her right hand. Frost stepped forward and took her by the wrist. She looked him in the eye, dropped whatever it was she was holding and allowed Frost to embrace her.

I heard sirens outside.

— twenty-two —

The hospital didn't help much with my four cracked ribs. There isn't much that can be done. A broken arm or leg can be immobilized. The only way to keep ribs from moving is to sit perfectly still – and not breathe. If I was a good boy, they told me, I might be okay by the holiday. I'm pretty sure they were referring to Cinco de Mayo, not Christmas.

I didn't help the hospital much either. I kept pestering them about what was happening downtown. For the most part, they didn't know what I was talking about. They gave up trying when I was in and out of pain med stupors. I kept asking about lost girls and ghosts.

They did put some calls through to my kids. We told them only the extent of my injuries and that they would probably release me on Monday. They said nothing about how I got hurt.

Late Saturday afternoon, I had my first visitor: Mike Coppola. He did most of the talking, understanding that I shouldn't and couldn't.

"There was a little damage to the set" he told

me. "Bob got it straightened up pretty easily. Chuck Wemyss is going to fill in for you. He's the only one who knows the scene. We'll announce that you were injured. He'll do fine.

"Our biggest clean-up was the guy you clobbered. You broke his nose. There was a lot of blood. There's still a stain, but the light won't be enough for anyone to notice too much."

I sort of made a face and gestured. He understood that I wanted more information.

"The police aren't telling me too much," he explained. "They are creating cover stories for the whole mess. Thank God. You might hear on the news that there was a break-in at the theater and that the two intruders got hurt in the dark. One fell into the pit; the other tripped over something. They may neglect to release the names."

I held up two fingers.

He went on, "There will be a small, separate story of a drunk suffering from exposure." He paused, then added, "No one else will be mentioned. Ever. The FBI insisted on that."

That was all neat and tidy. In Cedar Falls, two clumsy burglars and a careless drunk. An FBI case from New York would remain in New York.

"I know you're concerned," Bob said, showing his concern, "but that's about all I know. Except for a message from your friend Frost. He said that he knows you're in good hands and he and Aydyn will come to see you when they are satisfied with some other matters. He said you would know what he meant."

I did. It was something at least.

Mike started to leave but turned in the doorway.

"By the way," he said with an expression somewhere between worry and amusement. "Someone from the police wanted me to tell you that, if anyone asks, you fell off a ladder in your garage. Be more careful."

I was glad to have my own cover story, but I wish he hadn't said it that way. I almost laughed. Damn, that hurt.

I slept better than I had expected to. I was in a recliner. That would be my bed here and at home for up to six weeks. Calling an aide to help me to the bathroom was an anxious time. The pain of getting there and back was worse.

Sunday was a quiet day. Between medical business and induced naps, I tried to watch football. I couldn't even tell what teams were playing. My main thoughts were still about a girl I had only seen in the dark of the theater and the darker thoughts of my mind.

Sunday evening, I had two visitors that I didn't expect. The first was Agent Robert Remington.

Fortunately, he started with "the girl." He had no name for her. It wasn't his department. I wasn't too hard on him for that. I could tell that he wanted to tell me more and to help more, too. His part had been to sign an official FBI request that the girl's "care-giver" could stay with her in the hospital, to explain what was happening. A Ms. Littlefield would not let anyone touch her otherwise.

I had always like Aydyn. I was beginning to really love her.

Remington then filled me in on the culprits. Sheridan had recruited two registered sex offenders to help him. He'd been staying at one their houses. He promised to pay them with "special" videos. Drug dealers he'd caught did similar things. They keep track of who might have drug offenses. Then, they recruit them for local things. One of the animals Sheridan had found knew and recruited the third man.

Leon G. Humphrey, nicknamed "Humpy", had been kicked off three different college football teams. He played mean and dirty, even in practice against his own teammates. I had run across him on an insurance investigation in Minnesota. He had driven a pick-up truck into someone's bedroom. He claimed he only intended to hit the house. The guy in the bed, who had had a run-in with him earlier in a bar, thought otherwise.

The first two would face local and state charges. It was doubtful they would ever be released. Humphrey would soon be transferred to a federal prison hospital. He might walk again, but he would not walk free. The officer that Murphy had placed across the street from the theater, young Colton Jones, was dead. Humphrey had eliminated him.

Clayton Sheridan was already back in New York. Between bouts of hysterical blubbering, he was helping. He was terrified of prison. He knew that it was likely that he would spend the rest of his life in solitary confinement. If he was lucky. I still hoped it was a very dark cell.

Sheridan had been planning to take over Clauburg's operation for some time. He used the meeting with Christopher as the opportunity. He had no idea who Christopher really was. Thought he was just some blackmailer. If Christopher had been only that, Sheridan might have gotten away with it. The FBI wouldn't have gotten involved.

It could have been a lengthy report, but Remington wanted to let me rest and get back to Washington. He had two big cases to wrap up.

"Two?" I asked.

"Yes," he replied, obviously very satisfied. "The girl showed us where to find a small, red, metal box. Damned well-hidden. We wouldn't have found it without demolishing the building. It had a notebook and three thumb drives. A lot of scum is getting scraped off the streets."

"And the other?" I asked again.

"The man you knew as Christopher," he said, "there were things hidden at his house. Almost didn't find those, either. He was good at hiding things, tangible and intangible. There were a lot of weapons and cash.

"It seems his given name was actually John

L. Sullivan. Born in Illinois. Viet Nam vet. He had written down everything he'd ever done, in detail. Cleared up ones we knew, ones we suspected and three we never heard of.

"There was a lengthy confession. Seems he grew a conscience in later life. Just a little. Not enough to turn himself in, but he didn't want anyone else to pay for his crimes, or maybe take credit for them. He didn't really show remorse. He mentioned his 'extreme sorrow' as he put it, about a wife and kids. But he didn't mention any names or places for those. We have no idea what to do with that. Probably better to leave them alone."

"I think that would be best," I added.

Remington left. I wasn't entirely sure if I felt better or worse.

My case load was reduced. I had no murder to solve. Criminals were behind bars. Their victims would be taken care of the best way possible. I had only an insurance matter to clear up: the Davenport family.

Then, Aydyn came in.

I might have been speechless at her arrival, but the shock was just as painful as if I'd shouted.

"Oh, John," she said, obviously concerned. "How are you doing?"

"What are you doing here?" I managed.

"Frost insisted I come," she explained. "Alice is okay. Mrs. Murphy arranged for her to stay in the theater the first night. I think her husband threw his weight behind it. They had to check her out at the hospital. I stayed first. Frost is with her until I get back."

"Okay," I wheezed. "For now, anyway."

"Is there anything you need?" she asked.

"An explanation," I said as firmly as I was able.

"What...?" she stammered.

"Why did...you and Alice...come out when you did?" It was one question with pauses between shocks of pain.

"Oh, my," she gasped. "I'm so sorry for that. Alice and I were playing with stuffed animals. She loves those. Then, she told me she already had one. She'd left it where she had stayed before the costume rooms. Before I could think, she was off and running. I should have stopped her."

I thought Aydyn was going to cry.

"No," I tried to comfort her. "I think...she's too quick for you."

"Maybe," Aydyn was still fighting tears. "But I should have been more focused."

"Just remember," I whispered. "It worked out. She's okay. And...I think...she will be...."

"From now on," Aydyn finished it for me.

We talked for just a few more minutes. Aydyn was anxious to get back. I was about done anyway.

Sunday night was not as restful a night. The doctors were concerned about that. I told them I just had a lot on my mind, what with being incapacitated for Christmas and all. They still insisted on keeping me one more night. Afterall, I wasn't very mobile. I was alone in my house and my bedroom was on the second floor.

I told them I had a half-bath and a sleeper sofa in one room on the ground floor. I thought having an aide come by a couple of times a day would be good enough. They were skeptical, until Sean Murphy showed up.

The doctor and a nurse had gone to inquire about aides and what might be necessary when Murphy came for a visit. I certainly hadn't expected to see him on Monday morning.

I told him my problem, and he volunteered to help me out. It seems he would be having a couple of weeks of free time. He was on suspension.

"What happened?" I was shocked. Murphy was the best cop I knew.

"You know Luis, the bartender at "The Blue Moon"? he asked.

The bar was actually named "El Casa de la Lune Azul." Luis was more than a bartender. I always thought of him as one of Murphy's friends.

"Of course, I know him," I answered Murphy. "Great guy."

"Yeah. He is," Murphy said, sheepishly. "I punched him in the mouth."

"What?!" the gasp was painful, but necessary.

"I understand Remington told you about the red box," he went on. "We examined it right away at the station. They opened one of the thumb drives. I left. I needed a drink."

That, I could imagine. It was still a long way from a punch.

"Well, I had more than one," Murphy related. "Luis knew I was upset but didn't know why. He was trying to lighten the mood, talking about this and that, teasing some of the other customers. I didn't want any part of that.

"Some college kids came in. Luis knew them. They were legal. One kid came to the bar to place their order. Luis said something about the kid's date, something like, 'That's a cute little girl you're with.' That's when I punched him."

"If he'd said anything but 'little girl' I might have just left. Wrong words, wrong time. He isn't pressing charges, and the chief was very understanding – up to a point. Anyway, I'll have some free time on my hands for a couple of weeks."

After a pause that we both understood, I said, "Good. You can dig out all my Christmas decorations."

"Oh, God," he moaned. "And I thought the suspension was going to be my only punishment."

Murphy drove me home. We hadn't been there twenty minutes when I got a phone call. It was from Norm Corrigan.

"John," he boomed through the phone. "I just heard. Are you alright?"

"Not really," I said, with strain. "I have some cracked ribs. Hard to do anything."

"I won't keep you, then," he said. "I just wanted

to thank you for all your help. There's going to be a great Christmas for Davenport families."

I was silent. I didn't know what he was talking about.

"Are you there?" he asked, doubtfully.

"I'm here," I whispered. "I've been home from the hospital about twenty minutes. I'm still shaky and I think the pain meds have scrambled my brain."

"Oh, I'm really sorry, John!" He was, too. "I was just so excited when I got the envelope."

"What envelope?"

"Man, you really are out of it. Didn't you send me Christopher's obituary?"

I was silent again, more confused than ever. This time Norm waited for me to recover.

"If you got anything, my partner, Forrest Jackson, sent it to you."

"You mean, you don't even know about it?"

"I've been tied up in something else."

Now, it was Norm's turn to be stunned.

"Listen, John," he went on, in a kind whisper. "You just rest. It sounds like you need it. You call Jackson... Wait! Did you just call him 'partner'?"

"Yes," I said, as firmly as I could manage. "He's more than earned it. In fact, it seems he's been doing more than I have."

"He's doing a great job!" Norm said. "I mean that. I don't know where he found this, but it's wonderful! Don't you worry about anything. Just rest and have a merry, merry Christmas."

"You, too, Norm," I returned. "And a very happy New Year."

I think there is no such thing as just an emotion. Almost every one that I have had recently have been mixed – two, three, four! All mixed together.

What had Frost done?

My mail that day explained it. There was a manilla envelope with a note from Frost and a copy of what appeared to be an obituary:

Dr. Geoffrey R. Christopher, 71, died as the result of a tragic accident on North Main in Cedar Falls. Dr. Christopher, affectionately known as "Doc" to his friends in the Cedar Falls Community Theater was a retired psychologist and businessman. After practicing for a few years in a specialty hospital in Ohio, he left the medical profession to go into business, mostly investments. A former nurse colleague related that he had done so because he got too emotionally involved in his patients' lives, especially one very tragic woman and her children. Christopher had no family of his own and has left the bulk of his estate to various charities. Christopher had no family of his own and has left the bulk of his estate to various charities.

I stared at it for several minutes after I finished reading it, amazed, again, at Frost's computer wizardry. It looked so real.

– epilogue –

It was a long, slow time. By the end of January, I was mostly okay. I was no longer only in my recliner or in need of assistance. Of course, it was January and there wasn't much to do, either, except for one or two very special things.

I finally got to meet Alice.

It was a group meeting. They came to my house in a van. "They" consisted of Frost, Aydyn, Alice, Jane Murphy, and a determined, but kind looking woman introduced to me as Dr. Elayne Andress.

Alice didn't seem particularly nervous at all to be in a new house with someone she didn't know.

Alice is less than five feet tall, slim and graceful. Frost was right: she reminded me of a gymnast. She has a round face with dark Asian features. I took it that her heritage must be southeast Asian. Her eyes were dark and sparkling, and her smile delightful.

Her visit was much too short. Alice would be taking her first plane trip. Dr. Andress was one of the doctors at the special place that had helped Frost when he was young. She had been the one who had tried to help the girl that Frost had known at that time. Frost and Aydyn would accompany them, but Alice had been weaned from Aydyn's constant presence. All were more than hopeful.

"Alice had come farther than one might expect," Dr. Andress informed me. "It seems Drs. Jackson and Littlefield have had amazing success."

Frost deflected the high praise. "The credit belongs to Alice. She is the one who has made the journey."

Alice ran to hug him, something that would have been unthinkable two months ago.

Investigations into her origins were difficult. There was nothing in the Clauburg records about her, or any girls. They were insignificant to him except as a means to an end. Those records would eventually put seventeen people in prison.

Alice's memories were too vague. Her birth name, as she remembered it did sound Vietnamese. From it, Christopher had renamed her "Alice." Both names might, with a bit of a stretch, be translated as "strong woman." Authorities were looking into abductions from fifteen to twenty years ago. Alice probably fell into that age range.

Alice's more recent memories in combination with things Sheridan confessed led to the freeing of eight young girls. Most of them were not in the videos of the Box. Sheridan was leading the FBI to where he had taken others. We could only hope they were still alive. We also hoped some were as strong as Alice. We feared many were not.

After they left, I had those mixed emotions again. I didn't know whether to cry for joy or dance for joy. Or hope some more. I just sat.

Another month went by. Frost and Aydyn were back. Another play was in production. I was helping Bob again. All seemed normal, as if there is such a thing.

One day, I noticed that Bob was using the long-lost screwdriver with the dark green handle.

"Strangest thing," he said. "When I came to fix the set last December, when you got hurt, there it was just lying in the middle of the stage."

"Really?" I said, as if I didn't know.

Neither of us pursued it further.

A few days later, some of us were sitting with Pop Barnes. Most of them were actors, real actors, not off and on like me. We were playing a game. We would say a line from a play, nothing ridiculously obscure, and Pop would name the play. He rarely missed.

I told him mine, and he nailed it easily. Now, I remembered who Horatio was.

Frost had joined us. Mostly, he just observed, the people more than the game itself, as he usually does. He seemed to enjoy it. Pop noticed that he was very different from the others.

"Young man," he asked kindly, "have you a line for me?"

"Well, sir," Frost replied, "I am rather new here

and new to theater. Before recent months, I had read much but attended little."

"I am glad you are here," Pop said. "Try one, please."

"I am puzzled," Frost began. "I have had a line running through my mind during the time I have been listening. For the life of me, I cannot recall where I heard it. It seems like something I heard only recently, and yet it seems from long ago."

"That is very interesting," Pop said with a smile. "I often have that. Tell me yours."

Frost looked passed Pop toward the stage and said in a faraway kind of way:

"Oh, Doctor. You have not failed. My frail body is nothing. You have saved me. Me!"

Pop was absolutely stunned. I worried about him. His caregiver, a nurse, took his hand.

"I'm sorry," he said. "You startled me. I didn't think anyone knew that old thing. It's from an old chestnut of a play called, "Doctor Andrew's Dilemma." A young doctor thinks he has failed because he can't cure a young woman. She has turned bitter and cold. He can't do anything medically, but he removed her bitterness. It has only two good scenes. Most of it is almost unbearable for actors and audiences alike."

We had to end it. Rehearsal was due to start. Everyone went their separate ways. Only Frost and I and Pop and his nurse remained.

Pop was staring at the stage, at far stage left,

where Frost had been looking when he recited the line.

"Those were the words," he said, as a tear ran down his cheek. "The last line she ever spoke."